# BREATHE

BREAKERS HOCKEY #7

ELISE FABER

BREATHE
BY ELISE FABER
Newsletter sign-up
This is a work of fiction. Names, places, characters, and events are fictitious in every regard. Any similarities to actual events and persons, living or dead, are purely coincidental. Any trademarks, service marks, product names, or named features are assumed to be the property of their respective owners, and are used only for reference. There is no implied endorsement if any of these terms are used. Except for review purposes, the reproduction of this book in whole or part, electronically or mechanically, constitutes a copyright violation.

BREAKERS HOCKEY SERIES

Broken
Boldly
Breathless
Ballsy
Bewitched
Blowout
Breathe
A Breakers Christmas
Blazed
Bound

## ONE

Eva

"YOU CAN GO."

My pulse was pounding in my ears, my lungs still frantically trying to drag some air into my body, which was limp with pleasure...

Because I'd been pounded.

*Oh,* had I been pounded.

By a big, hard hockey player with stormy gray eyes.

Pounded so well that the sweat was still drying on my skin and my mind was still fuzzy from the orgasms—yes, *orgasms* plural. In fact, I hadn't even gotten the strength to pull the sheet up and over my naked body. Hadn't wanted to.

Because remaining naked might mean a round three with my big, hard hockey player.

Who'd cornered me when I'd been ready to head home and apologized for being a dick.

And then had given me *his* dick.

Well, he'd bought me a couple of beers first and some food and—

*Then* he'd given me his dick.

Which was...proportional and worth the hype, mostly because he knew how to use it, but also because he'd been generous and unwavering, and...*now* I was ready for round three. Not for talking. Not for processing how soft rumbling words that ordered me to spread my legs or lift my ass or take him deeper had made me feel.

"What?" I managed through my frantically working lungs, finally realizing in my lazy haze of pleasure that he'd said something. I tilted my head to look at him where he'd collapsed next to me.

His brows lifted. "You can go."

The first iteration of that finally processed...right as the second was hitting my eardrums. *Right* as I clued into the frosty expression that had settled onto his face, the way his eyes had gone from a scorching summer storm to a swirling, disorienting winter blizzard.

"What?" I asked again. A whisper this time, some feeling I didn't want to look too closely at beginning to swirl in my belly.

The shine of those multiple orgasms wearing off.

Shame creeping in.

All as those frigid eyes held mine, seemingly without a blip of feeling.

Just *cold*. So different from two minutes ago, from *two* hours ago.

But so much like the man I'd gotten to know in the locker room over the last couple of seasons. He hated me, and I didn't know why, and *because* he hated me, I'd found myself not willing to back down.

Antagonizing him back.

Not giving an inch.

An Eva Moreno special.

The man—the one I knew, not the generous lover of the last few hours—lifted a disdainful brow. "I think you heard me."

Okay, forget pleasure and limp limbs and orgasms that had blown my mind.

*Now* I was starting to get mad.

I pushed up from the mattress, clambered to my feet. "Do all of your apologies come with a side of orgasms?" I plunked my hands on my hips, not missing his gaze going to my breasts. *Fucking pig.* "Or," I went on dryly, "am I just one of the lucky ones to get both the hotshot hockey player's dick *and* the full asshole treatment?"

His eyes narrowed, mouth opening, but I spun away, not wanting to see the derision on his face.

Too much of that already.

I did a search of the room for my clothes, cataloging as quickly as possible, wanting to get the fuck out of there. No round three. No more of this man. God, I was such an idiot. *This* was the man I'd decided to end my streak with? This was—

A hand stroking across my ass.

Warm rough fingers. A presumptuous hold.

"What the fuck?" I snapped, straightening from where I'd bent to snag my underwear, snatching them up and whirling to face him.

He was sprawled back on the mattress, one muscular arm folded behind his head, the lines of the tattoo on his bicep barely visible. It was a graph and one that I didn't understand— and probably wouldn't, because the last I'd heard, Theo had just graduated with yet another science degree.

Something he did just for fun.

But I *had* licked my way across the lines, inhaled the spicy musk of him deep into my lungs. Now that line moved as he gave a lazy shrug. "You have a nice ass."

I wasn't proud of it, but I sputtered, totally at a loss for fucking words for once in my life and hating the disgust that skated down my spine because of it.

"You're unbelievable," I eventually managed to counter.

Pathetic.

As was my response to the sexy half smile in return—my pussy convulsing, thighs going a little shaky. "I'm only stating facts," he said silkily.

*Ugh.* Now he was just being an even bigger asshole.

Because...facts? *Right.* I certainly had enough in the booty department, but it wasn't anything to write home about, especially when it wasn't smoothed out by denim or camouflaged by lace.

Stepping out of reach, I glared at him as I tugged up my panties, snagged my bra. "What?" I asked, shrugging into it and trying to get the upper hand on this conversation. "No comment on my boobs?"

Another shrug. Another glimpse of the lines of that tattoo on his arm. "I've seen better tits."

He'd seen—

God, this man.

"Wow," I muttered, grabbing my T-shirt and yanking it over my head, following suit with my jeans and my Breakers-emblazoned sweatshirt. "Likewise," I lied, deliberately glancing toward his cock.

Even though it was a lie.

His cock was magnificent.

And, for the record, so were *his* tits. A set of perfectly squeezable pecs with flat nipples that I'd sucked on until he'd tugged me free and tossed me back onto the mattress, growling my name in a way that sent shivers rattling through me.

So, yeah. His *tits* were hot. His body was amazing. And his cock was glorious.

Better was that he knew how to use it.

Or *worse*—because it was likely that the man had ruined me for all other cocks.

Theo Young. Playboy. Professional hockey player. Ruiner of vaginas from coast to coast.

(And internationally.)

Grounded by my sarcasm, I shoved my bare feet into my sneakers, stuffed my socks into my pockets.

"Don't forget your purse."

A sly command.

One that was also an unnecessary jab because I'd already spotted it on the floor next to the dresser, its contents slightly spilled on the carpet, my phone two feet away.

I'd be up shit creek if *that* got broken.

But I hadn't exactly been thinking about cell phones and broken screens. Not with Theo tearing my clothes off and fingering me into an orgasm after a shockingly short amount of time.

"You're an asshole, Theo."

"An asshole who was just balls deep in you." And, as though to prove it, he pushed out of bed, condom still rolled down the mostly-rigid length of his cock and walked into the bathroom.

Giving *me* a glimpse of a nice ass.

Christ.

Shaking my head at myself, I bent and scooped up my shit, hating that I'd left my car at the bar, hating that I now had to call a Lyft and wait for it on a cold winter night, extending my walk of shame from the bedroom to the porch to the awkward silent ride with an aching pussy and a brain that wouldn't stop chastising me for being such a freaking idiot.

Fun times in the mind of Eva Moreno.

"Let 'em roll," I whispered. Down my back. To the fucking floor. Out of my mind and life and memories.

An exhale.

The shit feelings carefully shoved down, locked away.

Then I was slinging my purse over my shoulder, pulling up the rideshare app on my cell, and calling, "Thanks for the whole three good minutes!"

As far as exit lines went, it sucked.

But as things often went in my world, I took what I could get.

# TWO

Theo

THE HIT CAME at me far faster than I could dodge.

Because I was off my game.

Because my mind was on the woman I'd kicked out of my house early that morning.

Because I was exhausted—not just from the sex, which had been the hardest workout I'd had in years, just trying to keep up with her, but because I hadn't slept afterward. Or that afternoon when I'd tried to get my nap.

Then I couldn't eat.

And I'd fucked up on pregame soccer.

And now I was eating glass...and dirty ass snow as the player slamming me into the boards released me and I dropped like a sack of fucking bricks to the ice.

Lungs tight.

Body screaming.

I pushed back up to my skates and kept moving, focusing

on the play and not on the fact that all of my internal organs were protesting the collision.

That was hockey and I needed to get my shit together.

"Move, asshole," I muttered to myself, hauling ass to help out with the play, to support my teammate.

Walker took the puck into the zone and made a move around one of our opponents. He kept the puck, but barely, and then was stymied before he could get close to the net for a scoring opportunity, another player from the other team skating in and sweeping the puck into the corner.

I was closer, so I chased it down.

And got creamed against the boards again for my trouble.

Hockey was fun.

Hockey was the greatest.

Luckily, Marcel was nearby and he swept up the puck, kept the play alive.

While I spat out dirty ice for the second time in as many minutes—in *less* because I'd been out for this shift for less than thirty seconds.

*Forget it.*

*Get up on your skates.*

*Continue to move.*

*Keep on playing.*

Walker got the puck back, and he dropped it to Smitty at the point, opening some space up as I fought my way to the middle, sticking my ass in the goalie's face, trying to block his view, and succeeding somewhat...

Just as Smitty shot from the blue line.

The crack of my teammate's stick hitting the ice.

The crowd screaming.

The curses from the other team's goalie and defensemen.

Sharp crosschecks to my spine, chops to the backs of my legs, battling for every inch of space...

As the puck was flying toward me.

Flying *at* me.

No. Flying at my—

Pain radiated out from between my legs, sending them buckling and my face toward the ice for the third time that shift. Cold and heat mixed, frost on my face, burning pain in my pelvis.

The whistle blew.

The crowd cheered.

I peeled myself up from the ice.

Decided that was enough punishment for one shift and skated to the bench, cock throbbing, legs barely working, vision a haze of red. I made it, and, thank fuck, someone opened the door so I didn't have to climb over the boards, so I could just slide onto the metal bench, put my head down, and *breathe*.

And try not to think that this was karma for last night.

For Eva.

A punishment for being a dick.

One that was well-deserved.

A hard shove to my shoulder had me looking up into the eyes of the big—and for most hockey players, *that* was saying something—brute. Smitty, his beard wild and eyes amused, grinned over at me. "Forget to dodge?"

I picked up a bottle and squirted some of the sports drink-water combo at my asshole of a teammate. "You're not funny."

Smitty just wiped a hand over his face, droplets clinging to his beard. "That's a lie, and you know it. I am *eminently* funny."

I rolled my eyes. "That's a big word for a hockey player."

"I know," Smitty said proudly as he picked up his own bottle and sipped like he was a dainty fucker at afternoon tea, complete with lifted pinky finger. He winked at me. "I learned it from you."

Jesus Christ.

A man likes to learn, and it became a source of never-ending shit-giving.

Sighing, I focused on the ice and drank deeply from my water bottle, trying to ignore the ache in my balls. Smitty kept talking, but I didn't bite, just ignored the fucker who was my teammate and tried to do my goddamned job.

So, I played hockey—like shit.

And I focused on the game—poorly.

I tried my best—and it wasn't fucking good enough.

But right then, it was all I had.

Especially with balls that throbbed and guilt as heavy as two-ton bricks weighing down my shoulders.

Eyes on the ice.

Moving forward.

Ignoring the past.

That was the Theo Young way.

---

A COUPLE HOURS LATER, and with significantly less ice in my face, Smitty clapped me on the shoulder. "Tough break, man."

"I already told you," I muttered. "I'm fine. My junk is fine. Your shot isn't that hard, asshole. Get over yourself." A lie. Smitty had one of the hardest shots in the league, and my balls felt like they had swollen to the size of two watermelons. Hell, I was seriously considering going home and shoving all seventeen ice packs in my freezer down my pants.

No, this wasn't the first time I'd been hit in the balls, and it wouldn't be the last. I'd deal.

But it wouldn't be fun.

No sex for a couple of days.

Ice packs on rotation.

Moving on.

Smitty grinned. "No, man. I'm not talking about your balls" —a wink—"though if you need lessons in getting naked, I'll clear it with Kailey. I'm sure she won't mind me giving a few pointers a teammate."

Because the man never wore clothes if he didn't have to.

Christ.

"Fuck off, Smitty," I muttered.

"I'd rather go home and fuck my woman." Smitty winced, glanced down at my junk. "Not that you'll—"

"Christ, Smitty, my balls are fine!" I exploded.

Right as the locker room quieted.

Cool.

I ground my teeth together, shoved a hand through my hair.

"Speaking of..." Smitty tapped his phone on his thigh.

I froze, a sinking feeling in my stomach. That wasn't the normal Smitty shit-giving tone. That was...

"What?" I asked when my teammate didn't go on.

"Well"—Smitty cleared his throat—"you know it's not personal. It isn't ever with Eva. She just—"

That sinking feeling turned straight abyss. "*What* isn't?"

Was my tone sharp? Sure as fuck was. Did Smitty pick up on it? Un-fucking-fortunately.

Smitty ran a hand through his beard, winced again. "Maybe this isn't the right time." He started to put his phone away.

I glared. "*Smitty.* Tell me."

Wordlessly—and thank fuck for small miracles—Smitty passed over his phone.

It was an article.

No, it was a blog post.

*Playboy Player Pummels Prospects.*

By Eva Moreno.

My eyes went to the time it went live and my vision hazed.

Not twenty minutes after I'd left.

Fine. Whatever. I'd burned her.

And I'd certainly doubled down on burning me.

I should be happy. Tit for tat. It was done—

Except, then my eyes hit on the line,

*If only Young spent less time focusing on scoring in the bedroom, this author thinks he might contribute more on the scoreboard.*

Cute.

This coming from a woman who'd clearly do anything for content.

Including hockey players.

And what? It wasn't enough that she was commentating, that she had more access to us than most of the media? She regularly put *her* scores—no matter how she got them—to good use for fodder on her site.

And me.

*I* was fodder. Frequently enough to have my own tag.

*That* was a familiar feeling—familiar enough that any guilt about the night before disappeared.

And a *familiar* rage settled in its place.

# THREE

Eva

I HAD on my comfiest pair of socks, was wrapped in my oversized hoodie, and was catching up on some of the taped league games.

I needed content.

Luckily, the guys were providing it.

And not just Theo and his struggles on the ice—nor his glorious cock and asshole tendencies off it.

The Breakers *had* won that night, despite Theo's rough game. I'd already watched the replay, listening to the color commentator from that evening and had taken copious notes on how to improve my own performance during the games I had been picked up to do.

But beyond the Breakers, there were other games, and in them, some beauties of plays that I was able to pull highlights of to post on my social media (where I could fangirl over them properly). I'd also put together several captivating still photographs that made for engaging pictures on my site, and some funny behind-the-scenes moments that I couldn't wait to share both places.

And I had some comments to delete.

Also in both places.

Because that was normal, and I'd gotten popular enough that trolls liked to take potshots at me—because, heaven forbid, I was a woman who liked to talk about sports, and not just how athletes looked in their suits or the stylistic quality of their jerseys (though I had opinions on both of those aspects of the game and was a semi-firm believer in looking good meaning playing good).

But the trolls didn't often take exception to my *actual* opinions.

It was more of a blanket of misogyny.

Something I took advantage of—putting assholes on blast was one of my favorite things to do—but also something I didn't really engage in outside of making a TikTok showcasing their dumbass statements.

No arguing in the comments section.

But I *would* take more views and followers and a little bit of extra money in my pocket.

Because that was part of how I'd paid for school and food and groceries and the copious streaming platforms I needed to watch hockey—and it was still a good chunk of my income at this point.

And it helped my family, was the only way we'd been able to survive.

Well, not the *only* way.

But it was a big chunk of why.

Commentating was a dream—my *life's* dream—but it didn't pay all that great yet.

Especially when I'd only been picked up to do color on ten home games.

Hopefully, I would continue kicking color commentating's ass and get even more games next season but, in the meantime, I had to keep up with my other jobs.

Mostly because I liked to eat.

And drink.

And, okay, it was mostly eating.

I was a lightweight when it came to booze—hence my ending up with the Theo Young Special (wham, bam, don't let the door hit ya, ma'am)—so I was well aware that I couldn't drink a hockey player under the table. I *could*, however, give those big, bulky athletes a run for their money when it came to consuming calories.

And tacos.

Yum.

Tacos. With guacamole and sour cream and extra cotija cheese.

Great.

Now I was going to spend some of my hard-earned income on tacos. And chips. And guac.

Nothing to be done for it, I supposed. I wasn't going to cook, not when I was already cozied up in my socks and over-sized hoodie, and I sure as shit wasn't going to summon up the energy to put on a bra.

Getting my fingers working on my phone screen was the full extent of the effort I was willing to expend that evening.

"There," I murmured after tapping away for a few moments (and only a few because my favorites were saved there right at the top and I only had to click a couple of times to load up my cart and send off the order).

After tacos were incoming, I set my phone aside and went back to content gathering.

The doorbell rang sooner than I expected, but my stomach wasn't sad about that fact. "Score," I whispered as I set my laptop aside and got up to answer it, dawdling just long enough to give the driver time to head out.

No unnecessary socialization on my watch.

But when I tugged open the door, my bag of food wasn't sitting on my *Be a Good Neighbor, Stay Over There* emblazoned mat. Nope. That was empty and there wasn't any sign of tacos or guac or my delivery driver.

"Shit," I muttered, looking around again as though my tacos would magically appear.

Unfortunately, the only magical taco I had was between my legs—and I knew exactly how effective *that* was, considering it had gotten me kicked out of Theo's house before round three.

Sigh.

Closing the door, I moved back over to the couch, to my phone, opening the app and...seeing that my order hadn't even been picked up yet.

"What?" I whispered.

I frowned at the screen, as though that would change the fact that there weren't any tacos on my stoop. Then I pushed up from the couch again, moved into the hall, and started to tug open the door again.

Only...it wasn't closed.

There was an inch of open space between the frame and the wooden panel.

"What the fuck?" I muttered.

Wind.

It had to be the wind. Sometimes it came up through the corridor and pushed open my door if it hadn't fully latched. I tugged it wider, though, and poked my head out, searching for... some other explanation. Like why that one inch of open space had the hairs on my nape lifting.

But just as it had been a minute or two before, the corridor was empty, and all of my neighbors' doors were closed. And there were no tacos on my mat.

Sighing, realizing I'd been expertly doorbell ditched, I stepped back inside, firmly closed and locked the door this time —doublechecking for good measure—then went back to the couch, to my videos, to creating content for what had once been just a dream but was now an actual career.

I watched hockey.

I recorded herself in my messy ass hair and my oversized hoodie and no bra (not that anyone could see it with all of the extra material of that hoodie) and talked about hockey.

Plays and players and sick as fuck goals that amazed me.

Hits that took my breath away.

Goalies that robbed forwards and defensemen alike.

Coaches that made the wrong call in line pairings. Management who did the same when it came to trades and draft picks and who to leave in the minors and who was ready to come up into the big leagues.

I did my job.

I did what I loved and what fulfilled me.

I did it until my tacos came and I could pack it in, could shut everything down and watch some of my favorite YouTubers while stuffing my face.

After retrieving my tacos, the only thing I got up for was a beer.

And then another.

Because I found that the first beer reminded me of Theo, of the pleasure and the shame, but the second had my mind dulling blissfully, the memory blurred and fuzzy and like it had happened to someone else or I'd seen it in a movie somewhere.

The third beer...had all thoughts of Theo Young fading completely away.

Leaving me with my trashy videos and my buzzed mind and myself.

Just as I liked it.

# FOUR

Theo

THE BITE of cold in the air drifted in through the underground parking, clinging to my skin, pushing through my hair.

Like fingers.

Cool, tipped with pale pink nails that dragged across my scalp, the naked skin of my back, along my ribs, down my stomach—

My dick twitched.

Fucking stupid.

The organ.

My brain.

*All* of me.

Mostly because I was still thinking, dreaming, jerking off to the memories of my night a week before with a certain pink-nailed beauty, despite her posting that article that had led to no little amount of shit-giving in the locker room.

And online.

And from my fucking mother of all people. Though, that had been more safe sex talk than producing an on the ice lecture.

Worse because I'd had to promise my mother that I "wrap it up."

Fun times.

And still, I couldn't get that night out of my head. Nor excise the strong, beautiful, sexy as fuck, and surprisingly generous in bed woman from my thoughts.

She was totally wrong for me.

She wanted the dirt, wanted to make money off my life, exploit my story, and that was something I couldn't forgive even *if* I'd wanted to settle down. Which I didn't. Because that was... not something I wanted, not in the cards, not for someone like me, not for someone with my past.

Hell, it was a fucking miracle that bulldog of a woman hadn't dug *that* dumpster fire up yet.

Thankfully, she hadn't, so I still had a job, wasn't a total pariah online, and was able to keep my life and commitments light and breezy without any sticky, complicated spiderweb-like ties tangling things up.

*That* was what was right for me.

And no, I wasn't going to think about the fact that I could have royally fucked my life by nutting it to a couple orgasms, no matter how good of a fuck Eva was.

Because if I did, I'd never get the hell out of my head and then I'd be up for weekly sessions with Hazel, the team's sports psychologist. The last fucking thing I needed was someone else inside the mess that was my brain.

Light. Breezy. Uncomplicated. *That* was what I needed.

And anyway, I was out of town half the fucking year, training my ass off for the rest of it. What time did I have for a family, for—heaven-fucking-forbid—kids?

None.

Nor the mental headspace for it.

So, I stuck to hockey and fucking and hanging out with my friends. Never mind that those friends had families of their own—successful and happy units that weren't impacted by the same job I was doing, by the same excuses I was spewing.

They didn't have my past.

There.

Done.

Explanation enough.

Especially when it was after midnight and my legs were sore and aching, and I sported a cut on my cheek glued together by the team's doctor from eating the ice a-fucking-gain that game. My play hadn't improved much, and I'd have the scar to prove it. The cut itself still stung, but it was really nothing, small enough it hadn't even required stitches and I hadn't even missed a shift.

Glued up.

Back on the ice.

That was the life of a professional athlete—or at least, a professional hockey player.

Living and breathing the sport, fighting for the two points, practicing, finessing, studying, and working my ass off until the playoffs came around and then sacrificing everything for the chance at a Cup.

That was my life.

All I'd ever wanted. Really.

Even if watching my teammates have something different, something *more* made me—

"Theodore."

I froze, stomach sinking.

The voice—well, the man to whom the voice belonged to— shouldn't be here.

Like, really, *shouldn't* be here. There was security at the gate, and people had to be on the list or have a pass to access the underground parking. That meant players and staff were the only ones who should be here.

Not deadbeat fathers.

Gritting my teeth, I kept walking, brushing by my dad.

*Dad* in the loosest of fucking terms. Sperm donor was more accurate. Absentee father was perhaps slightly *more* accurate. Destroyer of worlds and evil incarnate...yeah, that was the *most* apt.

A hand slammed down onto my shoulder before I got more than a few feet away, jarring the breath out of me, making the soreness from the game surge through my muscles.

"Don't walk away from me, son."

Son.

Ha.

*That* was funny.

I broke the hold and shoved a hand into my pocket, tugging out my cell, jabbing at the screen until I found the proper contact. "Harry? Yeah, it's Theo. Can you send security down to the players' parking?"

My father—sperm donor, absentee, destroyer of worlds—started to protest.

But Harry—the team's head of security—was on top of his shit.

"I'm at the door," he said, and I could hear the other man moving. "I'll be there in thirty seconds."

"Thanks," I muttered, ending the call, and shoving my cell back into my pocket.

Then I kept walking, hoping my father would take a fucking hint and go away. He was good at that. I was the *best* at that.

Disappearing.

Blowing shit up and walking away.

Unfortunately, I was also a stubborn fuck, so it wasn't a surprise when the footsteps continued alongside mine.

"Son—"

The utter balls on my father.

I stopped again, turned to face the man who had provided one half of my genetic material. Which meant we looked too similar for my taste. Gray eyes. Brown hair. Though my dad's was threaded with strands of gray. But our noses, chins, jaws, even the muscular build of our bodies screamed of the familial connection.

No matter how much I hated it.

"I'm not doing this," I said. "I'm not doing it here or ever, really."

No hesitation, just blowing right by my words. "We need to talk."

Talk. *Now?* That was fucking hysterical.

"No, *Dad,*" I sneered. "That time has long passed. You need to go."

"I—"

"Theo?"

Saved by the security guard. Thank fuck.

"Harry," I said, turning back. "This is my father." Harry's face started to change, but I cut that off by adding, "He doesn't have permission to be here." A beat as I felt my father's protests begin welling up again, but I just held Harry's gaze. "Ever."

To his credit, Harry didn't falter. His expression went blank, his hand went to my father's arm, and he said, "I'll show you the way to the exit, sir." A glance flicked in my direction. "And have a word with Aiden."

The security guard who worked the gates.

"Thanks," I muttered, deliberately not looking at my dad, who was now struggling against the hold and objecting.

Loudly.

Fuck.

Never could just slide under the radar. Never could just let me have my peace.

Always had to come in and try to blow shit up.

"Let's go," Harry ordered, nodding at me before he turned away, fingers securely wrapped around my dad's arm, dragging him toward the exit, even as my father's protests grew louder.

"Christ," I ground out, shoving a hand through my hair.

Gripping.

Wanting to tear the strands from my scalp as frustration roiled beneath my skin. I exhaled, let my chin drop toward my chest, gaze going to my shoes, the brown leather gleaming. Studying the stitching while resisting the urge to chase after the pair and scream at my father. Standing there and just breathing through the annoyance of the intrusion, of the past coming out of nowhere and slamming a goddamned two-by-four across my jaw.

Then, finally, feeling like I had a semblance of control, I looked up...

Right into the coffee-colored eyes of Eva Moreno.

My breath stuck in my lungs even as my gaze dropped...to pink-tipped fingernails.

They were digging into the straps of her backpack.

Like they'd dug into my bare skin.

She gasped, the sound echoing across the concrete, and I watched those fingers tighten further before she spun on her heel and hurried away.

As though she hadn't just seen what she'd seen.

As though I couldn't see her there, couldn't see her hurrying over to her car and frantically yanking at the handle.

I was moving before I realized, storming after her, a hurricane of fury in my stomach.

This woman who wouldn't stay out of my head, who was always standing in the fucking corner waiting to write some damned story about me that would end up on her blog, that would go viral on social media, that would become material for my teammates to give me shit about in the locker room.

I caught her arm as she started to pull open the door, spinning her to face me. "What'll it be this time?" I snapped. "*Star Player Loses His Focus and Doesn't Contribute?*"

Her mouth dropped open.

"Or no, maybe you'll do a part two to *Playboy Player Pummels Prospects.*" I brought my fingers to my lips for a chef's kiss. "The alliteration on that one alone."

She tugged at my hold.

"Nah, you'll probably go simple with something like *Young Has Lost His Touch.*" I clucked my tongue. "Oh wait, I forgot. You've already used that title."

Pink on her cheeks. "That's not fair—"

"Let me save you the trouble, yeah?" I tugged at her bag, pulled out her cell. She always kept it in the front pocket, ready to serve as her recorder.

Hell, she was probably recording me right then, ready to break the story about my deadbeat dad.

"What are you—?" She fumbled to snatch her bag back.

But I was faster.

He'd already extracted her phone and jabbed at the screen.

Only it was locked and not recording and—

*Pft.*

Okay, so *one* time she wasn't after the story—

Of course, this wasn't the one time, even my rage-filled mind could recognize that much. I'd confronted her before, made some assumptions, and had been wrong in a way that had me apologizing.

Which had then led to both of us getting naked the week before.

My dick twitched again.

*Fuck.*

I exhaled, shoved her cell back into her bag.

She yanked the bag out of my hold, held it against her, nails digging into the fabric. "What the fuck, Theo?" she snapped.

"You chase the story," I said. "You know you do. You live and breathe and would do anything for it."

Her cheeks went bright pink.

"Anything," I pressed. "Including—" A flick of my hand between our bodies.

She paled and took a half step backward, bumping into the edge of the door and wincing, rubbing her arm when it started to swing closed.

Guilt immediately welled up.

I should apologize. I *knew* I should. This was another dick move. Accusing her of sleeping with me for a story...

But I couldn't bring himself to apologize. *Couldn't.*

Instead, I stepped closer, bent so my face was in hers. "You write about this, and I swear to God—"

"Fuck you, Theo," she hissed, jabbing a finger into my chest. "Just fuck you."

Turning, she jerked open the door, slamming it into my side in the process, but I relished the pain radiating along my ribs and torso, relished it because it eclipsed the burn of shame.

Her bag hit the passenger's seat.

Her ass hit the driver's.

The door closed, the engine revved, and...she was gone.

"Good," I muttered.

That was a good thing.

Except, why did it feel like shit?

# FIVE

Eva

"I HATE HIM," I whispered, my hand trembling as I shoved my hair out of my face. "I *hate* him."

I did.

Really, I did.

Or...I wanted to, anyway.

He was a jerk. He was arrogant. He had a revolving door of women and unfortunately that included me.

I just—

"No," I whispered, clenching the steering wheel. "He's awful. You hate him."

Right.

Precisely.

I hated him.

He was just an egotistical puckboy, and I had a shit ton of other things in my life to keep me busy and it didn't matter what he thought of me. I knew what I was about and understood my worth and he didn't—

My phone rang.

Thank God because I needed to get the hell out of my own head.

I tugged my cell out of my backpack, ignoring the fact that Theo had touched it last. I would not be derailed by a stupid, annoyingly sexy hockey player with a very nice—

"No," I whispered, plunking my cell into the cradle that was attached to my air vent and putting him out of my mind. "No Theo. No hockey players. Just drive." I took a breath and glanced at the screen, thinking that the universe was confirming my thoughts when I saw it was my sister calling.

No time for asshole athletes. I had a full life and a heavy load of shit that kept me busy, and one chunk of that load was calling right then.

Shifting my hold on the steering wheel, I reached for the cord that was dangling from the USB port, fumbling as I plugged it in (and cursing I hadn't gotten myself situated before pulling out in a huff from the arena's parking lot). Thankfully, I managed to plug it in before I missed the call—though my sister certainly would have just called right back—and swiped a finger across the screen.

The ringing synced up with the speakers for a heartbeat before the call connected.

"Hey, Dommie," I said over the road noise.

A brief pause then, "You sounded good tonight, big sis."

I froze, my eyes sliding closed briefly as the pride washed over me. Not something I'd heard from my parents, not when my dad had been alive, not now from my mom, who didn't understand what I did in the least. So, as the oldest, I'd been the one to give affection and love and, yes, pride to my siblings, to show them the tenderness and care I had craved. That Dommie was giving it back...

I cleared my throat of the sudden emotion. "Thanks,

kiddo," I murmured before focusing on the important topic at hand. "You good?"

A longer pause then, "Um."

Shit. My stomach twisted and I hated that my throat went tight for a second time, that my hands were shaking again, albeit for a whole different reason.

Not a hockey player.

My family.

And that was worse.

It was always worse—

*Breathe.*

I clenched the steering wheel, ignored the trembling in my hands, and cleared the emotion from my throat again. "Tell me, sissy," I ordered.

"Mom's doctor called."

*Breathe.*

Why hadn't they called me? They were supposed to leave my siblings out of this shit. They weren't used to navigating insurance companies and pharmacies and doctor's offices. Then they panicked and created drama or worried over nothing when I could handle it.

When I *always* handled it.

"Did she call you?"

"No, she called the house. I heard the contact come up on the caller ID"—our mom was old school and still had a home phone that announced who was calling—"and Mom was going to ignore it, so I picked up."

Yeah, that wasn't a good sign.

"What did she say?"

Silence that went on long enough to send my pulse skyrocketing, my hands clenching so tightly on the steering wheel that I was shocked it didn't creak in protest. But my voice was steady when I pressed, "Dommie, honey, what did she say?"

Another blip of quiet, but my sister did eventually reply, "She says the medication isn't working."

Fuck.

*Breathe.*

"Okay, that's not unusual. Sometimes they have to change up her dosages."

"She's at the highest dosage the doctor feels comfortable using," Dommie whispered.

*Breathe.*

"That's fine," I said, even though it didn't feel fine, even though it felt very *not* fine. "Are there any alternatives?"

"Yeah," Dommie said.

Relief. It was a heady motherfucker.

"But—" My sister broke off, sighed.

Relief. It was heady *and* could disappear like a puff of smoke in the sky on a windy day.

There and gone in an instant.

"But what?"

"But," Dommie whispered again, "it's expensive."

Of course it was. "How expensive?"

"It's not covered by Mom's insurance, and they won't."

"You mean the doctor tried to file a prior authorization?"

Silence. Blank. Dommie's voice small when she murmured, "I think she mentioned something like that. They submitted paperwork to say Mom needed it, but her insurance denied it, and then they denied it on the appeal too."

Of course they did. Because what was the point of insurance companies actually covering anything for their clients without a fight?

"Do you need me to fill out some paperwork?" I asked. "Appeal that decision?"

"I...don't know," Dommie said. "Apparently, they've been trying to do that for a while. After the first time, the doctor appealed three times and was denied every time."

I slid to a halt at a red light, just resisted the urge to rub my temples. "I'll call the doctor in the morning, work out if it's worth it to keep fighting."

"Really?"

"It's Mom. Of course I'll do that."

I'd gotten damned good at filing insurance paperwork, at fighting and spending hours on the phone to make sure our mom got the care she needed.

Worry in my sister's words. "It's just...the doctor says it's been months, sissy. Months that the medication hasn't been working and Mom and the office have been appealing. If she doesn't have medication, she can't get better and we m-might l-lose—"

"Breathe, honey. Just take a minute and *breathe*."

Dommie, for once in her stubborn-filled life, stopped and listened to me.

Even though I was fighting my temper.

Because, Christ, my mom never changed. Hiding this shit from me, from us.

Again.

This was what had gotten us all into this mess in the first fucking place, what had nearly broken me with the weight of responsibilities that never should have been mine.

What had driven me to make decisions I couldn't regret because they'd saved my family.

But decisions that I resented.

Especially when I had the feeling I was about to add another to that tally.

I exhaled silently, pulled forward when the light changed, glancing behind me before I changed lanes. "Good, Dommie," I said softly when my sister's breaths came slow and steady. "I'll call the doctor in the morning. If she thinks that process with the insurance is going to take a long time or be a losing battle, I'll get her to put in a prescription and I'll pay for it out of pocket."

"But she says it's expensive and there's no...what do you call it...general type?"

I turned into my apartment complex. "Generic?"

"Yeah, there isn't a generic."

Great.

I stifled a sigh. "It's fine, Dom. Promise."

"But fall tuition for Gabe is going to be due soon and—"

Now I *did* rub my temples, though thankfully, I managed to keep my sigh silent. "I'm working for the Breakers, remember?" I said lightly after I'd pulled herself together. "I have plenty for the tuition and whatever meds Mom needs. You just focus on your classes and work and let me worry about the rest of it, okay?"

"It's not fair that you have to—"

"Dommie," I broke in, pulling into my parking spot, suddenly too exhausted to break this down any further. "I'm good. I promise," I added when my sister would have pushed. "But I just got home and it's late, and frankly, I'm tired. Can we talk after I speak with the doctor?"

My sister's uncertainty drifted through the airwaves.

But to her credit, Dommie agreed. "Okay, big sis."

"I love you. Talk soon, yeah?"

We hung up, and I dropped my head onto my steering wheel.

Breathed.

Maybe let a tear or two escape.

Then I went into my apartment, dug into the back of my closet, and...I got to work.

I had a prescription to pay for.

# SIX

Theo

"ARE you sure you don't need me to pick you up some—"

I groaned, threw myself back against the couch. "For the love of God, Mom. Please lay off about the condoms."

She slipped a coaster beneath my beer. "I was just going to ask if you needed me to pick you up some fruit." A tilt of her head toward the kitchen. "It's a wasteland in that fridge."

"Boy's got beer and milk," my stepdad, Roger, said. "That's enough to keep a grown man going."

"He's a professional athlete," my mom protested. "He works hard and needs good nutrition to fuel my body."

"Does that not include beer?" Roger asked, plunking his own beer down onto the coffee table next to mine.

My mom sighed, slipped a coaster beneath it. "No, that doesn't include beer."

Roger glanced at me, shrugged as if to say, *"Women. What can you do?"*

I chuckled and took a sip of my beer, happy that things

were different now, that my mom was happy and had some good in her life.

It had taken a while.

It had just been the two of us for long enough that I'd worried.

Now, though, she had Roger and Lana and Rose. Who were currently raiding the "wasteland" that was my fridge. It might not have fruit, but like Roger had pointed out, it had beer and milk.

And tapioca pudding.

Personally, I couldn't stand the stuff, but from the moment my sisters were old enough to eat the lumpy dessert that was cloyingly sweet enough to make my teeth ache, they'd gone crazy for it.

Which was why I heard the plastic drawer in my fridge slide open and twin squeals of delight.

Even though they were in high school, a freshman and sophomore, respectively.

"You spoil them," my mom said softly, settling in with a glass of red that I'd picked up especially for her.

Because she deserved spoiling too.

It was why I was having them stay, even though my fridge was a wasteland (that was what DoorDash was for, helping hockey players with empty fridges left and right). I'd made breakfast reservations in the morning and then had a spa day planned for the girls, a tee time for me and Roger. Guest rooms were made up. VIP treatment arranged at the arena. No, I hadn't gotten around to a big grocery shop, but I had put the time in to make certain they all knew how important they were to me.

Because they were my family.

I'd never felt like an outsider, even after the truth had come out about my dad and my mom had gotten remarried to Roger, the girls coming along shortly afterward.

It would have been easy for them to shut me out—biology trumping half-siblings.

But they hadn't. Not Roger. Not Lana and Rose.

I was lucky, and I knew it. Blended families were complicated, especially when it came with the baggage of my gem of a sperm donor.

My parents—and for all intents and purposes, Roger was more of a parent than my biological father ever had been—never made it look anything but easy. Even when money was tight, and the story was everywhere, and we'd had to deal with my bio dad's shit more times than I could count.

So, yeah, I was lucky.

And I knew it. Which was why I made up spare beds and stocked tapioca pudding and set up massages and mani-pedis.

My family lived in California.

It was a trek to come back east to Baltimore, especially with how busy the girls were. But they'd flown in for the game anyway—even though I was getting on a plane straight after the matchup the following night—and it was a tight turnaround for them to get the girls back to school for Monday.

That was just what they did.

They carved out time for me.

So I could spoil them.

And next time I'd order in groceries. Including some fruit so that my mom wouldn't worry. Hell, who was I kidding? I was going to come home on Wednesday and my fridge would be full of fixings for a multitude of balanced meals along with the equivalent of a freaking fruit orchard.

Because that was my mom.

Taking care of me, even though I was a grown adult.

Which meant that I'd probably also have several boxes of condoms squirreled in various locations throughout my house.

Bedside table. Bathroom. Pantry.

Wherever else she thought the need might arise.

Because she cared about safe sex.

Because she'd never been shy about discussing it with me.

Because she was very concerned about my "Lothario ways" after that article Eva had posted on her blog.

Yup. She was a subscriber, and she loved all things Eva Moreno—especially the broadcast games with Eva doing color commentary. And even though my mom was protective of me, she didn't hold any ill regard for the pink-nailed beauty.

One would think that the articles lambasting her son would bother her.

But apparently, Eva Moreno could do no wrong, even if it meant calling me out.

My mom had just shrugged and said that Eva had a point and I needed to support my defense more.

Was this the truth?

Yes. Unfortunately.

Did I want her to have my back no matter what, even if it was unreasonable and she was ignoring the fact that Eva had brought up good points about my game? Yes.

I didn't want logic.

I wanted outrage, and then to swiftly excise Eva from everyone's minds.

Unfortunately, that wasn't going to happen. Not in my family and not on the team.

The front office knew what they had. My mom appreciated Eva's straight shooting and knowledge of the sport. Roger thought she was hot (he wasn't a sports guy so had to take my mom's opinion of her hockey knowledge as fact). And the girls thought that Eva was the prettiest and funniest and most real woman on social media.

Of course, they didn't know I'd fucked her, that I knew *intimately* she was one of the prettiest women around—and not just her face.

Her tits that I'd lied to her about. Her ass that I hadn't. That pussy that had my mouth watering even now.

Gorgeous, all the way down to her skin.

It was just *inside* that she was a fucking shark.

Still, I wasn't going to burst my mom's bubble. She didn't need any more fodder for that article, and I didn't want to examine too closely why it was out there.

The guilt would come back.

It was much easier to be pissed that she'd crossed a line than to think about all the lines *I'd* crossed.

Logic, see?

Snorting to myself, I smiled when the girls came back into the family room, each with a spoon in hand and a tub of tapioca tucked under one arm. Lana had a roll of paper towels beneath the other and Rose had what they'd gone into the room for in the first place.

Nerts.

The card game of champions.

As in, only *one* of us would survive as champion that evening.

And it would be me.

Because I was the oldest sibling and a professional athlete and—

"Oof," I grunted when Rose dropped into my lap, nearly upending my beer and cramming herself between her and her dad.

She smiled up at me beatifically. "What?" she asked innocently. "Gotta get my spot."

I growled jokingly and tugged at a strand of her hair. "Evil."

"I know." Rose dropped the cards on the table and nudged them in my direction. "Will you shuffle for me?"

"And me," Lana said, shoving herself into my other side, already working at the lid of her pudding.

"I know I taught you two how to shuffle," I pointed out, tugging open the top of the game and extracting five decks of cards.

"You did," Rose agreed.

"So, you can shuffle your own cards."

"Then who will we blame when we lose?" Lana asked innocently.

I'd been extending a pack toward Rose, but that had me turning back toward Lana. "Really?"

Another beatific smile.

A shrug.

I glanced at my mom—saw she was fighting a smile of her own as she shuffled a deck for herself. Roger, at least, took pity on me, snagging Rose's cards. "This way she'll blame me and Lana'll blame you."

I lifted a fist.

Roger bumped it. "Us men gotta stick together."

"Damn right we do," I agreed, opening the cards.

Lana hissed. Rose booed. My mom—having been around hockey players far too often—talked some serious trash.

We shuffled and dealt and played.

And got competitive.

Because that was the Young way.

The game got *intense*.

Because that was *also* the Young way.

And over the next couple of hours, I lost. Terribly.

Normally that would be frustrating, but I was with my family and Lana and Rose were goofs who had victory dances for winning a hand and they spent hours trying to get me to try the pudding, even though I couldn't stand the stuff no matter how many times they forced me to "just have a taste."

And Roger had a sly sense of humor that always got everyone laughing in between rounds.

And my mom was happy, her wine glass refilled more than once.

And I found with all the laughter and happiness and teasing, with all the chaos...I didn't think of Eva.

Not once.

Not until I went to bed and the house quieted around me.

*Then* the memory of her body pressed against mine meant that sleep eluded me for hours.

And that my dreams—when I finally managed to drift off—were filled with pink fingernails and soft whispers.

# SEVEN

Eva

I SLIPPED OUT from the arena, leaned back against the wall.

I'd color commentated that evening, and it had gone well, so much so that the voice of the play-by-play, Tommy Hilkens, had told me he would be surprised if they didn't invite me back for even more games next season. I'd barely withheld my squee, had barely resisted the urge to lift my hand so Tommy could smack his palm against mine, had barely stopped myself from jumping with joy and embarrassing myself in front of the broadcast crew.

Thankfully, I had held it together long enough to smile, gather my shit, and take off my mic.

Then I'd hauled ass for the bathroom and squeed sub-audibly (who knew who was listening through the door or walking by and might overhear?).

There. Done.

Happiness banked. Relief stoked.

I needed more games to pay for the medication because I'd

spoken with the doctor a couple of days ago and the insurance company several times since then and even if insurance did eventually approve the prescription, it wasn't going to be soon.

But my mom needed it, so I'd gone that morning and picked it up.

And paid for it out of my pocket.

And fuck, it was almost crippling.

Anyway, Tommy's news was good news—because more games meant more money.

Which was a good thing.

It was *always* a good thing when I had a mom to take care of and three siblings to look after and tacos to eat.

That was why I'd only made a quick stop to the locker assigned to me off the broadcast booth, picking up my purse, my notebook, and my trusty set of pens before I'd headed for the players' locker room, intending on asking all the questions I'd spent hours preparing the night before, had been thinking about during every spare moment during the game.

The playoffs were just around the corner. The race was getting tight.

And I needed content for my blog to stay relevant.

Only...Theo was down there.

I'd heard his voice echoing out into the hall as I'd approached the room, eyes on my notebook, already uncapping my pen, my recording app open on my cell.

Ready to work.

Yet unable to take another step forward.

That I could identify his voice over the din of other noises was concerning, but there had been a lot of concerning things about Theo from the very beginning.

Like the fact that he'd snapped at me during our first interview, and I'd gotten mad...then hadn't backed down.

Like the fact that I *should* have distanced herself when I'd begun to actively seek him out for interviews more than the other guys.

Like the fact that proving myself to him had become critically important to me for some reason.

Like...the fact that we'd fucked.

And it had been life changing and I could *not* stop thinking about it.

Hence the escaping and avoiding and trying not to think about how the man was built, and that his cock was magnificent, and he knew how to use it—and how his lips and teeth and tongue and fingers had felt—

He'd blown my mind.

I hated that.

Almost as much as the fact that he'd moved right on.

Ouch, yeah?

But he was Theo Young. He had a revolving door of women and an allergy to commitment—or at least an allergy to committing to just *one* woman.

And I was just one woman.

An average one at that, with more than enough baggage to send the average *man* packing.

Let alone a man like Theo Young.

So why couldn't I just put him out of my mind? Why did it feel like I'd now been ruined for all other men?

Maybe I should switch to women. I liked a good set of boobs, could get behind curves—

Ha.

Who was I kidding?

I liked hard and built and thick.

And Theo.

I'd really liked him. That glimpse he'd given me of himself over beers, how he'd held me close and talked to me gently. And...it stung that he hadn't even let me stay the night. Hell, that he hadn't even let me catch my breath. He'd fucked me senseless, sent me on my way, and yeah, being blown off hurt, but it wasn't exactly a surprise. I was me. He was him.

"Sucker," I whispered, eyes stinging.

I'd been dumb. That was all. I'd thought the night was something else.

And so...I needed to get over it.

Time to get on with work—which, uncomfortably, was in the Breakers' locker room.

Now was the time to prove he didn't affect me, to ignore what happened, to demonstrate that he meant nothing to me, that sex wasn't something I continued to think about (lies!).

Lies or not, I had grit.

"You have grit," I repeated aloud—just to prove that fact to myself—as I shored up my spine, preparing myself to go back in. I was going to interview him like normal, to report on him like I always did.

Were all my stories nice and kind?

No, but that wasn't because I had a personal vendetta—no matter what the man thought.

I told it straight.

That was it.

And yeah, so what if I'd sucked the guy off, and he'd still been ready to fuck me senseless? So what if my pussy had throbbed for two straight days after we'd fucked, and so what if I'd left his bed feeling like I'd run a marathon—something I didn't bother with because exercise, blegh.

Fucking.

That was all we'd had.

There wouldn't be any catching of feelings. Definitely no repeat performances. Just...moving on.

So, no, not all the stories I wrote about Theo were nice, but that wasn't because we'd fucked. I just...didn't shy away from tough questions, and he'd made it clear that my tough questions, that my reporting in general, made him unhappy.

But, I repeated, *moving* on.

Making the best of it. Doing my job.

Getting opportunities I'd dreamed of and staying busy enough that dealing with Theo Young would continue to get easier.

Unless he eviscerated me in front of Smitty and Cas and Raph and Julie and Lake Jordan again.

Made me feel like the lowest kind of scum.

Something that, surprisingly, was harder to get over than never having his dick inside me again, never tasting his skin, or feeling his big body come over mine.

He didn't like me.

He didn't respect me.

And I'd *still* gotten wet in the face of all that derision. One little apology, a couple of beers—

And I'd gotten naked.

I was despicable. And pathetic. And desperate. And—

The heavy metal door swung open so fast that I didn't have the chance to stop it, to dodge it. The panel of steel slammed into me—nose to toes—and then the pain was flooding my senses, sending me to my knees on the concrete.

Hurt cascading through me.

But then there was warmth—*liquid* warmth. Blood gushing out of my nose, dripping down...onto my blouse.

Shit.

Not the expensive silk blouse I'd borrowed from my sister.

It cost who knew how much—and I was terrified it would be a lot, considering that Dommie had expensive taste and saved up to only buy the best of the best.

That wasn't the worst of it.

Nope.

There was something even more terrible than the thought of having to replace an overpriced shirt, than the pain in my kneecaps and my face and my hands and my chest and my toes.

It was the *voice*.

"Shit, I'm sorry," the man said, frantic hands on my arms, my shoulders, my waist. "Are you okay?"

The voice.

I heard it in my fantasies, my dreams, my nightmares.

Rough and soft, like velvet sandpaper, if that was even a thing.

And I supposed it was.

At least in Theo Young's world.

# EIGHT

Theo

FOR A SECOND, I didn't process who was on her knees, white blouse stained crimson, bloody hair sticking to a gushing nose.

Then Eva was pushing up to her feet, was shoving out from my hold, spinning away.

Her shoulder hit the metal panel of the door with a sickening thunk that had my heart squeezing and gut sinking, but she didn't stop, just kept her hands clamped to her face as she sidestepped the steel door and took off through the parking lot.

Leaving her phone and pens and purse scattered on the ground, her notebook face down on the concrete, pages bent this way and that around the spiral of metal.

"Eva!" I growled, taking off after her, catching up in just a couple of steps.

"I'm fine," she said, the words muffled with her hands over her face, the blood still gushing, dripping down her chin, her throat. "Go away."

"Stop," I snapped, snagging her arm.

A violent jerk had her breaking free again.

Hurrying away again.

"At least wait while I get your stuff—"

She froze, hands slipping away from her face for a second.

But that second was enough to have guilt tearing through me, scouring my skin from the inside out. *I'd* done that.

"Shit, Eva, I—"

Her hands shifted, covering herself again, moving away again—only this time she was heading back for the building, bending and gathering her stuff with one hand, the other still clamped to her nose and mouth.

I hurried over, started shoving stuff into her bag, wondering why she didn't have her backpack because it seemed impossible that the sheer number of pens would fit in the small black leather bag, let alone the notebook whose pages I carefully smoothed and straightened.

"Just leave it," she muttered when I struggled to shove yet another pen inside.

"I've got it." But Jesus fuck, *how* had this woman fit this much shit into her purse?

"It's fine," she snapped, yanking it out of my hold...and dumping the contents for a second time.

"Christ," I growled, reaching for the spread of pens—

"I'm fine! I said I'm fine, and I fucking *mean* it." She snatched her purse from me, started shoving the contents in one-handed.

I grabbed a handful of pens. "You're bl—"

"I'm fine!" She snatched a pen from me. Then another. Getting blood on my hands, but I'd had her tongue in my mouth, my tongue in her pussy. A nosebleed didn't worry me... aside from the fact that it was *still* bleeding, and she was worried about pens.

Instead of fighting her and prolonging the nosebleed, I just handed over her belongings.

Which she expertly packed, even with one hand.

Women were amazing.

She stood, hitched her purse over her shoulder, fingers of one hand still pressed to her face, and glanced down.

Her shoulders slumped, eyes closing for one long moment.

Then she sighed.

Turned away.

Maybe I would have let her go, ended the painful—for her, certainly; for me, painful in the sense that I felt guilty for hurting her—interaction.

Maybe I *should* have just let her go.

Okay, I definitely should have let her go. Put us both out of our misery. Gone back into the locker room, got my shit, and left.

But...she stumbled.

With her purse over her shoulder and her hand over her face, she wavered, caught her toe, and nearly went down.

I was already moving, catching her before she ended up on the ground again.

"What are you—?"

I'd stopped thinking. I'd stopped caring about what I should or shouldn't do. I'd stopped caring about anything except for the fact that she was bleeding and hurting and had almost gone down a second time.

A heft had her in my arms, her body cradled against mine.

She smelled like flowers...tinged with iron.

Because of me.

"Put me down," she snapped, wiggling against me, squirming against my hold.

"Shut up," I ordered, turning back for the door, tugging it

open, ignoring her protests, ignoring the fact that the last time I'd opened it, I'd hurt her.

That I'd been upset.

That I'd been *pissed* and she'd gotten caught in the crosshairs.

And she had been hurt.

God, I was such an asshole.

"Don't tell me to shut up," she gritted out.

"Then stop fighting me when you're ready to fall on your face," I growled. "You're hurt. You're bleeding. Let me take care of you."

"First"—her words were icy bullets—"I can take care of myself."

I sniffed, not willing to give on this, even though it was quite clear that Eva was more than capable of looking after herself...if she hadn't been reamed by a door two minutes before, that was.

"Second," she went on, not acknowledging my scoff, "even if I found myself in a situation where I *couldn't* take care of myself, the last person on Earth I'd ask for help from is you."

I couldn't fault her logic.

"Third," she sneered, "*you're* the reason I'm bleeding in the first place!"

Since that was the truth, I didn't argue, just kept walking, ignoring the looks people were giving me—I didn't often carry bleeding, protesting women through the hallways of the arena. Luckily—since Eva was the one doing the protesting and she was doing an excellent job of it—she didn't notice the looks she was getting, didn't notice that we were drawing no little amount of attention.

Which meant that everyone would be privy to this scene in the hallways.

In minutes.

Maybe seconds.

And they'd be nosy fuckers—Smitty especially, but the rest of them would be equally as bad.

And...there would be questions and shit-giving and...

I'd slammed the door into this woman's face.

No, it wasn't on purpose, but I still needed to make sure she was good.

So, I kept walking, kept carrying her, striding through the maze of hallways until I found the room that I needed.

It wasn't empty of everyone but the person I needed—my luck wasn't that good. The training room, especially after a home game, was always busy, and even though it was jam-packed with my teammates (though thankfully not Smitty), I knew I was lucky my family wasn't here for this game. They were safely back in California, busy with their own lives and not aware of door-slamming and bloody noses.

For now, anyway.

Who knew what they'd hear through the grapevine.

The grapevine that was currently staring at me, mouths hanging open.

Sam—our head trainer—moved first, bustling over to me and Eva and taking one look at the latter's face before ordering me over to one of the tables. "Set her there and be careful about it."

"I'm fi—" Eva began.

But Sam...Sam was a scary motherfucker. She was smart, tough, and took absolutely no shit from anyone. And she was used to ordering stubborn hockey players around. One petite, curvy—albeit stubborn—sports blogger and color commentator wouldn't scare her.

Case in point?

Eva's protests shriveled up, and she didn't move when I set her on the black faux leather-covered table.

"What happened?" Sam asked as she bustled back over, first aid kit in hand.

"I walked into a door," Eva said before I could own up.

Sam froze, gauze in hand, brows lifted. Then shook her head and gingerly peeled Eva's hand free. "Seriously?"

A shrug paired with a self-deprecating smile that looked positively gruesome with the blood staining her face. "I never said I was graceful." She propped her elbows beneath her. "Can you help me stop the bleeding?"

Sam's eyes flicked to mine.

"She might have had some help running into the door," I admitted.

Sam's brows lifted further.

"I wasn't looking and pushed open the door too hard and—"

"I was standing behind the door," Eva interjected, sounding oddly like she was defending me. When she had absolutely no reason to do so. When she should be holding my feet to the fire and milking this for every headline she could.

*Playboy Player Pounds Peaceful Passerby.*

"That was my first mistake. And it won't be my last, I'm sure," she added lightly. "Next time, I'll run into a doorknob." She winked at Sam. "Try to make things interesting."

I exhaled, suddenly wanting to throttle her.

She was hurt and making jokes.

Sam studied us both then shook her head. "I'm not sure I want to know. You"—she jabbed a finger in my chest—"get an ice pack. You"—a jerk of her hand toward the table—"settle back and let me take a look—"

The door to the training suite slammed open, bouncing against the wall in a way that had me wincing and Eva jumping.

"Yup," Eva muttered, "exactly like that."

Sam sighed.

Smitty prowled into the room like the gossip seeker he was, shit-eating grin spreading on his face when he spotted the scene. "What's this I hear about blood?"

# NINE

Eva

"I'M NOT A FUCKING INVALID," I grumbled, pushing against Theo's chest.

His grip didn't loosen.

At all.

Even though I was pushing with all of my strength.

Admittedly, my arms were puny when it came to dueling with Theo's, but I worked out. Lifting tacos to my mouth counted as exercise, right?

Definitely.

Biceps curls for days.

But not a workout that would help me in that moment, though, what with Theo carrying me up the stairs.

If I fought too hard—and for some reason managed to overpower him with my puny arms—we might tumble down the stairs. Then I'd have to write a blog post about his injuries and fudge over my involvement in them.

Plus, it would hurt.

Sigh.

So, I pushed, but not hard. And waited as he carried me, as he paused at the top of the stairs and glanced down at me, both brows lifted.

"What?" I muttered, deliberately looking away, my heart skipping a beat with his face so near.

He huffed out a breath. "Are we still fighting about this?"

"Fighting about what?" I asked, genuinely confused.

I blamed it on being cradled against his chest, his arms tight around me, his mouth close, and his spicy scent surrounding me, filling up my senses. My brain had gone to mush because my pussy was on high alert and—

He jiggled me.

Sharply enough that the haze of need in my mind was dislodged. "What?" I snapped.

"Tell me which door is yours, stubborn woman."

Oh. Fighting about *that*.

"If you put me down, I could just walk to my own door and both of our nights could be done."

His arms tightened, and I braced, ready to be jiggled again. But he just sighed again and started forward.

"What are you doing?"

"I'm going to knock on every door until I find one that no one answers."

"What?" That made no sense.

"And then I'm going to dig your keys out of that purse of yours and unlock it."

That was just...dumb. "It's after midnight," I pointed out. "People aren't going to answer their doors."

A shrug, my body bouncing against his in response. "Then I guess I'm going to pry those keys away from you sooner than expected."

"I—" I shook my head. "Why don't you just look at my ID?"

He froze, hands tightening on my body. Then his lips curved up. "Good idea."

"Wh—*ah!*" I was suddenly on my feet, my purse plucked from my hands, his big one rooting around inside the black leather. "Hey!" I snapped. "Stop that. Get your hands out of—"

He pulled back, my keys dangling from one finger. "Found them."

But even as I was still sputtering about his gall, he stuck his hand back into my purse and yanked out my wallet.

"Hey!"

He undid the snap, stared down (presumably at my ID in the plastic-covered holder), and I watched his lips curve. "Number six, huh?"

I made a disgusted sound. "It has nothing to do with you, asshole."

"Tell that to another number six, yeah?"

I rolled my eyes. "You realize that six is a defenseman's number, don't you?"

He scooped me up again, purse hitting my stomach. "You realize that, long ago, I started as a defenseman."

Shock rippled through me. "Really?" I asked, the word coming unevenly as he carried me down the corridor and stopped in front of my door.

"There's something Eva Moreno doesn't know about me?" He stuck the keys in the lock, shifting me from arm to arm like I weighed nothing, then he turned them. The bolt disengaged and he shoved open the door. "Well, color me surprised," he added sarcastically, stepping over the threshold and moving to the couch.

Placing me on it gently.

Carefully.

My heart squeezed, and I bit the inside of my cheek.

That was the memory of his dick raising its head, the magical taco between my legs trying to convince me that our night hadn't actually been a mistake.

*Take off your clothes*, it coaxed. *See where this night can go.*

I knew exactly where it could go.

Been there, done that, got the signature guacamole.

"I know enough about you," I told him, pushing up when he moved away from me, when he turned and crossed the room to close and latch the door.

"Yeah?" he asked softly. "Do you?"

"Do you doubt that?" I countered.

"Nope." The p at the end popped with that pronouncement. "But I've also realized how little I actually know about you." He leaned back against the closed door. "So, what gives, Stubs?"

Putting aside *Stubs* for the moment—which I, unfortunately, had a thought regarding what it was short for—I glared at Theo. "I have no idea what you're talking about."

"Don't you?" His eyes flicked around the space.

A moment of panic had my head swiveling, my gaze searching for something incriminating that I might have left out. But, just as quickly, I saw that everything was just as it should be. Couch, relatively clean space, bland furnishings, an obscene amount of throw pillows because I could never resist the home goods section at Target.

Normal.

Except for...

"What?" I asked, moving to the ring light and quickly folding it up. "A girl needs good lighting."

He smiled sardonically. "For when you talk about hockey in your pajamas with your hair a mess?"

"So, you *do* watch me," I teased, surprised to see his cheeks go red. Surprised that his gaze dropped to his feet and didn't lift again. "I thought you hated reporters," I found myself commenting into the silence that fell between us.

Gently.

Me. *Gentle?*

What the fuck?

Unfortunately, before I could kick myself too much for that, his head popped up and I couldn't take my gentle back and—

"I *do* hate them," he said softly.

That settled heavily in my stomach.

Okay, no, that made me feel like shit.

Something that was becoming far too familiar when it came to this man.

"Oh," I whispered.

"My sisters think you're the greatest," he said, pushing off the door and stepping close to me. "Did you know that?"

Mutely, I shook my head.

"Not only do they love that you give their big brother crap, but they think you're so *real.*"

I paused, considered the words, the tone, the way his gray eyes were piercing straight through mine. "And," I said softly, "the implication is that I'm not real because I sometimes use a ring light to film my videos?"

One big shoulder lifted then fell. "*I* didn't say it."

"Right," I muttered. "But I did."

Another shoulder lift, another drop.

Cute.

"Why?" I found myself asking, even though I should be showing him the door, should be putting us both out of our misery.

Letting us both get to bed.

His head tilted to the side. "Why do I hate you?"

Ouch.

I rocked back on my heels, breathed silently, cursing myself for the fact that stung as I did some studying of my own feet. "Right," I whispered, shaking my head, knowing that I'd had more than enough punishment for one evening. "It's time for you to go—"

Fingers on my cheek, sliding down my skin, cupping beneath my jaw, drawing my head up.

And he was there again, close and strong and male and...

Hating me.

I could see it in his eyes.

But only for a second, only for a moment before his mouth was closing the distance between ours, his lips hitting mine, tongue sliding inside to tangle with mine.

Hot. Wet. Hard.

A little rough. One hand on my hip, drawing my body flush to his, and I didn't pull back, didn't draw away like I should have. Instead, I just allowed him to part my lips, to kiss me senseless, to melt my body.

For his.

For *him*.

Heart pounding, desire liquid between my legs, I reached for him, my fingers going to the bottom of his shirt, drifting beneath, brushing the molten skin on his abdomen. Needing him, wanting him, *touching* him—

He tore his mouth from mine, leaving me standing there, chest heaving, legs shaky.

Pussy needy.

"I'll tell them you use a ring light," he rasped.

I blinked, brows drawing together, and opened my mouth.

But he was already turning away, already walking across my living room. *Then* he was already at my front door.

Opening it.

Walking out.

The door clicked closed behind him.
Leaving me alone.
With my ring light.
Alone.
Like always.

# TEN

Theo

"BEAT UP ANY INNOCENT WOMEN TODAY?"

I paused in my set, fingers clenching on the dumbbell I cradled against my chest.

Like I'd cradled Eva.

And it felt just as light, just as inconsequential as her weight had been as I'd carried her up those stairs, along the corridor, through her front door.

It would get heavy though, the weight of the dumbbell, the weight of her.

It always did.

Until I had to let it go, let it roll to the ground, and move on to another exercise.

Move on to another woman.

"Fuck off," I muttered, moving again, ignoring Smitty hovering, that damned shit-eating grin in place on his face.

Like he'd just made the funniest joke ever.

Like he was the cleverest bastard on the planet.

Fucker.

Smitty didn't *fuck off*, though, and he didn't pick up on the fact that I was deliberately ignoring him. He just stood right beside the incline bench I was laying on. I had hooked my feet around the supports at the top, and then, with the dumbbell hovering above my chest, I sat up, lay back, and then sat up again.

Over and over again.

Until my abs burned and my arms shook and the voices in my head disappeared.

Unfortunately, *Smitty* didn't disappear.

Just stood there, chattering about nothing and everything—okay, it was about something, and something important, a program his wife was writing that would be licensed for free to school districts, helping neurodivergent kids learn.

Smitty was dyslexic, and he did a lot of work with charities that supported kids, not only those with dyslexia, but those who had other challenges too.

So, Smitty might be annoying, but he was a good guy with a big heart.

Which was why I didn't drop the dumbbell on my teammate's foot. Well, that, and also because the fucker probably wouldn't feel it. And I supposed, the team needed the hulking brute on the ice, and they needed me full strength.

Not with a broken toe.

So, I kept hold of the dumbbell and did sit-ups and listened to Smitty prattle.

"You know that flat abs aren't required for hockey players," Smitty pointed out.

Maybe not, but women liked them.

"Not all of us can be barrel-shaped," I pointed out in return, lips quirking even though my abs and arms were burning.

A smack to my balls that nearly had me dropping the dumbbell.

"Asshole," I grumbled.

Smitty grinned then said, "Kailey likes my body."

"Congratulations," I muttered, "I'll have the gold medal made up."

A snort, but thankfully Smitty didn't hit me in the balls again. He just picked up a dumbbell of his own and started going through his own off-ice routine.

His mouth didn't stop, though.

Of course not.

He kept talking, and I kept ignoring him. Well, kept ignoring any and all overtures trying to direct the conversation toward Eva. I didn't want to talk about her, didn't want to think about her and her body or that sweet cunt of hers or the fact that she'd had a pair of black eyes when I'd watched her leave her apartment that morning.

Sitting in my car, gaze glued to the stairs that led down from her apartment, watching as she hurried across the pavement and got into another car.

Because hers was at the arena.

Because I'd forced her to accept my ride home—arguing there right in front of everyone—and I'd expected her to...

What?

Ask me for a ride when she didn't have my number?

When I'd left her like I had...after kicking her out like I had...after *acting* like I had.

Apparently so.

Because I'd almost gotten out of my car and demanded she let me drive her to her car.

I hadn't been able to sleep once I'd realized I'd left her stranded, had gotten up way too early in the morning, intending on waiting for a reasonable hour and knocking on her door.

And then, knowing I *couldn't* knock on her door, couldn't risk spending more time with her.

More time thinking about her.

But I'd stayed. I'd stayed and I hadn't gone home, even though it was—

"Stupid," I muttered.

"I'm rubber and you're glue," Smitty declared, not missing a beat in his squats. "Whatever you say bounces off me and hits yo—"

I tapped *him* in the balls, busting up when my teammate grunted and nearly dropped the weight he was holding.

Not caring that I'd been an idiot.

Not when I'd finally found a way to shut Smitty up.

Not when I'd gotten my teammate back.

Not when I was thankful Smitty turned his attention elsewhere as I moved through the remainder of my exercises—sit-ups, extensions, squats of all kinds (goblet, split, sumo, pistol), footwork, cardio. And after, stretching, an ice-cold bath, and a visit to Sam. Then I'd showered, gotten dressed, and was just heading out of the practice facility when I came across a cluster of my teammates looking at a phone. Not Smitty and Raph, Cas or Marcel, but a few of the younger guys. Barely twenty, one of them still eighteen, and all living the life sharing a house and a parade of women.

Not that I could comment.

That had been my life. Well, not the sharing a house. I didn't want any part of that. Guys were gross and especially guys who were under the age of twenty-one and living in a fuck palace and couldn't be bothered to so much as wash a dish.

Hence why I'd always lived on my own whenever possible.

"What's that about?" I asked Walker, slowing to a stop and nodding at the gathering.

Walker rolled his eyes. "One of the rookies subscribed to an OnlyFans. Apparently, the girl's got the best body they've ever seen."

"What? They don't get enough pussy as it is?" I asked.

A shrug. "They might be professional athletes, but they're still idiots."

I shook my head. "Even in my worse days."

"Hey," Smitty said, coming up behind us, the big brute a sneaky fucker when he wanted to be, "sex work is real work."

I groaned. "I'm not saying it isn't. I'm saying"—I nodded at the group of man-children—"that them cackling like hyenas and forming their own circle jerk over a pair of tits and a nice body is ridiculous."

"Supposedly, she sits on cakes."

That threw me for a second. "Uh, what?"

"The OnlyFans girl. She makes her money by sitting on baked goods."

I felt my eyes go wide. "Seriously?"

Smitty lifted and dropped those big shoulders in a shrug. "I mean I'd check for myself, but I like my balls where they currently are."

"Kailey's got you that tied up?" Walker joked.

"I love her," Smitty said. "There's nothing to be tied up. But"—he tilted his head toward the rookies who were still moonlighting as cackling hyenas—"you *could* go let me know if that's true."

"Dude." I huffed out a laugh. "Not a chance in hell."

Smitty turned to Walker, lifted a brow.

"I'm on a diet," Walker rebuffed.

I snorted.

Smitty grinned, saluted us. "To everyone raising their very own freak flag and letting it fly."

"To baked goods, you mean," I quipped.

Though, I could do with less freak flag flying in the locker room.

"To red food dye and fondant?" Walker added with a smirk.

I tapped my chin. "Shouldn't it be like...to Devil's food cake or something?"

"Oh, or red velvet." Smitty rubbed his stomach.

"I think *we're* the idiots," Walker muttered.

"Either that, or hungry," Smitty said, his stomach rumbling and supporting the second half of his statement.

"For cake or knowledge?" I asked.

Smitty lifted his hand, tilted it back and forth as though to say, *"A little of this. A little of that."*

Walker huffed out a sigh, shook his head, and turned away, though his mouth was curved. "Right. On that note, I'm out of here."

"Gonna buy a tub of icing?" I asked innocently. "Experiment?"

Though, that wasn't a bad idea.

Icing could be fun...especially with a certain curvy, troublesome blond.

Walker shook his head again, and waved a hand, but he didn't stay to engage with us on any additional joking about baked goods, and, as he left, he didn't poke his head into the circle and confirm the OnlyFans rumors. He just walked out of the locker room and into the hall and didn't come back.

I should have gone with him.

That was something I realized approximately two point two seconds later.

Because Smitty turned to me, and that shit-eating grin was back. "You know that I'm the team's matchmaker, right?"

"Self-appointed, you mean," I muttered, grabbing my wallet and shoving it into my back pocket, hurrying now so I could make my escape. "Because I think Beth and company have strong opinions to the contrary."

"Oh no," Smitty said. "Don't try to distract me. Beth and I are in full agreement on this."

"On the fact that you both need to stop interfering in other people's lives?" I asked, more than a little hopefully.

Smitty dropped his head back and laughed. "You're hilarious."

"There's nothing hilarious about this," I ground out.

"About you being so far gone for Eva that you can't see your hand in front of your face?" Smitty grinned. "I don't know. I find it totally hilarious." A beat. "And so does Beth."

One would think that Raph's fiancée would be busy planning their wedding.

Unfortunately, the tiny dynamo was good at multitasking.

As was Smitty.

Except for when it came to one thing.

The big man was terrified—

"Did you know that wombats poop in cubes?"

Smitty's mouth clicked closed in almost comical fashion, his skin going pale. "Don't you dare, man," he threatened.

"What? Talk about the fact that they're marsupials, but their pouches are backward when compared to—"

A shake of his head, Smitty's eyes panicked. "Don't you talk about those beady-eyed fuckers."

"There are several species of them—"

Smitty clamped his hands over his ears. "La. La. La. La. I can't hear—"

He went on, but I took advantage of my teammate's distraction—*cough*, terror over wombats—and snagged my jacket.

Then got the fuck out of there.

Not engaging in the matchmaking talk.

And not confirming anything about baked goods either.

# ELEVEN

Eva

I'D OPENED the door to my apartment and was expecting tacos.

Again, I was to be disappointed.

Because it was a hockey player.

Though, not the one that had been skating around my mind, slamming into the barriers that surrounded my brain. Rattling boards and glass alike.

The one on my stoop was bigger, brawnier, and had a beard that could have been on a package of paper towels.

Thicker than Theo's.

Okay, Smitty was thicker than Theo overall—

Which sounded dirty.

I just meant that he was one of the biggest guys on the team and standing on my doormat, he took up entirely too much space.

Not as much as Theo did, though, come to think of it.

*He* filled my apartment with his presence, my insides with—

"Did running into that door rattle your innards?"

I blinked.

Smitty snapped his fingers.

I blinked again.

His expression became concerned. "No, seriously, Eva. Do you need to see a doctor?"

*Jesus Christ. Get it together, Moreno.*

"No," I said quickly, rubbing a hand over my hair. "I'm fine. I'm just tired."

"And have a pair of black eyes that rival a hockey player's?"

My mouth hitched up. "Rub it in, why don't you?" I allowed the rest of my smile to form and leaned back against the doorframe. "I'm fine. Really. It was an accident, and I can't say I slept all that well last night"—because it had hurt and because of...well, other things—"but I'm fine today. Just ready to gorge myself on tacos and then go to sleep."

"Tacos?" he asked hopefully.

"Don't you have a girlfriend to go home and eat tacos with?" I countered dryly.

He made a face. "She's at Cheese Night Extravaganza. I have to eat tacos by myself."

"What's a Cheese Night Extravaganza?"

"Why don't you let me come in and I'll tell you?"

This wasn't the first time Smitty had shown up at my apartment door. He'd come a few weeks back, after Theo had—

Well, after Theo had torn me a new asshole in front of more than a few Breakers, a Breakers' significant other, and a player from the Sierra. Julie. Cas. Raph. Walker. Smitty. And Lake Jordan. They'd all witnessed Theo ripping into me, leaving me bleeding—figuratively that time—on the ground.

Smitty had shown up the next night.

I'd pretended to be together then too.

I frowned, that thought fading when I noticed. "What's that in your hand?"

He straightened with a jerk, one arm tucking further behind him. But I'd seen it and, now come to think about it...I sniffed.

"You have my tacos!" I exclaimed, lurching forward and seizing his arm, yanking it toward me, the brown grease-stained bag crinkling.

Smitty winced. "I caught the delivery guy on the stairs."

"Thief!" I accused.

"I'm not going to eat them." He winced again. "Or, anyway, I'm not going to eat them without you."

"They're *my* tacos."

"Okay, so I'm not going to eat them alone, and while *we're* eating them"—he waved the bag-holding hand between us—"together, I'll order more tacos. So many tacos that you won't even know that you've shared *these* tacos and—"

God, I really couldn't hear him mention tacos one more time.

I stepped back, waved him in. "Come on, trouble. Make yourself at home on my couch." I fixed him with a glare. "But there will be no complaints about my choice of TV show."

I had more games to catch up with.

And then I had a date with my favorite polygamist trash TV program.

He lifted the hand with the tacos. "On my honor as a consumer of delicious crunchy tacos."

I narrowed my eyes.

A shrug. "I might have peeked inside the bag."

"*And,*" I added with a glare. "You'll be ordering more tacos right now."

He nodded.

"And guacamole."

Another nod.

"And extra nachos."

More nodding.

Satisfied, I allowed him to pass, shut and locked the door, and went to get some plates from the kitchen. "Do you want a beer?"

"Do hockey players like their skates sharp?"

I huffed out a laugh at sheer cheesiness and shook my head. But I grabbed two beers, tucked the plates under my arms, and then went back into the family room, plunking onto the couch next to him.

"I really *am* okay, you know," I said softly.

He'd already unwrapped a taco, ate half of it with one bite, his other hand typing on his phone.

(And hopefully ordering more tacos).

"I know," he said, after a moment, pointing the screen in my direction, and to my relief I saw that he was putting in an order, one that was significantly larger than what I'd made.

When I nodded, he tapped the screen to add a few more things then hit the button to submit.

"If you know, why are you here?" I asked after he'd passed me one of the wrapped tacos.

"You were hurt." A shrug. "I don't like it when women get hurt."

I sucked in a silent breath, turned my focus to my food. "Oh," I whispered.

"Hey," he said softly, tilting my head up with a finger under my chin, and his eyes told me that he saw too much in *my* expression. "Eva," he added. "I—"

"It's fine," I said quickly. "I'm just sad that you're plowing through my tacos."

He snorted but didn't bite on my joke. A first for him.

And I found out why a moment later when he said, "He didn't mean to do it, you know that, right?" A quiet question that sneakily took my breath.

I forced a smile. "I know. And really, I shouldn't have been standing behind the door in the first place. It's not Theo's fault that I was in the line of fire."

Smitty studied me, quietly, gently, *deeply*. Then he tugged a strand of my hair. "You realize that you're stuck with us now, don't you?"

"Because I have Breakers-induced black eyes?" I asked lightly.

Another tug before he finished off the taco. "Because you're part of the team."

I scoffed. "I make TikToks and give Theo a hard time."

"Exactly." He grabbed out more tacos, plunked one on my plate, unwrapped another. "That's more than half the guys on the team do."

He said that so confidently—and did it with such focused taco consumption—that I had to laugh. "You're terrible."

"No, I'm Smitty."

I laughed again.

Cheese factor one million.

Speaking of, I needed to find out what the heck a Cheese Night Extravaganza was. But as I opened my mouth to ask, he nudged my plate toward me. "And *you're* downing that taco like a champ because I have ten more coming our way."

I grinned, and picked up my plate, got to work on consuming my taco, and I did it—funnily enough—smiling.

Because...

Stuck with Smitty, with the Breakers...that actually sounded kind of nice.

And it *was* nice. That night, anyway.

We watched hockey. We watched my favorite polygamist TV show.

He helped me make a TikTok.

But now Smitty had gotten word that Cheese Night Extravaganza—apparently an event where much cheese was consumed amongst the ladies of the Breakers—was over, and his woman needed a ride home, so I was clearing our plates (and storing the four tacos we hadn't managed to finish in the fridge for leftovers the next day) and Smitty was slipping on his jacket after he'd deposited the empty beer bottles in my recycling bin.

His eyes went to the kitchen counter. "Is that cake?"

I frowned, glancing between the counter and the big hockey player. "Um, yes?"

The pink bakery box made that fairly obvious, I thought. But...hockey players were confusing, especially when my answer made him grin for some reason. "What kind?"

"Of cake?"

A nod.

"Red velvet," I said.

His smile widened. "I love red velvet."

Smitty was weird, but he'd bought my tacos and made my night nice. And...well, even if it didn't last, I felt like I was part of something for that night anyway. So, I didn't bother trying to make sense of all his weirdness, just grabbed a knife and folded back the top of the box.

"Here," I said, cutting a piece and scooping it onto a paper plate. Then another because he couldn't go home to his woman with cake and not bring enough to share.

"You sure?" he asked, but I noticed that he eagerly accepted the plates after I'd wrapped them in cling film.

"I'm sure," I said. "My sister works at a bakery. She brings me extras all the time, and I can't finish them."

Smitty grinned. "You're my new best friend."

I rolled my eyes, but I was grinning too.

And I was still grinning long after he'd left.

Stuck with Smitty as a friend.

Yeah, that wasn't a hardship.

# TWELVE

Theo

LAKE JORDAN WAS a pain in the ass.

He was big, strong, and fast, and his hands were unrivaled.

Swear to fuck, every time I thought I was past the fucker, Lake would somehow get his stick in front of me or between our bodies and he'd get it on the puck, disrupting the play outright, or disrupting it enough to make me fuck up and bobble shit—

"I thought I was done seeing you this season," I grunted, shoving Lake back and finding myself pinned harder to the boards as we dug for the puck, a clump of skates and bodies and sticks.

Lake shoved me a little harder. "Not my fault you don't look at the schedule ahead."

I hated playing here, at the Sierra's home rink in Tahoe, hated being up at altitude, the way it made my lungs feel a little tight. Like I couldn't suck in enough air to fuel my muscles, my body, like I couldn't skate fast enough.

Lake Jordan didn't have the same fucking problem.

Of course not.

"Move the puck, boys!" the ref called.

Like that would make us move, make us give up position and risk the other team getting the puck.

From my perspective, I was fine being squeezed against the boards until the whistle blew.

We were in the Sierra's end. A whistle would mean a face-off in their offensive zone, a chance to score, and a line change to get fresh players on to do it.

So, I didn't move.

Not willingly, anyway.

More players joined in, the mass of bodies shifted, and the puck loosened up, squirting between my skates. Luckily, I managed to kick it over to Walker as the scrum continued, and my linemate scooped it up, started hauling ass toward the net.

Players broke apart.

A Sierra forward gave chase.

But Walker had legs, and I only had one defenseman to get around.

The Sierra goalie slid forward, cutting off the angle, taking away much of Walker's space in a fraction of a second with just one levelheaded play.

Fucking goalies.

I shoved Lake back, managed to actually break free of the fucker for a change, and skated hard toward the net.

Lake was on me in a second, but I wasn't going after the puck, wasn't intending to be anything more than a distraction, a potential option the Sierra needed to defend against.

And it worked.

The defenseman saw me coming, adjusted marginally, taking a position that would allow him to better cover both Walker and me.

Lake, skates crunching as he came up behind me, cursed.

But it was too late.

That minute shift gave Walker some space to maneuver.

And, more importantly, it gave *Marcel* space. Marcel who'd been in the scrum with me and was tearing toward the net.

Marcel, who was open and unencumbered and...

Who Walker spotted too.

The puck flew across the ice, hovering over sticks, landing flush on Marcel's tape. He was already hustling—and he was *fast*, dragging the puck around to the left, cutting back in, making a move that was so fast I had a hard time tracking it.

The goalie did too.

The only one who *didn't* seem to have the same problem was Lake, who skated toward Marcel like a bull chasing down a flash of bright red cloth.

Too late, though.

I slid to the side just enough to make contact, just enough to slow down the big fucker, just enough to buy Marcel a half second more time.

I ended up on the ice—since Lake didn't fuck around and I wasn't in a position to brace myself effectively for the contact— but for once, I didn't give a fuck. Because my position on the ice gave me a prime view of Marcel dragging the puck back to the right and flicking it up.

Over the goalie's shoulder.

I popped to my feet, skating in and crashing into Marcel. "Fuck yeah!" I slammed my fist into my teammate's back. "Fuck *yeah!*"

Our celebration was short-lived though, and the Sierra came in and cleared out the front of the net, knocking me and company back away from their goalie.

Knocking me on my ass.

Swear to fuck.

If I didn't start keeping my feet, I was never going to hear the end of it.

"At least buy me a beer first," I muttered as Lake extended a hand, yanking me up to my skates. I couldn't be mad about the shoves, about the contact. We'd been in the crease and near the Sierra's goalie, and if there was one thing that most hockey players got tetchy about, it was protecting our goalie.

"Stay out of the crease," Lake muttered back, "and I won't need to open my wallet."

"I hear you don't do that anyway."

Lake glared.

I smirked at him. "Don't you make girls go halvsies?"

"Christ." Lake dropped his hand as I was halfway up, and I had to scramble to not go down again. "I knew it was trouble when Jules fell for one of you fuckers."

Grinning, I started to skate by him. "Because we're better?"

A flick of his gaze up at the scoreboard—which showed that, even with the goal, the Sierra were still ahead. "Is that what this is?" he asked, skating toward his bench.

Not minding the lighthearted (somewhat, because I still couldn't stand the fucker) chirping, I continued to skate next to Lake on the way to our respective benches. "Or is it because we know too much about the illustrious Lake Jordan—underwear model, sock spokesman, and face of a well-known but shit-tasting vodka company."

"My vodka is delicious."

"If you say so. I'm not a fan of swill made from potatoes."

"Swill." Lake shoved me again, eliciting a cheer from the crowd, who probably assumed Lake was taking offense about the game and not his vodka company. "What are you? A fucking pirate?"

"*Argh.*"

Lake snorted, and thank fuck neither of us were mic'd up for that game.

That was a shit impression, for one, but I knew if Smitty had overheard, my stall would be full of pirate shit.

Eye patches. A stuffed parrot. Peg legs.

I could see it now.

Internally promising myself to never make that sound again, or use the word swill, I started to skate past Lake to end this interaction before it got out of hand.

Or *further* out of hand anyway.

"You know what?" Lake called when I started to step through the door and climb onto the bench.

I glanced back, lifted a brow.

Lake's mouth was curved. "I *will* buy you that beer. A full calorie one even." A beat, his grin growing. "It might put some weight on you. Help you keep your feet."

The Sierra bench erupted in laughter.

Smitty, skating to my end of the Breakers' bench, snorted, but my teammate was my teammate, so he didn't miss a beat when he chirped back, "Your vodka tastes like shit!" A glance back at me. A nod, like he'd done good and was proud of himself for standing up for his teammate.

Of course, Smitty ruined that with a wink, with mouthing, "*Argh.*"

I sighed, shook my head, and focused on the game.

I kept my feet, and we pulled out a tie then went to a shoot-out.

And lost.

Because...fucking Lake Jordan.

Later, after I'd showered, it wasn't too much of a surprise— because Lake fucking Jordan—to find a bright orange box with a well-known white swoosh sitting on the bench in front of my stall. I opened the lid to find a pair of Jordans, along with a note with the name of a bar and a time.

*P.S. Since you're so light on your feet, I figured
I'd give you something to keep you flying.
-L*

"Christ," I muttered, shoving the note back into the box, slamming down the lid.

Hockey players.

Swear to fuck.

They were annoying as shit.

# THIRTEEN

Eva

IT HAD BEEN a week since tacos.

A week without seeing Theo in person.

I'd watched the guys play in California and then in Denver, losing in a shootout the first game, pulling out a definite win in the second.

Now they were home and I'd been commentating—and so busy doing it that I hadn't made it down to the locker room.

So, I still hadn't seen Theo in person since the door-to-face incident.

He was playing better though.

No more articles about him on my blog—well, he'd been in a compilation of good plays on my social media, but whatever had been messing with his head seemed to be resolved.

Ever since that game in Tahoe.

He'd probably got some while on the road.

Which stung...and had me wondering if he'd kicked the woman out before round three.

Probably.

Or maybe not. What did I know?

He'd fucked me and disposed of me like trash. He'd said he didn't like me and kissed me. He was a dick to me in front of people I respected. He fought to take me home because he'd actually hurt me...and then he hadn't checked up on me once since then.

"You're an idiot," I whispered.

"Just so you know," a voice said in my ear, "your mic is still live."

"Right."

We were at a commercial break, and I'd stepped off the set to refill my water, but I'd need to step back on in about ten seconds. Step on and be ready to contribute to the postgame commentary with pithy interjections and plenty of teasing byplay.

The guys I worked with on this segment were funny and quick and former players.

They knew how professional teams functioned. Intimately.

It meant they were stiff competition for me, and I needed to be ready to hold my own at all times.

Not thinking about Theo.

Not even thinking about how much I despised him.

Really. I despised him.

Or that was what I was trying to hold on to. Because if I didn't despise him, if I somehow *liked* him despite how he'd treated me, then I might as well burn my feminist card and put on an uncomfortable underwire bra.

And a too-tight thong.

Because what type of self-respecting woman would I be?

One who wanted to solve the puzzle of Theo Young, who wanted to reconcile the glimpses of nice with the asshole.

But...circling back to self-respecting.

Because I deserved more than just a glimpse of nice, of care.

I deserved...everything.

I'd seen the way that Smitty looked at Kailey. Had seen the protective instincts that seemed to garner each and every one of Cas's movements. Like his body was so in tune with Julie's that his world orbited around hers without thinking.

Like she was the center of *his* universe.

Marcel and Pru were no different. And Beth and Raph were the same.

Oliver—even though his injury meant that he no longer could play—was equally as protective of his woman and team psychologist, Hazel.

And even though I rarely interacted with Luc, the GM of the team, I'd seen enough. He acted like his wife, Lexi, hung the moon.

Was it wrong to want that?

No.

I sighed silently.

No, I wasn't wrong to want it—that devotion and love and partnership. But I also knew it wasn't that simple, that I wasn't the kind of woman who would ever be in a position to have a relationship like that.

At best, I'd end up with someone like my father.

Or maybe, that was at worst. Because I wouldn't put up with someone like that in my life.

I'd seen what it had done to my mother, to my siblings, felt the sting of it myself.

At best, I'd end up with a meaningful career and a nice house.

That would have to be enough.

With that grim—even though I was pretending it wasn't—

thought, I took a sip of water, checked my lipstick in the reflection of a monitor, and marched back on stage.

I had money to earn.

I had medication to pay for.

I had a job to do.

And it didn't involve trading in happy endings.

---

DESPITE MY LACK of happy endings—or my disbelief that one was in the cards for me—I managed to focus on my job.

And I was happy with my performance.

So was the rest of the crew if their smiles were any indication.

My other commentators had even invited me out for a beer.

Something I'd needed to take a rain check for.

Because I was on Mom Duty.

A checkup and some blood work to see if the medication I was paying for out of my future house fund, paying with my heart and soul and dignity, was working.

It had better be.

So, no beer. Not when I had to be up in a handful of hours, and I still needed to work—go through enough of the material I had set aside to review—to come up with some content for my blog and socials.

And I'd do it that night because I wouldn't sleep for a while yet.

Physically and mentally, I was tired.

It was late, after midnight, but sleep wouldn't come. It never did. I'd lie awake, staring at the water stain in my ceiling from the apartment above and go over everything I had said that evening—from the pregame show to the post game and every moment in between—rating it as good or bad or indifferent.

Analyzing.

Knowing I could do better.

Trying to shove away the imposter syndrome.

Beers would have helped.

Staying up later, dulling the edges of those emotions, the failures that wanted to creep in would have helped.

If I could have gotten that drink before going home, staying up to work half the night, not falling asleep until the tendrils of dawn were creeping across the sky, it would have been better. No, it would have been ideal.

But I couldn't.

I had *responsibilities*.

And yes, I said that like it was a four-letter word.

Sometimes being the oldest child sucked. Sometimes being parentified sucked.

Sometimes—

"You need to stop moping, Eva," I muttered, lifting a hand to the security guard manning the booth at the entrance of the underground parking. I turned out of the lot, started to head toward home, but barely got a block before I saw...

"Ugh," I groaned, eyeing the piece of paper tucked beneath my wiper.

I paused, debated, but it was late and dark, and I wasn't going to get out of my car.

So, I hit the wipers instead, let the paper fly off my windshield.

Littering was better than dead.

Nodding to myself, I continued down the road, slowing to a stop at a red light, taking off again when it turned green, and—

"What?"

I glanced down at the steering wheel, trying to discern the odd pull.

The entire car was pulling to the right. Hard, enough that I was really fighting to stay in my lane just to go straight.

"Fuck," I muttered, letting up, slowing to a stop beneath a streetlight and putting my car in park.

I glanced around before I got out and rounded the hood, my phone in hand.

One look told me enough.

The front passenger's side tire was flat.

"*Fuck,*" I muttered again, barely resisting the urge to kick the useless lump of rubber and steel. I walked back around the hood, reached for the handle, intending to get back in my car and call a tow truck.

Only something made me pause, the hairs on my nape prickling.

I stopped, stared into the shadows, trying to pinpoint what the fuck it was...

Right as a man materialized out of the darkness.

And headed straight toward me.

# FOURTEEN

Theo

I WAS FINALLY FEELING good about a series of games.

I was pulling my weight, and a nagging injury—a sore ligament in my wrist—had been cleared up thanks to Sam's militant care.

Plus, I'd gotten a goal and an assist that night.

And we'd won.

*And* I hadn't been an asshole, or spent an overly large amount of time on the ice.

So, there wouldn't be anything on Eva's blog.

Though, to be fair, there hadn't been much about me on the blog for a while now.

She was—as Smitty had pointed out—tough, but fair.

I still could have done without the playboy comments in the first place, but I supposed I had to take my victories where I could get them. There wasn't an article on her blog or TikTok about me slamming a door into her face, no videos of her documenting her black eyes.

The only shit-giving had come from the guys.

But that had been usurped by my new nickname.

Air.

Fucking Lake Jordan.

Sighing, I turned out of the lot, waving at Walker as my teammate and friend got into his own car—a ridiculous sports car that would have had my knees crammed up to my chin if I tried to sit in it, but it fit Walker just fine.

Mostly because he was in shape, but at just under six feet (and five-ten if someone was actually measuring), he was on the smaller end of heights for the team.

But the sport was getting faster.

Players were smaller and lighter, and we couldn't all be big brutes like Smitty.

Though I figured there would always be a place for a big motherfucker or two on a professional roster, especially when we had to protect our goalies and star players.

Meanwhile, I was confident in my current position.

I was producing again. I was back on my game.

And I hadn't gotten yelled at by Coach for at least two games.

So, yeah, I was doing okay.

Even with the new nickname.

Shaking my head, I turned out of the lot, driving down the quiet street, enjoying the silence after the buzz of the crowd, the talking filling the locker room.

Which meant it was the perfect time for my phone to ring.

I snorted, glanced at the caller ID and answered. "Hi, Mom."

"That was a good play tonight, baby."

"Thanks, Mom."

"But you need to make sure that you're in a better position

to support your center on the breakout. You're getting lazy, baby, and that's not like you."

As always, she had the finger on the pulse of what was going on in my game.

"You're right, Mom." In fact, it had been one of the things that Coach had discussed—cough, yelled—at me about a couple of games back.

"It's better than it was," she added quickly, always trying to sandwich the critiques with a positive, "and you've been really good in the neutral zone."

I chuckled. "Coach should put you on the payroll."

"I can tell you boys to shoot more and make sure it hits the net," she teased, referencing two of the favorite things hockey fans liked to yell. "How much will that get me?"

"Top billing," I teased back, pausing at a red light. "How's everyone back home?"

"The girls are busy as always. I'll be so glad when Lana can drive and I don't have to play taxicab anymore." She huffed out a disgruntled breath, but I knew she loved it, knew she loved being there, being the glue that kept our family running. "Did you know that, collectively, they have twenty-six volleyball tournaments this season. Twenty-six! That's half the freaking year! And can they play on the same team? Oh no, of course not! They have to play on two teams each. I don't think I've spent a free weekend with Roger since we got married!"

"You love it," I reminded her.

A huff. "You know I do." A beat. "Plus, I made a color-coded chart to keep organized."

That had me grinning as the signal flicked to green. "Color-coding is optimal."

"Of course it is."

I laughed. "When I come visit this summer, I'll hang with the girls and you guys can take the weekend."

"Really?"

"Yeah—" I paused, gaze hitting on a car parked on the side of the road, hazards on, and headlights breaking through the dark.

"You don't have to do that, baby. I'm just complaining."

"It's—"

I paused again. It was dark, but the headlights were on and the car was parked beneath a streetlight and as I passed by, I...

Realized I knew that car.

Cursing, I flipped a U-turn.

"What's that, baby?" my mom asked.

"Sorry," I said quickly, making another U-turn so I could pull behind the car. "I've actually got to go."

"Everything okay?"

"Fine. I'll call you later, okay?"

We exchanged goodbyes and I hit the button to disconnect just as I stopped behind the car. A second later, I had the door open, was walking up...

To Eva.

Who had her back pressed to the driver's side of her car, palms flattened on the metal panel, gaze glued to the shadows.

"Eva?" I asked softly.

She jumped, hand lifting and clamping to her chest. "Theo," she whispered, hurrying over to me.

She never hurried toward me, not unless it was with a recorder in her hand and a tough question on her lips. But she hurried this time, hurried and didn't stop until she was right next to me.

"What's wrong?"

Her stare went over her shoulder, to the shadows on the side of the road.

"Is there someone there?" I asked.

Her head jerked back toward me, and I watched her tuck

away the fear, the worry, watched her shoulders straighten and chin lift slightly. "I thought I saw someone," she said, voice so even I knew what it hid, would have known what it hid, even without having watched her tuck her emotions away. "Clearly, it's just late and I need sleep."

It *was* late.

But she didn't look tired.

Her eyes were clear. Her body held with a rigid sort of tension that told me she was not only alert but had a heightened awareness of her surroundings.

Yet, the chances of the stubborn woman actually coming outright and telling me what was up were slim.

To none.

Okay, most certainly *none*.

"Why'd you stop?"

A blink, as though surprised I hadn't continued along the previous line of questioning. "What?"

"Why'd you pull over?"

She blinked again. And I watched, again, as she focused, as her expression went neutral. "I have a flat," she said, gesturing with one hand toward the opposite side of her car. "I'm calling a tow truck, so feel free to continue on with your evening."

I might have.

If she didn't glance to the left again, across the nearly empty street to the shadows where two buildings were positioned closely and a narrow alley was mostly shrouded in darkness, I might have.

But she *did* glance over into the darkness.

And...I did something that was either really dumb or exceptionally nice.

Maybe both.

I could have waited for her to call a tow truck, waited until it came and she was safely on her way—even if she argued the entire time.

Only, I was learning about Eva Moreno.

Learning that arguing just made her hackles lift and her stubbornness rear up and—

That was why I moved to the back of her car, tugged at the hatch.

"Pop it," I ordered when it didn't open.

"What?"

"Pop your trunk."

Then when she didn't react, didn't acknowledge me, I closed the distance between us, snagged her keys, and hit the button to open the trunk.

*Then* I got to work.

# FIFTEEN

Eva

IT TOOK me far too long—and much longer than I was happy about—to react to Theo taking my keys from me and opening the trunk of my car.

Digging around inside of it.

"What are you—?"

Something clanked, something else hit the pavement, and I finally got my shit together. With another glance over at the shadows, I finally got my ass in gear, hustling to where Theo was pawing through the belongings in my trunk, a la a bear searching for crumbs in amongst the worn carpet.

And certainly finding them.

Keeping my car clean wasn't exactly high on my list of priorities.

It was on my mom's though.

Which meant that anytime I drove my mom and didn't want to get a lecture about an organized car meaning I had an organized life—hilarious, considering the state of my mom's house before I did my weekly clean of it—I dumped everything from the inside, everything that might be under the laser-like purview of my mother, and tossed it in the trunk—papers, notebooks, trash, empty drink bottles, candy bar wrappers, fast food bags.

Usually, I couldn't give two shits about it.

I was an adult. I had a messy car.

There were worse habits to have.

Hell, *I* had worse habits.

But also, usually I was the one elbows deep in my trash (when it got bad enough that I felt honor bound to clean it). To have someone else digging through the crap in my trunk was embarrassing, least of all having *Theo* digging through it. He already thought I was the Scum of the Earth, and now he—

Why did I care?

He thought I was scum, so he might as well add *keeps a messy car* to my list of faults.

Reporter. Blogger. Influencer.

Dirty trash person.

I didn't care.

I moved to the trunk, glared at him. "What the fuck do you think you're doing?"

He shoved some of my crap to the side, paper bags crinkling in protest, then yanked at a tab, hard enough that the plastic started to rip off.

"Hey!"

But he kept yanking and the plastic kept coming off and—

*Oh.*

He set the cover to the side, and I was left looking at my spare, a jack, and one of those L-shaped wrench thingies.

He glanced at me, rolled his eyes, and reached back into the trunk, yanking out the jack and wrench, setting both beside the flat before coming back for the spare.

Before I could speak—before I could come up with anything to say—he lifted the spare tire out of the trunk and went back to the side of my car.

"I—"

He was on the ground.

In his suit.

Kneeling and positioning the jack, using the wrench thing, spinning it so that the car started rising off the ground.

"I—"

He leaned back, ripped off his jacket, tossing it on the hood of my car.

"Theo—"

Fingers working at the buttons at his wrists, rolling up his sleeves. But before I could do more than gape at the sinewy forearms he'd revealed, he was moving again, lying on the ground, sprawling out next to my flat and—

*Oh.*

More forearm action.

This time working at the bolts that held my tire in place.

One. Two. Three. Four. Five.

The tire slid off.

The spare went on.

One. Two. Three. Four. Five.

*So* much forearm action. They were toned and thick and covered with a light dusting of hair.

And they were working that wrench like—

*Thunk.*

He popped to his feet, kicked the jack out of the way, and my car plunked back to the asphalt. "There," he said, "now we can both get home." He bent, picked up the jack, the flat tire, and the wrench, and carried them to my trunk, dropping them in without care.

"Hey!" I snapped, even though I'd already mentally established there was nothing inside to ruin.

"You know"—he paused, glanced up at me—"you *could* say thank you."

I *should* say thank you.

He'd saved me however long it would have taken for a tow truck to come, and he'd saved me from the—

I glanced to the shadows, almost convinced now that no one had been there in the first place, that my imagination was getting away from me, that...

It didn't matter.

My spare was on.

We could both go about the rest of our nights. I'd sleep, take my mom to her appointment, add getting my tire fixed to my long-ass to-do list.

"No comment?" he asked.

I opened my mouth.

"Or you don't like that I did something for you?"

No, I didn't. *Really* didn't. "I—"

"Or maybe you don't like it when people ask *you* questions for a change?"

I didn't like that either.

But it was late, and I was tired, and I didn't want to have this conversation here. I didn't want to have this conversation at all. Not now. Not fucking ever. I didn't want to watch the derision spread, to feel its sting. Not again.

I reached for the top of the trunk, slammed it shut. "Thank you for changing my tire."

"There," he cajoled. "Was that so hard?"

I spun back on my heel, glaring at him. "Seriously?"

One shoulder lifted, dropped, mouth curving sardonically.

"You know, I've been taking care of myself for a long time."

A pause, his gaze going from where he'd installed the spare tire and back to me. "And doing such a good job of it."

"I had a fucking flat," I snapped. "I was going to call a tow truck."

"And how long was that going to take?"

"As long as it fucking took."

He snorted. "Is that why you were petrified and pressed up against your door when I pulled up? Because you were calling that tow truck?"

Asshole.

"No," I gritted out. "I was just making sure there wouldn't be another door accessible for you to slam into my face."

He flinched.

Shit.

Why did that make me feel guilty?

Probably because I should be thanking him for changing my tire, so I didn't have to wait for that tow truck.

"Look," I said on a sigh, dropping my chin to my chest, my gaze on my feet, my shoulders and neck and head aching as fatigue sank heavy into my bones, "thank you for stopping and changing my tire. Now, we've both had a long night, can we just go home?"

Silence.

Long enough that I looked up again.

He was staring off into the shadows, jaw flexing, but as though he sensed me looking, his gaze came to mine, eyes unfathomable.

My pulse picked up.

I wanted to step closer, but I found I couldn't, felt like my feet were glued to the surface of the street.

He took a step closer.

Another.

Then lifted a hand, caught a lock of my hair in between his thumb and forefinger, and rubbed.

Back and forth. Back and forth.

I released a shuddering breath, but didn't move, didn't tell him to stop.

A half step forward, Theo bringing the toes of his shoes in line with mine, those fingers still rubbing gently.

Back and forth. Back and forth.

"We should go home," I whispered.

Willing myself.

Willing *him*.

He bent, head coming close to mine, his words soft, almost a kiss against my lips. "What if I don't want to go home?"

# SIXTEEN

Theo

SHE ROCKED BACK on her heels, shock clearly visible beneath the bright streetlight overhead. "What?" she whispered.

I should turn around, should get in my car and go the fuck home.

Call my mom back and listen to her break down my game.

Sit on the couch, drink a beer, go to sleep in an empty bed.

Or go to a bar, find someone to bring home so that I didn't have to go to that empty bed alone.

I wouldn't let them stay of course. I never did.

So, at some point I would be sleeping alone and—

For once, I didn't want that.

I wanted...Eva.

Safe and at my side and looking at me not like I was a total asshole, but like she had when I'd apologized, when I'd kissed and touched and stroked. Like I had when I'd gotten out of my car and she closed the distance between us.

Like she didn't hate me.

I didn't deserve that. I deserved the disdain, deserved the loathing.

I just...didn't want it.

*Fuck.*

My head was so fucked up. This was why I didn't do shit like this, why I didn't do connection. It made me want...things I couldn't have.

"Never mind." I shifted, walked around the trunk of her car, tugged at the handle on the driver's door, and pulled the metal panel wide. "You should head home."

But she didn't move, just stood there, head down, eyes on her feet.

Then slowly, her head came up, eyes connecting with mine. "What if you don't want to go home?"

My lungs squeezed tight, voice raspy when I forced out. "Get in, Stubs."

She tilted her head to the side, frowned. "What's with you?"

"Nothing," I said, fingers tightening on the handle. "It's late. I'm tired and covered with who knows what was on the street."

"Why wouldn't you want to go home?" she pressed.

"Get in."

There was a chill in the air, a breeze that ruffled her hair, drawing the strands forward, splaying them across her face, making my fingers itch to touch the silken threads again, to tuck them behind her ear, to plunge my hand into the strands, draw her to me. "Theo," she whispered, "why wouldn't you want to go home?"

Because I couldn't be alone with myself, with my thoughts.

Because I couldn't allow myself to be anything different.

Because that would...

End in catastrophe.

"I want to go home," I lied.

Her lips curved. "Liar." A beat, her letting that sink in. Then she stepped a little closer, near enough that I could smell the floral scent of her shampoo, could feel the heat of her body. "I don't understand you," she whispered. "You hate me, and yet you're here."

"I don't hate you."

The words were torn out of me, ripped free before I could stop them.

Her response was one brow lifting. "You've said the opposite."

"I've said a *lot* of shit."

And that was something I shouldn't have said, something else that muddied the waters, but I didn't even know what was going on in my head.

I just...knew that I didn't want to get back in my car and drive away.

There.

Jesus fuck.

I'd admitted it, yeah?

I wanted to spend more time with Eva. Hell, it wasn't even really a want. It was need and longing, confusion and hatred, silken bonds that had formed without my permission, mistakes and panic and...

I wanted Eva.

And I was tired of fighting it.

So, for one fucking night, why couldn't I have it?

"What's going on in your head?" she asked softly.

"A tornado of bullshit."

More words pouring from me before I could stop them, could process what they revealed and bury them deep.

But then they were out there, and they'd revealed too much.

I braced, waited for her to press, to demand I keep sharing.

I reveled in that, knew it would help me shore up the walls, reinforce my defenses. I could say she was just like them, that she was just a reporter who wanted the story.

I could—

"Follow me," she whispered.

Now I rocked back on *my* heels. "What?"

She shifted, sliding between my body and the car, setting every one of my nerves alight with need, with memories, with wanting for this woman. My thoughts and emotions were a tangled fucking mess, but one thing was never in question.

I wanted Eva Moreno.

Wanted to taste those lips of hers again, wanted to stroke my tongue along hers, wanted my mouth on her skin, trailing along her throat, over her breasts, worshiping her between her thighs, the slick evidence of her desire on my taste buds.

Sex was easy.

But sex with Eva wasn't.

It was an avalanche of confusion.

One that didn't get better when her body brushed mine as she moved and sat down in the driver's seat.

"Theo?"

I'd been staring at the spot she'd just been in, that light brush of her body against mine nearly propelling me down the slope where confusion and need warred.

Her calling my name had me jerking, my head twisting to the side.

Those coffee-colored eyes on mine.

"Yeah?" I whispered.

"Get in your car and follow me."

I DIDN'T CALL my mom.

I didn't turn on the radio.

I didn't go home.

I didn't do anything except get into my own driver's seat, turn on the engine...and follow Eva as she drove through the streets of Baltimore, as she navigated the freeway, the on-ramp and the off-ramp. As she pulled into her apartment complex.

At any point of that drive, at any point during that navigating, I could have turned off, could have gone home.

*Should* have gone home.

But I didn't.

And when Eva paused, rolled down her window, and pointed at an empty guest parking spot before pulling ahead to the one numbered for her apartment, I didn't turn around, didn't head out of the lot and drive home.

I parked.

Got out.

Walked to the staircase I'd carried her up barely two weeks before.

Waited for her to get out of her car, for her to cross to me.

Waited as she paused in front of me, her purse slung over her shoulder, cell in her hand, body in front of mine, eyes...

I didn't want to look closely at her eyes.

But I found myself falling into the deep brown depths, studying the pools of chocolate and coffee, the threads of gold.

Her hand lifted, and I found my lungs freezing again, my body going completely still as that hand came up and up and—

Her fingers brushed along my jaw.

Stroked through the short, bristly hairs of my beard.

We stayed like that for a long time, long enough that the

cold of the night began to bite through the layers of my clothes, that quiet began to get loud.

The rustle of the wind through the trees bordering the parking lot.

Hoots of an owl in the distance.

The swoosh of an occasional car passing by.

The hum of a heater, the slowing click of my engine as it cooled, crickets having their nighttime conversations.

Gossiping. Talking shit. Whispering in lovers' ears.

Losing my fucking mind.

Losing myself in the depths of Eva's eyes.

A door slammed and we both jumped, our gazes breaking apart, our bodies creating distance seemingly without thinking —or at least unthinking on my part.

She took another step away from me. Then one more, turning away from me.

My stomach sank.

She should go up to her apartment. *I* should go home.

But when she paused and glanced over her shoulder, asking softly, "Are you coming?"

I couldn't do anything except follow her up the flight of stairs.

And into her apartment.

# SEVENTEEN

Eva

"I'D BE LYING if I said this was how I expected you to spend your spare time."

I shrugged, dumped the flour into the bowl, even as I felt the embarrassment clinging to my cheeks, heating them. "My sister works for a bakery." Another shrug. "She taught me a few things and"—my cheeks felt even hotter—"it relaxes me."

"Hmm."

I was an idiot. A big effing idiot.

Had been that big effing idiot from the moment I'd seen the uncertainty drift across Theo's face, easily discernible in the streetlight overhead.

As easily discernible as the confusion, the worry, the insecurity.

It called to that part of me—the one that wanted to make the puzzle pieces of him fit, that wanted to make it all make sense.

And now he was here. In my apartment. In my kitchen. Making sugar cookies.

When I had to get up in less than six hours to take my mom to the doctor's.

So...idiot.

"Add the butter and sugar to the mixing bowl," I ordered, instead of allowing myself to focus on my idiocy.

At least I'd get cookies out of this.

He scooped a measuring cup into my sugar container, doing it not quite like a pro—not that I was one either—but doing it with a confidence that told me this wasn't the first time he'd spent time measuring ingredients.

"What have you made before?" I asked.

"Hmm?" he replied, peeling back the paper on a stick of butter and shaking it into the bowl of the mixer, the latter of which he turned on.

To the right speed.

"You know how to use a mixer," I said. "And how to measure ingredients. Do you cook a lot at home?"

He paused, hand dropping to his side, rotating back to face me as I sifted the dry ingredients. Then he laughed and the sound settled somewhere in my belly. It was a warm sound, a nice one I'd only heard directed toward other people.

That it was for me—the warm, nice sound...

I exhaled. "Why's that funny?"

He grinned, moved over to me. "My mom called my fridge a wasteland the last time she visited."

A chuckle. "So, I'm guessing that's a no on the cooking at home front."

"It's a no"—he tilted the flour container so I could scoop out another cup—"but I did bake a lot with my mom and sisters growing up."

"The ones who are going to be disappointed in me because I use a ring light?"

He winced. "I think I've well established that I can be an asshole."

"To me," I said softly, sifting the last of the flour.

"What?"

"I think that we've established you can be an asshole to *me*."

Theo had been putting the lid back on the flour container, but my statement had him freezing, had him wincing again. "Yeah," he whispered.

"I don't get why," I whispered back. "I mean, I know you're not a fan of reporters—"

"I hate them."

I sucked in a breath. "You hate me."

He froze again, fingers clenching on the flour container. "No," he said softly, "I don't hate you. I *want* to, but I can't."

The last was barely audible.

"I just—" I sighed. "Theo, I don't get it. I know I'm hard on you and the guys, but I think I'm fair—"

"You are," he said.

"So, is it me or is it my job?"

"It's not you."

"It's just what I do."

He spun away from me, moved to the mixer, and shut it off. Then he dropped his hands to the counter, hung his head. "Yes," he whispered.

That shouldn't sting.

It wasn't like he said it cruelly.

It actually sounded rather pained, admitting that.

"Why?" I asked.

Silence, long enough that I was certain he wasn't going to answer, or that he was going to blow up and be mean to me again, or that he was going to run screaming out of my kitchen and pretend I'd never asked, that he'd never been here at all.

An exhale, sharp and pained. "I can't talk about it."

"Theo?"

I watched every muscle in his body seize, brace, and I paused for a heartbeat, waiting for him to lash out, to run.

But it was almost as if he was expecting the same.

For me to turn.

For *me* to hurt him.

And that said enough, didn't it?

For this particular moment, that said enough.

"Can you add two eggs?" I asked, deliberately changing the subject.

He exhaled and it was longer this time, longer but no less pained. "Yeah," he murmured. "I can add two eggs."

And he did.

Cracking the first one on the counter, turning the mixer on and blending after adding it to the bowl, then repeating the same movements after cracking the second.

Knowing what he was doing.

Not lashing out.

Admitting some portion of the truth—even if it wasn't all of it.

"I started baking because my sister had a bake sale at school and my mom forgot," I blurted.

He glanced up at me.

"My parents were..." I shook my head. "Well, they weren't good together."

"Fuck, if I don't understand the weight behind that statement," he muttered.

I paused, pocketed that bit of information. "But I've heard the guys talk about how in love your parents are."

"My mom and stepdad," he said softly, giving me more

information to pocket, taking the bowl of flour from me and adding a portion of it to the mixing bowl. "My real dad"—a glance in my direction—"you saw that gem of a human in the parking garage a few weeks back."

I inhaled.

"He's the definition of toxic."

An exhale. It *had* seemed that way. "I'm sorry," I whispered.

A shrug. "That's life."

I nodded when he held up the bowl, silently asking me if he should add more. "It's not life," I said as a little dust cloud of flour floating up around the metal rim. "Or it shouldn't be, anyway."

"No," he said after a moment, "it shouldn't be."

"But I'm glad you have your mom and stepdad."

He dumped the last of the flour in. "I'm glad I do too." He set the bowl on the counter, looked up. "Why weren't your parents good together?"

I sighed. "Typical shit. Married young. Too many kids. Always struggling from paycheck to paycheck. Then my dad got sick, and things were even tougher. My mom picked up extra jobs. I picked up the slack at home."

"Like with cookies for the bake sale."

My mouth tipped up. "Yeah, like with cookies for the bake sale."

"What happened?"

I shook my head. "The usual stuff that happens with a busy family and overworked mom. Things slip through the cracks. My mom was supposed to make cookies, but ran out of time, so then she was going to buy some at the grocery store, but she got off late and the bakery only had one box of crappy-looking cookies left." I shrugged. "So, we got online and I found a baking blog and...the rest is history. My sister and I were hooked on making cookies in the middle of the night"—my lips turned up further—"though now she does it before dawn and for half the morning before heading off to school, and I was hooked on blogging."

"*That's* how you got your start?"

"Yeah. Well, that and when my dad was alive, we watched a lot of sports." He'd controlled the TV with an iron fist. "But he especially loved watching the Breakers. So, between late-night baking with my sister and hockey games with my dad, I stumbled into my career."

"That's pretty cool."

"Is that begrudging respect I detect?" I asked lightly, even though my pulse had sped up.

"It's not begrudging," he said, voice soft but with a thread of warmth that matched his laughter from earlier. "It's not begrudging at all."

Surprise had my mouth falling open.

A thumb tracing over my bottom lip. "I hate that you're surprised by a compliment."

I *was* surprised, but I wasn't dead. And I hadn't lost my spine. "Then do better," I told him bluntly.

Another flurry of emotions on his face.

Another mix of confusion and angst and frustration.

Then he nodded.

"Okay."

# EIGHTEEN

Theo

THEN DO BETTER.

It was so fucking simple.

And yet it was the hardest fucking thing.

And...I owed it to her.

"Here," she said softly, as I was sitting in that truth, reaching past me and picking up the bowl. But when she dumped the contents on an unrolled length of opaque white paper, folded the ends over, and patted the disc flat, I frowned.

Because the disc then went into a zip-top bag.

And then she tucked it into the freezer.

Were we not going to have cookies then?

Was she done with me and my bullshit?

"Um," I muttered when she handed me the metal bowl back.

"Wash that, yeah?" she asked, turning away and opening a cabinet on the far side of the kitchen.

Okaaay.

But I didn't comment, just moved to the sink and started washing the bowl. Warm water. Soap. Scrub-a-dub-dub. The bowl was clean.

As I was setting it in the drying rack, Eva was back from the cabinet, a series of bowls on the counter, powdered sugar and a series of small cylindrical containers with white lids next to them.

"Here." She handed me a bag of toothpicks.

"What?" I asked, taking them.

"Pick your color," she told me.

"My—"

She nudged a container toward me.

Kelly Green.

Oh.

I started looking through the containers—and there were a lot of them. "Are we not going to bake the cookies?"

My mom and I had made chocolate chip cookies, snicker-doodles, even those little crinkled chocolate ones, but we hadn't made sugar cookies, or not ones that needed Kelly Green food coloring to finish them off.

Eva picked up a container, unscrewed the lid and dipped a toothpick inside. "The dough needs to chill."

Right. Okay, I knew that was a thing.

"How long does it need to chill?"

A glance up at me as she scraped the toothpick in the bowl, stirring it and turning the powdered sugar and milk concoction a bright pink. "Until tomorrow."

"But—" I clamped my teeth together, shut my mouth.

I was here instead of alone. She was being nice to me when I didn't deserve it.

If I didn't get freshly baked cookies out of this time, then them's was the breaks. I'd shut my mouth and pick my color.

A giggle. "And now he looks like I broke his favorite hockey stick."

I lifted my gaze, caught her smiling over at me.

She held up a plastic container, popped open the lid. "Don't worry," she teased, "I have plenty of treats for you." Perfect squares and rectangles and ovals filled that box. "But you have to work for your dessert." A nod to the containers of food dye. "Get on it, Air."

I scowled at her, but picked a color at random, dipped a toothpick in like she had, and got mixing.

A Breakers blue.

"Good," she said, and pulled out a clear plastic bag, slopped some of the icing I'd been mixing into it, and passed it over to me. "Ready for your lesson in cookie decorating?"

"Why am I very afraid?" I asked lightly.

"Don't worry. If you mess up, it'll still taste good."

Since there was a lot of credence to that, I spent the next little bit mirroring exactly what Eva did.

Snipping the end of the bag with scissors (though I did it too far up the bag if the sheer volume of icing that globbed out was any indication). Tracing the edges (messily). Waiting for the border to dry while grabbing another cookie and doing the same.

I got better at it as I went on.

But I was wearing a good amount of icing.

So, maybe I wasn't getting better at it.

Maybe I was getting worse.

I was definitely losing focus as time went on, and that was mostly because I couldn't stop myself from looking at Eva.

At the way she nibbled at her bottom lip as she bent over the cookies and expertly applied the icing.

At the way her hair slid forward, teased at the tops of her cheekbones.

Her shirt gaping and giving me a glimpse of skin.

The way the slacks she was wearing tightened over that lush ass of hers every time she moved.

Okay, so I was definitely getting worse.

And...so was she, I realized when the icing dripped over the edge of the cookie I was failing to focus on and proceeded to get all over my hands.

Her breath caught, and I froze, my finger on my lips, tongue darting out to taste the icing I'd made a mess of.

"Theo," she whispered.

"Yeah?" I whispered back.

"You're making a mess."

The words settled in my belly, in my cock. My eyes darted to where she'd been working, saw that her neat decorating had devolved into...

"You're making a mess, too."

Her throat worked, gaze dropping to her hands like she just realized what she'd been doing. "Yeah," she said softly, "I guess I am."

She set the bag on the counter, reached for the roll of paper towels.

I moved before I realized it, catching her hand before she could make contact with the paper.

"Wha—"

I brought her fingers to my lips, flicked out my tongue, tasting that frosting, taking that smear of pink sweetness into my mouth and wishing it was a different bit of sweet pink.

"Wait," she murmured.

I froze again, but she didn't pull back, just pressed our palms flat, laced our fingers together. Then slowly, infinitesimally, she lifted our connected hands to her mouth, traced over my skin with her tongue. "Why is there something sexy about a big hockey player with frosting on his hands?"

My cock twitched.

Hell, it was past twitching. It was hard and pressing against my zipper and—

"It's clearly not finesse," I blurted.

She froze, her mouth on my hand, lips parting over my pointer finger, the hot puffs of her laughter coating my skin like that frosting.

Then those lips closed, and my finger disappeared into the depths of her mouth.

Hot. *Wet.*

Sliding deep and then not, popping out from between her lips. "Maybe you don't have finesse with a piping bag," she whispered, stepping closer, her breasts brushing against my chest, her thighs rubbing against mine. "But I know you have it other places."

I froze. "Eva."

She brought another finger to her mouth. "What?" she asked when she'd slid it out, clean of the frosting.

"What are you doing?"

One shoulder lifted. Dropped. "You're here. I'm here. Is there a reason we can't...enjoy making cookies together?"

Making cookies.

I chuckled, the uncertainty fading. Heat blooming. This made sense—the desire and need, my hard cock and the fire in her eyes. All of that made so much more sense than decorating cookies and talking about my family and—

Her body shifted away, weight dropping back onto her heels.

Need dimming.

Expression closing down.

Shutting out any progress I'd made, setting alight the bridge we'd begun rebuilding.

I stopped thinking.

Snaking out a hand, catching her wrist, yanking her body back flush to mine.

Then my lips were on hers, tasting the frosting, adding to the sweetness of her, adding to the addiction of her.

Fingers in my hair, smearing icing through the strands, on my nape, my jaw, through my beard.

I didn't give a fuck.

Because I was moving, wrapping my arms around her and lifting her up, setting her on the counter, rattling bowls, knocking over those little containers of food dye.

She gasped and I took advantage, licking across her lips, into her mouth, kissing her until my lungs threatened to explode, until her thighs were wrapped tightly around my hips, her pelvis rubbing against my cock, making me...

A tug at the buttons on my shirt.

"Off," she gasped against my mouth.

That was a great fucking idea.

I tore at the buttons, ripped at the ones on her blouse, yanking at the material until our shirts were on the floor and her—

"Christ," I muttered. "Your tits should be illegal."

Her mouth curved, arms wrapping around her middle, plumping the globes, threatening to spill them out from the confines of satin and lace. A flash of pale pink. A jiggle that had me going harder.

"I thought you'd seen better?" she asked, reaching behind her.

God, I was such an asshole.

But I didn't have time to dwell on that further because the waistband loosened and she shifted, the straps falling down her shoulders.

I sucked in a breath.

She let the bra fall.
And...I stopped thinking.

# NINETEEN

Eva

I WATCHED his face change and shivered, desire a fire sending my insides alight.

This was stupid.

But also...he'd looked so fucking hot holding that piping bag, standing there, making a mess while concentrating so hard. And he'd shared, given me a couple of pieces to slot into place, and...I wanted him.

Always with a low-level hum when he was around.

But when he was in my space, giving me that warm laugh, the teasing conversation, the self-deprecating humor I craved, that I'd only seen from other reporter's highlights or happened to overhear...it was cranked up to a thousand.

Vibrating through me—

No, *burning* through me.

Knowing he didn't hate me, not really.

Understanding that it wasn't even truly my job—that it was something from his past messing with his present.

Did I still want to know every detail?

Yeah.

Was I content enough with what he *had* shared to put it aside?

Also, yes.

Especially with those big hands mirroring my movements, squeezing the bag, sending icing onto the cookies and his skin and occasionally the counter.

Too much strength for fine detail work.

But enough finesse to make a good effort at it, no matter what he said.

Putting the time in. Trying hard. Even if it was accepting a turn in his evening that he couldn't have expected.

Being...Theo Young.

And so, as I watched him, I'd increasingly wanted the effort, the focus to not be on my cookies—

But on me.

On my breasts and my mouth and between my legs, putting those strong hands and thick fingers to good use.

Now, my ass was on the counter and we were both naked from the waist up, so I supposed I was successful in *that* part of my evening.

Then he picked up the piping bag.

My lungs seized, heat blossoming in my belly.

"Beautiful," he whispered, squeezing on the bag, sending icing dribbling over my front. Over my breasts, dripping down to cover my nipples, to splatter on my belly.

"Theo—"

The bag hit the counter and I gasped when his mouth closed over my nipple, sucking deeply, sending pleasure spiraling through me. But I barely had time to process the sensation of his tongue and teeth and lips working in tandem before his hand was moving, trailing sticky circles over my abdomen, tracing them lower.

Until his fingers were working at the button on my slacks, tugging at the tab on my zipper.

Until his fingers were slipping beneath my underwear.

Slipping between the slick folds of my pussy.

Another gasp, my hand going to his wrist, not sure if I was trying to drag him closer or pull him away.

But all it did was have his mouth break away from my breast, his body push away from mine.

He lifted me from the counter, but before I could manage so much as a protest, my pants were down my legs, swept off my feet with my shoes and underwear. Leaving me naked with icing dripping off my skin.

"Hands on the counter," he ordered roughly, spinning me around and pushing me back against the cabinets, wrapping my fingers around the beveled edge of the granite. "Don't move."

Chest pressed to the cold surface, bottles and bowls scattered about, icing smeared every-fucking-where, I shivered.

But obeyed the gruff order.

How could I do anything else?

A warm, rough hand pressing between my shoulder blades, sliding down my back, curving over my ass.

Down the backs of my thighs.

Up between them.

A thumb pressing to my clit, slipping through the liquid evidence of my desire.

Then inside, just barely, the thick digit circling lightly at my entrance, not sinking deeply into me. Not giving me what I wanted.

I arched back, seeking more, wanting more, *needing* more.

He bent, voice in my ear. "Hold still."

Another gruff order I obeyed without question.

And he rewarded me, pressing that thumb inside me, deep and forward, grazing my G-spot, rubbing over those internal ridges. "Theo!"

He pulled out and I gasped his name again, hips moving now, desperate for purchase.

But he just placed a hand between my shoulder blades, ordered me to, "Hold still," again.

I hated orders, hated the presumption of them, hated the way they tried to control me...except in bed.

In bed, I didn't mind.

Especially when I knew this man could deliver on them, when I could just go along with the flurry of pleasure and not have to fight for it, not have to take care of it myself.

Oh God, it was nice to not have to take care of it myself.

"Good girl," he murmured, nipping at my earlobe, lightly tapping at my ass.

I arched against the contact, just to show him that even though my nerves were on fire, my body was quivering with need, I wasn't completely without spine, hadn't completely lost my head. "You'll be a *good boy* if you stop fucking around and make me come."

A chuckle in my ear. "I'll make you come," he said, tongue dipping into the shell of my ear, "but not until you beg for it."

"Yeah," I said, and if the word was breathless, I was pretending it wasn't. Because the gall of this man was...well, it was hot as hell, but it was also annoying. Orders were one thing. A cocky asshole was a whole other. Hot but too far. Or maybe it was just far enough. Maybe it made me wetter than I'd ever been before. Maybe it had me lying anyway, telling him, "That's not going to happen."

"Hmm." A nip to my jaw. "I think it will."

Then he was reaching past me, picking up one of the piping bags, this one filled with blue icing.

He lifted it, and I felt the sticky, sugary substance start to dribble over my skin.

It was wasteful, would certainly leave my skin dyed blue.

And I couldn't care less, not as the liquid dripped onto my back, slightly cool on contact, but warmed by his fingers and tongue as he rubbed it into my skin, as he lapped it off my skin.

He let it flow over my ass, between the cleft of my cheeks.

Felt his tongue follow the ribbons of liquified sugar.

"Theo!" I gasped as he jerked my hips back and knelt between my legs, positioning himself between my body and the lower cabinets, the icing trailing over my flesh, his tongue in my pussy, circling my clit, thrusting together with his fingers as he began to lick and suck and generally drive me fucking insane.

Up and up until my hips were jerking, grinding against his face and fingers.

Then stopping, giving me nothing more than the hot puffs of his breaths until my orgasm began to slip away.

And then working me without mercy again, driving me up the edge.

And stopping.

Then up.

Then...stop.

"Fuck," I hissed when he paused again, when I had nothing of purchase, no friction, nothing but the heat of his breaths.

Which was steady.

While mine was...nothing close to steady

A long, slow lick. "You just have to ask for it, Stubs," he cajoled.

I shuddered. "You mean, I just have to *beg* for it."

His finger trailed through my folds, dipped into my entrance. "Yeah, baby. I just want you to beg for it." That finger slammed home and he began to fuck me with it, hard and fast and without mercy.

Until he stopped again.

And that was the point my control snapped.

I pushed hard against the counter, knocking him back. He fell to the floor, and I was on top of him in an instant, moving with a speed I didn't recognize, didn't know I possessed. My hands went to work on his slacks, yanking at the button and zipper, shoving them down his thighs until his cock popped free.

"Maybe I'll be the one to give the orders," I panted.

His fingers weaved into my hair. "You don't want that," he rasped. "You like my orders."

Heaven help me, but I did.

"So, suck my cock, baby," he said, those fingers pressing lightly, coaxing me down. "Suck me deep."

I shuddered again and then my lips were around him, tasting the bead of salty desire on the head of him, feeling the velvet and steel along my tongue, pushing against the back of my throat. I wrapped my fingers tight, used my hand and mouth in tandem.

And then, just to give him a taste of his own medicine, I stopped.

Grabbed that bag of icing.

And dripped it over his cock, took my time tasting it on his skin,.

"Eva," he groaned, fingers tightening, hips jerking up.

I pulled back, slid my tongue over him. "Maybe *you'll* beg for—"

I didn't even finish the taunt before I was on my back, before he was thrusting into me, cock hard and hot and stretching me almost to the point of pain.

But it was a good stretch, a good burn.

He didn't give me any time to sit in the feel of him.

He just...fucked me.

Deep and fast and across the kitchen floor, until I had to brace my hands over my head, so he didn't fuck me into the cabinet, until there was no need to beg for my orgasm.

It was barreling down on me like a fucking Mack truck.

And he was right there too.

I could see it in the lines of his face, in the taut muscles of his jaw, in the gleam of sweat all over his skin.

"Come for me, Eva," he ordered.

Another order.

Another one I liked.

"Harder," I ordered back.

His eyes darkened, mouth turning up before he bent and nipped sharply at the underside of my jaw. "Fucking trouble," he muttered.

But his hips moved faster, and his free hand went to my hips, holding me in place as he fucked me.

"More," I ordered.

He groaned...and maybe he liked me giving orders too.

Maybe he didn't mind letting me be in control—

He ground deep and I gasped, neck arching, head digging into the tiles.

Okay, nope.

Not thinking about being in control.

Not thinking about orders. Not *thinking* at all.

Because it was there.

My orgasm. Blazing through me like fire in my veins, scorching me with pleasure that went on and on and *on*.

Until I was just ash in the aftermath.

Until he called out my name and every stroke as he came broke me apart a bit more.

Dust in the wind.

Changed in a way that shouldn't be possible.

Filled with pleasure that left me limp and fear that was slowly eating its way through my insides.

Never had I felt like this before. *Never*.

And that was the only explanation for why I said what I said next.

# TWENTY

Theo

"YOU CAN GO."

My heart was pounding like a motherfucker, and it felt like every bit of energy had been sucked from my body.

So, I didn't immediately recognize what Eva had said.

This was right.

This, with this woman, was right.

I felt it in my fucking bones, and it terrified the shit out of me.

That I wanted her more than I'd ever wanted anyone, more than I'd wanted her over the last couple of seasons. That I didn't think I could stay away...didn't think I could do the right thing and let her go.

I hadn't been able to do that since our first night together.

Hell, if I was being truthful, I hadn't been able to get her out of my head from the first moment I'd laid eyes on her, from the first time she'd asked me a tough question, her pen in her hand, notebook in the other, cell on the bench next to me, recording my response. Expectation in her eyes, determination in her expression, stubbornness in the set of her jaw.

I wouldn't be able to do it *now*.

Cookies after midnight and grace after a door to her face.

Kindness and not pushing and the sound of my name on her lips, her tongue.

The clasp of her body around my cock. Her nails biting into my scalp. Her scent in my nose.

I wouldn't let her go.

I *couldn't*.

"What?" I murmured, brushing her hair back, noting it was sticky with icing.

We needed a shower.

Yeah. A shower would be great, I thought, mouth turning up.

A hand on my chest, pushing me back.

Thinking that I was squashing her, I pulled back, slipping from the heat of her body, pushing back onto my knees.

"You can go."

I froze, the words finally processing. "What?" I asked.

Stupidly.

She climbed to her feet, a fucking goddess on display, blue streaks of icing across her skin.

Skin I'd touched and licked and kissed.

Skin I saw more of when she spun on her heel, started off down the hall. "See yourself out, yeah?" she tossed over her shoulder. "And don't forget to lock up."

Then she kept moving.

Down the hall.

Away from me.

After telling me I *could go*.

What the fuck?

And no, the irony didn't sit well with me, sinking heavy into my gut, adding a whole other layer to my guilt.

I was a fucking asshole.

I knew that.

But I also wasn't going to walk out her front door, wasn't going to leave her. Not now. Not. *Fucking.* Now.

I was an asshole, but I wasn't going to leave.

I was an asshole, but I was done fighting my need for her.

I was an asshole, but I wasn't going to walk away.

*That* was fucking done. I'd come home with Eva knowing that things were going to be different, and maybe this was all a mistake, maybe—probably—it would all blow up in the end. She would look closer at me, know that I was a shit show she couldn't invite into my life.

But...I was here now.

And I wasn't walking away.

Wasn't *going* to walk away.

*Couldn't* walk away.

A door closed in the distance, and I heard water turn on. She was taking a shower—not a surprise considering the amount of icing on our bodies. It was already drying, already flecking off onto the floor.

Making a fucking mess.

Worth it.

Even without tasting the cookies.

After yanking up my pants—but not bothering to button or zip them—I moved down the hall, past two closed doors that I opened—revealing one to be a closet, another a bedroom. There was another door at the apex of the hallway, this one closed as well, and behind the thin wooden panel, I could hear the water running loudly.

Jackpot.

I tried the handle, a blip of pleasure running through me at finding it unlocked—as idiotic as that was—and pushed at the door. It opened silently, a gust of steamy air hitting my skin. A pair of socks sat on the rug—the only article of clothing I hadn't actually stripped off her—and I could see the barest glimpse of a silhouette behind the gray and blue-patterned shower curtain.

I shoved down my slacks, left them in a pile next to those socks, and pulled back the curtain.

And froze.

Because, fuck, she was hot, all that slick skin on display, her arms lifted as she massaged shampoo through her hair, suds and water sliding down her beautiful, naked body.

Then her eyes shot open, and she gasped. "What the fuck, Theo?" she snapped, swiping at her eyes, choking a bit on the water.

I wound an arm around her middle, tugged her back against my front.

That ass.

Fuck, I was hard again.

And I knew she felt it, knew it by the way her breath caught and her body arched against me, ass rubbing against my aching cock.

"You're dirty," I murmured, running my hands over her breasts, down the curve of her stomach, stopping at the apex of her thighs.

She released a breath but didn't push against me. "I asked you to leave."

I slid my hand a little lower, just teasing the edge of the swollen bud of her clit. "I know," I murmured, "but I'm staying."

Her breath caught again, and this time it wasn't paired with an arch against my body. Then she stiffened, spun in the circle of my arms, and glared up at me. "You have big balls."

I glanced down, back up, one brow lifting. "I mean..."

She made a disgusted sound, gave me her back again, stepping forward and taking the full stream of water, leaving me on the cold end of the shower, goose bumps lifting on my skin. Soap on a loofah, more suds on her body, but I figured I'd pushed her enough, figured I'd pushed my luck enough. So, I just shut up and stood there as she washed her body, washed her hair.

Stood there until she huffed out a sigh and handed me the loofah. "You hurt me."

My fingers clenched on the mesh, sending soap suds to the floor of the tub. "I know," I whispered.

"No," she whispered back, "you *really* hurt me. Not just that night."

My fingers convulsed. "I know."

"Not just with the door."

"I know."

"And not even just with being a jerk in front of Julie and Smitty and Lake and Cas."

I winced. "I know."

"And not just—" Her voice broke, and she looked away, shoulders lifting on an inhale, dropping on an exhale.

"I'm sorry," I whispered.

Her head came back up. "I don't know if that's enough."

"I know," I said, but I moved closer to her anyway, turning her and running the loofah over her back, getting a spot she'd missed, wiping away the blue smear. "I know," I said again, rotating her back so the water flowed over the soap, taking the bubbles and stain with it. "But I'm here now."

She froze, shook her head. "I should kick your ass out of this shower."

"I won't go." I bent, brushed my lips over her jaw. "You know that."

"Idiot," she mumbled under her breath. "*I* am an idiot."

But before I could respond—could agree with her—she took the loofah from me and began soaping up my body, rinsing away the icing, the food dye, the bubbles.

I couldn't lie.

My cock was already hard, just from seeing her all slick and wet. With her hands moving over my body, touching me, stroking me—

I was moments away from blowing.

Something she seemed to recognize because she lifted her leg, positioned the head of my cock at her entrance and...

Then I was inside.

Wet. Hot. Tight.

I reacted without thinking, spinning us and pinning her against the wall of the shower, thrusting hard and fast, but exploiting everything I knew about what she liked, grinding against her clit, angling her pelvis for maximum contact, pinching her nipple hard.

She gasped out my name, pussy fluttering around me, telling me enough.

She was close.

Which was good.

Because I was close too.

I kept thrusting, clenched my teeth, held back my orgasm.

"Fuck," she hissed, pussy convulsing around me, head flying back as she came apart on my cock, body going limp so quickly that I had to lock my knees so we didn't end up in the bottom of the tub as I came right behind her, the heat of the water, the intensity of my orgasm, the sensation of her body against mine enough to send my head spinning.

Then I was coming down, and her arms were wrapped tightly around me.

*She* was wrapped around me.

Under a stream of water that was growing cooler by the moment.

Eva stretched, glanced up at me, mouth curved, fingers brushing along my beard. "I thought I was the stubborn one."

I grinned, pressed my forehead to hers. "You started it."

She giggled.

In my arms, her body flush to mine, an orgasm that had nearly broken me still firing little jolts of pleasure through my nerves. But not as much pleasure as that soft laugh in my ears, as the feel of her in my arms.

And I knew that not walking away might have been the best decision I'd ever made.

## TWENTY-ONE

Eva

I DIDN'T KNOW what to do with this.

Didn't know what to do with Theo holding me gently as he slid back the shower curtain, lifted me in his arms, and stepped out onto the fluffy gray rug.

A second later, I was on my feet, a towel being wrapped around my body, another draped over my hair, rubbing lightly to dry it.

"Do you need to blow dry it?" he asked softly.

"Um..." I was still processing the gentle hands toweling off my hair, my body. "What?"

"Your hair is wet," he murmured. "Do you want to blow dry it?"

"I"—I blinked, *focused*—"no, I'll wrap it up."

Which probably didn't make any sense to him, but he didn't argue with me, just kept his hands moving on my body until I was dry. Only then taking the time to dry himself off.

My heart squeezed.

And, yup, I was definitely an idiot.

One sign of sweet, caring Theo and I was melting, dissolving, *wanting*.

More.

Him.

Turning away before I could say or do anything stupider, I grabbed my heatless curls wrap that TikTok made me buy and set about winding my hair. It was either wear this to bed or take the time to blow dry. And I was tired.

My body was limp and lax with pleasure.

Blow drying wasn't going to happen.

And I wouldn't have time in the morning to deal with the disaster that would be my hair if I went to bed without doing anything to it.

A finger in the light socket would have nothing on me.

So, heatless curls it was, and if, in the meantime, I looked like a Victorian—or whatever the era was—wannabe, then so be it.

Theo was here.

Theo wouldn't leave.

Theo could deal with my lazy hair routine.

"Done?" he asked when I'd finished wrapping and clipping.

"Almost," I said, feeling awkward and too intimate, but not willing to let him see that as I slapped on some moisturizer and eye cream, rubbed a lotion that was expensive, but worth its weight and one of my few beauty indulgences I made because of the gorgeous silken way it made my skin feel and the soft floral scene it left behind. After drying my palms on a towel, I snagged my toothbrush, used it. Then, because it seemed clear that he had no intention of leaving, I opened the cabinet beneath the sink and offered him an unopened sample I'd gotten from my last dentist appointment.

Still feeling awkward and too intimate.

But...also unwilling to leave the bathroom when he brushed, watching him like he'd watched me. Studying him. *Feeling* him in my space.

And...not hating it.

Okay, I liked it. Probably more than I should.

Just as I liked it when he took my hand after he'd finished brushing—after rinsing out the sink without me having to ask, like the strange man he was—and led me down the hall. Into my bedroom.

"Spying?" I asked softly.

He shrugged, drew me closer to the bed. "I had to track a woman down."

"Through the entire one bedroom and bathroom of my apartment," I replied dryly. "How challenging."

"You know what they say about hockey players."

My brows came up. "What *do* they say about hockey players?" I asked, curious now.

"They can't find anything unless it's encircled by glass and boards."

I snorted. "Do they say that?" I stepped to the dresser, pulled out a pair of underwear and a tank top. "Do they *really* say that?"

"No," he said, chuckling, coming up behind me and wrapping his arms around my middle. "Skip the clothes and keep a naked man company?"

My fingers faltered on the drawer, but I didn't argue, just slid the clothes back inside, allowed him to draw me toward the bed, to settle me beneath the covers.

To reach over me and flick on the bedside lamp.

To give me a glimpse of his gorgeous ass—freaking hell, but hockey players had the *best* asses—bouncing as he walked to the door, flicked the switch to turn off the overhead light.

Then he was striding toward me again, his front equally as sexy in the soft glow of the bedside lamp as his back had been. God, the man had a beautiful dick, and a sleekly strong body, and thighs that were thick enough for me to ride.

Just get me a cowboy hat.

He slipped in beneath the covers, tugged me close, and leaned over me again, this time to turn off the lights.

And...this was awkward.

Listening to the sound of him breathing, trying to make it so my own breath was quiet even as I felt like I was huffing like a hippopotamus.

Did hippopotamuses even huff?

Was hippopotamuses even the proper term for more than one hippopotamus?

Was I spiraling?

Yup.

Did I know how to stop?

No.

"I didn't use protection," he said softly.

I stiffened. Because he hadn't and that was stupid and...I exhaled.

Think.

*Breathe.*

"I have an IUD," I murmured. "And I don't make a habit of unprotected sex."

His arm tightened. "I've never been with a woman without a condom." He stroked his fingers along my arm. "And I'll get tested too, just to be safe, sweetheart."

Sweetheart.

Fuck, that was...

I was back to huffing like a hippopotamus again.

"Tell me about your siblings," he said, still softly.

My heart squeezed at the gentle tone, and I found myself asking, "Do you really want to know?"

A pause, long enough that I began holding my breath.

Then his fingers slid along the bare skin of my shoulder, his words barely above a murmur. "Yeah, baby, I really want to know."

My heart did that squeeze again.

But my tongue loosened, and I started to tell him about Dommie, who worked her ass off in the bakery while going to college, didn't date, and loved expensive clothes. I told him about Gabe, who was the typical middle child who got lost in the shuffle but was a great artist and kicking ass in art school. I told him about Jer, who was saddled with the worst name of all us siblings—Jeremiah—but was the coolest of all us and didn't care. Because he was the baby and everyone doted on him, even if he was just barely passing his junior year.

I told him about my dad dying and how he hadn't taken care of himself, but that, still, his heart attack had taken us all by surprise, especially when it seemed as though he was finally getting better.

And I told him about my mom and the way she'd disappeared on us, the grief turning her mean and infantile in equal intervals and how she'd taken a page out of our dad's book with the whole not-taking-care-of-herself thing.

I told him about struggling to pay rent and fighting to make it through school and not eating so that Jer could get new shoes.

I told him how this apartment was the first thing I'd done for myself when my blog started making money and how it was the best thing I ever could have done.

I told him...about me.

The small, hidden parts that didn't belong to anyone but myself.

And he took possession of them, carefully, gently, protectively.

And...for the first time in a long time, for the first time since I could remember, I felt safe.

Safe enough to allow my eyes to slide closed.

Safe enough to sleep in this man's arms.

---

I woke to my phone ringing, eyes bleary and body still vibrating with aftershocks of pleasure.

My bed was empty and—

*Buzz. Buzz.*

Right. Phone.

I rolled toward my nightstand, seeing that my cell had been plugged into the charger—something I hadn't bothered with the night before.

*Buzz. Buzz.*

Right. Really. Phone.

I snagged it from my nightstand, swiped, lifted it to my ear. "Hello?"

"I need my coffee," my mother groused. "Where are you?"

"I'm—"

My gaze went from the window—the sun peeping up over the horizon—to the clock on my side table.

*Fuck.*

I was late.

I tossed the covers back, flinched against the cold, and darted across the room, yanking open a dresser drawer and tugging out clothes as fast as my mind would process them. Underwear. Bra. Leggings. Socks. A T-shirt.

"Have a cup of coffee at home," I told my mom, wrestling my way into my leggings. "I'll be over in ten minutes."

"But I want a latte," my mom snapped. "The coffee you bought for the house is shit."

It wasn't shit.

It just wasn't a latte from a coffee shop.

"I'll buy you a latte after your appointment. Look," I said over the protest that began to ring in my ear, "I'm getting in the car. I'll see you in ten, yeah?"

Then I hung up, knowing I would get an earful, but too late to worry about it.

Too late to process that Theo was gone.

Too late to process that he'd cleaned up before he left, that my kitchen was spotless, and there was coffee waiting to be brewed in the pot.

I didn't notice any of that until much later.

Until after my mom's appointment.

Until after I'd found out that the medicine wasn't working as well as the doctor had hoped.

Until after I'd pulled out my ring light and some of that icing in order to make enough money to pay for the next round of tests the doctor wanted to order.

And lunch and lattes for my mom.

And a better coffee maker so I didn't have to keep my mother in expensive lattes.

And a replacement blouse for Dommie because the dry cleaner hadn't been able to get all of the blood out.

And—

Life.

I used my ring light and got on creating content.

So I could live my fucking life.

And I did it in a clean apartment thanks to a hockey player who'd hated me...and now—

Just confused me.

# TWENTY-TWO

Theo

MY CELL BUZZED, and I practically ripped it out of my pocket, trying to see the screen.

"Whoa there," Smitty teased, chowing down on his pancakes in a way that I didn't understand.

Devouring them so quickly, there was no way my teammate could possibly be tasting them.

Such a fucking waste of good pancakes.

"You're a monster," I muttered, glancing at the screen, disappointment a goddamned tsunami crushing my insides when I saw it was my mom and not my...

Well, not Eva.

I'd thought she would call, would maybe thank me for the orgasms...or at least for cleaning up the kitchen.

Though, I'd probably eaten too many cookies in the clean-up process.

That was bound to piss a woman off.

She worked hard, invited me in, and I'd trashed her kitchen and eaten her food.

So...*not* smooth.

"I'm not the one who nearly decapitated a teammate trying to get to his cell." Smitty shoveled another bite in, spoke around the pancakes, the words slightly muffled. "Got a hot date?"

I glared at my friend...okay, teammate, especially when Smitty had that gleam in his eyes.

He was going to be nosy as fuck.

He was going to be *annoying* as fuck.

His matchmaking powers were making a reappearance—or maybe they never fully went away.

So, I glared.

And I did it to buy myself time to come up with an excuse for nearly taking Smitty's head off while anticipating a message from Eva.

Luckily, my mom's text provided me that excuse.

I scowled at the words on the screen, showed them to my teammate. "My sister is dating a fucking hockey player."

Smitty glowered, full protective mode snapping right into place. "Lana or Rose?"

"Lana."

That scowl deepened. "She's too fucking young."

"Yeah," I muttered, jabbing away at the screen. "No fucking kidding. And look at this asshole"—I held up the phone again, showing them the picture my mom had sent of a base-ball-hat-wearing, floofy-haired motherfucker who had a cocky smile—"look at that fucking smirk."

"When do we go back out to California?" Smitty asked, and I knew he wasn't joking.

"If we make it to the finals," I muttered—and if a California team did the same. I jabbed at my phone screen, telling my mom that my sister had better call me as soon as Lana got home from school.

*With* the hockey player on the line.

So I could make the proper threats.

Considering that my mom's only response was that sideways kiss with a heart emoji, I wasn't feeling all that confident Lana would call.

"Christ," I muttered, shoving my phone back into my pocket. "A couple of weeks ago, she was excited because I'd bought her a tub of tapioca pudding."

Smitty, a huge bite of pancakes dangling from the tines of his fork, froze and shook his head. "Seriously?"

"What?"

He shook his head, shoved the bite into his mouth. "We need to work on your gift-giving skills."

"She loves it," I protested. "Both of my sisters do."

A sigh. Another bite into that big fucking mouth. "Pathetic, man. You need to show your sisters you care, show that you're thoughtful. Not that you'll buy them senior center food."

I scowled. "Is this where I remind you that I was being thoughtful because they *love it?*"

Smitty just shook his head, and, probably taking pity on me but also probably more than tired of hearing us bicker, Walker broke in with a story of the younger guys getting caught looking at that cake-sitting OnlyFans account again. "So now Coach has instituted a no phone in the locker room rule."

"Probably for the best," I muttered. "It's like those three"— the young, not even twenty-one-year-olds—"haven't seen a naked woman before."

Not that I hadn't had my own fun with baked goods just the night before.

I'd just...well, I preferred to have baked-good fun with a woman in my arms rather than jerking off to the screen—or adding to my private spank bank standing shoulder to shoulder with my teammates.

"Have you seen those awkward fuckers?" Walker said. "They probably haven't seen a real naked woman, let alone touched one."

We all busted up, knowing that the kids were cool—albeit kids—and that they pulled plenty of action.

It was just...

They were kids.

Though, this conversation—or at least the one about showing the women in my life that I cared—was food for thought.

I'd cleaned Eva's kitchen, put coffee in the pot, had made sure that she didn't wake up to a mess, but I hadn't left a note, hadn't told her that I was leaving.

We were up late. I hadn't wanted to disturb her.

But after our night together, after how I'd treated her—

Fuck, I really should have left a note.

She probably thought I was being an asshole again, probably thought—

Smitty darted his fork out, tried to snatch a chunk of my pancakes.

"Seriously," I snapped, blocking him. "What the fuck?"

Smitty shrugged and pulled back his fork to where it belonged—on his own fucking side of the booth. "You're wasting Donna's pancakes."

"*You're* looking for an ass beating," I threatened.

"Children," Walker said on a sigh. "Eat your own pancakes. You"—a nod at Smitty—"keep your own fork on your own plate. And you"—he pointed at me—"stop thinking about wanting to murder the asshole your sister is dating and eat your food. I want to get on the ice sometime this century."

We were eating pancakes before practice.

This was bad in theory and bad in execution.

We'd be bloated and slow as fuck.

Luckily, it was an optional skate and we were only going because Walker wanted to try out the new stick our equipment guys had found for him.

We could be bloated and slow and still dick around with our sticks.

I froze, mentally shook my head at myself—the euphemisms, thank God I hadn't spoken them aloud—and focused on my pancakes.

And on glaring at Smitty.

Because that was almost as good as the fluffy deliciousness of Donna's.

LATER, feeling far less bloated thanks to fucking around on the ice for an hour or so, I left my teammates, showered, and pondered what Smitty had said.

The fucker was annoying.

But he was happily in love.

And Kailey was happily in love with him back.

So...clearly he knew at least some of what he was spouting off about.

So...how to show Eva that I cared?

I didn't think leaving her before she woke up, without a note, was good practice. I also didn't think that eating her cookies and barging into her shower was the way to go.

The problem was that I didn't know how to be romantic.

Ever since I'd been old enough to even look at a woman with interest, I'd purposely kept it light and transactional. Getting in there. Getting off. Getting out.

Obviously getting off wasn't the problem.

It was the whole getting *out* portion of events that was hurting my brain.

Mostly because I wanted to stay *in*.

But how? I hardly knew Eva, and most of the time I'd been an asshole. How did I make up for that? How did I puzzle out what would make her happy? What would entice her to not want to kick my ass out the door? And...what if I put the effort in and she dumped me anyway?

The benefit to just fucking was that there was no vulnerability.

With Eva, with all the shit she was conjuring up in my head, in my heart, there was way too fucking much exposure.

"Theo."

"Fuck," I muttered, grinding my teeth together, picking up the pace.

This wasn't happening.

"Son." My dad grabbed my shoulder, yanked me to a halt.

I broke the hold, kept walking. "How many times do I need to make it clear that I don't want you here?"

"I'm married."

"To how many women?" I asked snidely—asked *stupidly*, considering it would only extend this interaction.

A scowl. "Don't be an asshole."

"Rich coming from you," I muttered, yanking at the handle on my car, pulling it once to disengage the locks, again to open the door.

My dad put a hand on it, tried to slam it closed. "You need to meet Gloria."

I caught it, kept the metal panel open. "How old's this one?"

"That doesn't matter."

Which meant young.

Fuck.

"What does," my sperm donor went on, "is that you're going to have a new brother or sister."

Jesus *fucking* Christ.

I resisted the urge to rub my temples, even though my head was throbbing. "Look," I said, "You made it very clear years ago where I fit on your priorities. Some shit can't get fixed." And obviously my dad hadn't changed. Making new families. Moving on. Leaving the pieces behind without a second glance.

My father crossed his arms. "I just want to have a relationship with my son."

"And how many of them do you have now?" I asked dryly.

Anger on my father's face. "That's not fair—"

"I've heard that somewhere before," I sneered, tapping a finger to my lips. Because I *had* heard it. Too many fucking times to count. But I focused on the present, on why my father was coming around again. The only reason I ever did. The reason why I would never fucking *ever* allow my sperm donor a place in my heart again. "Just like I know the only reason you're here now is because you have some crisis."

My dad scowled.

"So"—I tapped my lips again—"what is it this time? A test that her insurance isn't covering? A deposit for an apartment? Money for diapers or a push present or a babymoon?" I crossed my arms, having had to Google the last two over the years after enduring exactly these types of interactions. "Oh, maybe I need to kick in for a baby shower. Right? Isn't that my *duty?*"

"That's not fair," my dad protested. "I don't want anything."

I just lifted my brows, waited.

My dad sighed, dropped his hands to his sides. "Her car—"

And there it was.

Toxic. Drama. Incapable of caring for the people he supposedly loved.

And I had that DNA coursing through my veins.

"Things never change, do they, Dad?"

"You need—"

I didn't *need* to do anything. Which was why I got in the car, closed the door, and drove away from the shit show that was my past.

# TWENTY-THREE

Eva

I WAS in the broadcast booth, staring down at the ice, and my stomach was somewhere in the proximity of my shoes.

Something was wrong with Theo.

Very, very wrong.

I hadn't heard from him yesterday—though the calling card of a clean kitchen, coffee waiting to be brewed, and my icing-covered clothing in the washer was one of the nicest things anyone had ever done for me.

Definitely the nicest thing a man had ever done for me.

He'd even swept the floor. Something I hadn't noticed until I'd gone to throw away the remnants of the cake my sister had given me and found cookie crumbs in the trash. And dust and my own hair...because I wasn't the best housekeeper and maybe it had been a while since I'd swept under the edges of my cabinets.

And because my hair shed like a mofo.

I probably had a thick undercoat like the mutt of a pup we'd had growing up.

Chewy had shed like she had an entire other dog beneath her fur.

I—

Theo stepped off the ice, moved down the hallway, paused just out of sight of most of the arena.

But not out of sight of me way up in the booth.

Which was why I saw him pause, press his hands against the wall, and hang his head.

Yes. Something was very, very wrong with Theo.

Turning from the sight of him, I tugged out my mic pack, set it on the desk, at the spot I always occupied while on the air. "I'll be right back," I told our director.

"It's almost time—" Mark began.

"I know," I said, "I'll just…" A shake of my head. "I'll be right back." Avoiding Mark's eyes, I hustled out of the room, hitting the stairs and doing it quickly, knowing I needed to get my ass back up to the booth before it got too close to broadcast time or I'd risk looking like a complete fuckup and would gamble with—

My dream.

My future.

This was probably stupid.

Definitely stupid.

And yet, I still pounded down the flights of stairs anyway.

Down the stairs, through the halls.

To the other hall, skidding to a stop on the black skate mat six feet from where Theo was standing, still with his hands on the wall, still with his head hanging.

I paused, some part of me telling me this was stupid, that this was a big mistake, that I shouldn't be here, risking my dream. But I moved forward anyway.

Because something was wrong with Theo.

Because he'd swept up crumbs and packed away my cookies.

Because he'd listened to me talk about my siblings and held me when I slept.

Because he'd apologized, and he was upset and—

What-fucking-ever. I was here now.

Shoring my spine, girding my loins, bracing myself for the return of the asshole, I closed the distance between us.

"Hey," I said softly when I was within arm's reach of him.

He jerked, head shooting up, palms flying off the wall, body spinning. Flying toward me.

What the—

His arms wrapped tightly around me, dragging me toward him, pulling me against him. One second, I was standing in the hall, the cool air from the rink making my skin tingle, and the next, I was pinned between his body and the wall.

His jersey was rough against my arms, his equipment pressing into me in strange ways, hiding his muscles, making him harder in some ways, softer in others.

A hand obscured by a hockey glove cradled my head, protecting me from the heavy concrete blocks that formed the walls of the arena. His other was pressed to my cheek, the leather palm soft on my skin.

His forehead dropped to mine.

And he held me.

Silently. Firmly.

As the sounds of fans filling the stands, the soft cracks of sticks and chatter from the guys on the ice warming up drifted down the hall.

But those were the only sounds aside from his breathing.

Which was unsteady.

"Theo," I finally said. "Honey, what's wrong?"

He just shook his head, continued to hold me.

So, I just wrapped my arms around him in return, held him as tight as he was holding me, and waited, trying not to worry about the time, trying not to do anything but give him a little bit of what he'd given me the night before last.

But as time ticked on, I knew this bubble of privacy we had was going to be punctured.

Warm-ups would end.

The guys would come down the hall, heading to the locker room for last-minute game preparations and...I would need to get back upstairs to the broadcast booth, preferably before I put my job at risk.

"Theo," I murmured, covering his hand with my own, gently peeling his glove-covered fingers from my face.

He lifted his head, gray eyes stormy.

"Talk to me, honey," I ordered.

He sighed, pulled back slightly, leaving me cold, the air from the rink filling the space where his warm body had been.

I waited.

Braced.

*Breathed.*

And prepared to be shut down.

Instead, he lifted the hand that had been on my cheek, shook off his glove, the leather and suede concoction hitting the floor with a soft *thud*.

Then he sighed again. "I'm being fucking ridiculous," he muttered, that hand landing softly on my cheek again—sans glove—before sliding back along my jaw, dipping into my hair, running lightly through the strands.

"Why are you being ridiculous?" I pressed when he didn't go on.

A muscle in his jaw flexed. "It's stupid, seriously." He dropped his hand, gently slid the one from behind my head free, and started to step back farther, the cold from the rink seeping in, his eyes tracing my body. "I know you need to get up to the booth."

"Theo."

His gaze came back to mine.

"When have I ever let that shit slide?" I asked with a lifted brow.

Some of the thunderstorms faded, and I watched, heart skipping a beat when one corner of his mouth tipped up. "Never."

Then his mouth flattened out and he bent to pick up his glove.

I thought he'd turn to go back out on the ice, or maybe to retreat to the locker room.

Instead, he spun so his back was to the wall and reclined next to me, feet on the mat, shoulders on the concrete, sighed again. "My dad's an asshole."

That...wasn't what I'd expected him to say. "I used to have one of those," I said dryly. "I have to say—and I'm fully aware this makes *me* an asshole—but my life is much less complicated now that he's dead."

He sucked in a breath.

I winced, realized too late that was probably far beyond what I should have shared in the span of polite conversation.

Then he started chuckling, rotating to face me, his bare palm coming to my cheek again, sending my pulse skittering. "Fuck, if I haven't thought the same thing myself more times than I can count."

"Not very charitable, are we?" I asked.

"Fuckers don't deserve charitable," he muttered. "Especially after what you told me."

I *had* told him—not everything, but enough that he did know what my parents were like.

"I am sorry, though," I whispered.

"I know," he whispered back.

"So...what did your parental asshole do this time?" I asked after a couple of moments passed.

"He's getting married." A roll of his eyes. "Again. And making more kids he won't take care of."

That was...yuck.

But also, by the way Theo recited it, that wasn't unusual.

So, what had upset him this time?

"He wanted money. Again."

I grimaced, but also...that sounded like more recitation.

I braced again, waited.

"And when I turned him down, he called my mom this morning and tried to guilt her into talking to me."

Shit.

"And then he messaged my sisters, who aren't biologically his, just to fuck with them." A beat. "Because he knew it would fuck with me."

Double shit.

"And then when I told them to block him, he circled back to me and threatened to go on social media and tell the world what a terrible son I was."

Okay, yeah, *that* would do it.

# TWENTY-FOUR

Theo

HER FACE CHANGED, pity lacing those coffee-colored eyes, and a bolt of anger surged through my middle.

A month ago, I might have let it loose.

This woman was just like *them*.

Another fucking vulture trading in other people's lives.

Only...she wasn't like that, wasn't like the people who'd reveled in the drama of my pain.

She was Eva, and she was taking time out of her day, time when she should be hauling her gorgeous ass up to the booth, getting ready to talk hockey, getting ready to do the job she'd been hired for, the job she had been working hard for. Not standing in the hall, goose bumps on her arms—yeah, I could see them on her skin, could see the faint outline of her hardened nipples beneath her blouse (also, yeah, I was a fucking pervert).

"Shit, honey," she whispered, and I'd be lying if I said that her calling me *honey* did nothing for me.

It did a lot.

It made me *feel* a lot.

A lot of relief in knowing I'd made the right decision to not go home when she'd ordered me from her apartment.

A lot of—

"I'm sorry your dad is such an asshole," she murmured, stepping closer, pressing her body to mine, flattening her palm against the back of my hand where it still rested on the silken skin of her cheek. "If it's any consolation, people always see through that bullshit."

No. They didn't.

Which was why I was so fucked up.

I'd lived that shit. I knew what people thought or said or commented from the safety of their homes. Or gossiped behind backs while saying something completely different to my face.

I knew that if—or when—my dad put this bullshit out into the interwebs, some people would always believe I was a deadbeat son who made millions of dollars and didn't want to help my dad out.

But I also understood I didn't have control of this situation.

Didn't have control of my dad dive-bombing my life.

Again.

I didn't tell her that, though. Just said, "Thanks, sweetheart."

Her mouth quirked up.

"What?" I asked.

"No Stubbs?"

I cocked my head to the side. "I figured you were being sweet, so I'd better reward that."

"Don't get used to it. Stubborn is my middle name." She waggled her brows, making me chuckle. "Which is why you've been trying to make Stubs my nickname, right, *Air*?"

"Absolutely," I lied.

It was because I was lame and couldn't come up with anything better.

She smiled at me goofily.

God, that hit me right in the feels, filled my stomach with... fuck, if I didn't have butterflies (something I was never going to say aloud). "Thanks," I told her softly.

"For what?"

"Making me feel better."

Her expression softened. "I didn't do anything."

She had, and the fact she didn't see that sent butterflies through my stomach again. Softened my heart...right before I had to get on the ice and go crush the other team into oblivion. "The fact that you think that tells me enough."

"To find a new nickname?" she asked lightly.

"What, you don't like *sweetheart?*"

A shrug, though her eyes were dancing. "Sweetheart is perfectly...acceptable."

I rocked back on the heels of my skates, my chuckle filling the air. "Acceptable?"

She shrugged again. "Yup." A beat. "Albeit, not super creative."

"Is this your way of telling me that you need me to put some effort into nickname creation?"

"I would never dare to tell someone that." She grinned. "Nicknames are created organically and not to be argued with."

The rules of a hockey locker room.

That she knew that—

This woman was fucking amazing.

And I really needed to come up with a better name for her.

I clucked my tongue. "Great."

"What?" Her brows lifted in question.

I tugged a lock of her hair. "Now I've got to go play hockey with a bunch of assholes while I'm feeling all warm and squishy inside."

Her face...fuck, *warm and squishy* had nothing on it. The way she looked at me, her expression, the gentle in her eyes—all of that arrowed straight to my heart. All of that had me falling for her—no, falling *in love* with her—right there in the bowels of the arena, my teammates on the ice behind me, the stadium filling with fans, one of the support staff or my coaches able to walk in on us at any moment.

I didn't get the chance to put that into words, to have to *find* the words, before she spoke.

"Here," she said, taking my hand, the bare one, and tugging it toward her. She bent over it, and I felt her fingers work at my wrist, soft, featherlike touches that reminded me of other soft touches in other places. Touches that had my dick twitching in my jock.

I shifted slightly—since it wasn't the most comfortable thing —having a hard dick while wearing a cup.

"This is supposed to help you focus," she said softly, glancing up at me, taking my mind off my dick, fingers still working on my skin. "Gabe, my middle brother," she added, and I nodded, silently telling her that I remembered. "Gabe makes these. He's really into art, but also spirituality. The colors and beads are supposed to help with focus and bring good luck. They're rose quartz and amethyst, so not really your colors and I know it's all probably fake, mumbo jumbo but"—she shrugged—"it's brought me good luck."

Not falling.

Diving.

Into love with this woman.

"Sweetheart," I rasped.

Her cheeks went pink, and she glanced away. Then back,

lifting her chin, straightening her shoulders. "It's not a big deal."

I touched the swathe of pink, that blush growing by the second. "It's not nothing to me."

"Theo," she whispered.

Sliding my fingers down, I cupped her jaw. "It's not nothing to me," I repeated.

A breath in, holding it for long enough that I worried she would pass out, but then she exhaled, turned her head in my hand, and pressed a kiss to my palm. "Okay," she murmured. "It's not nothing." Another exhale. "I hope it brings you good luck." A pause as she captured my hand, peeling my fingers from her face. But she didn't release me, just squeezed lightly and smiled at me. "And focus."

"Fuck," I muttered, my heart rolling over in my chest, offering itself up to this woman.

"What?"

"So not helping me with all that *warm and squishy*."

Laughter in my ears. Mischief in her eyes.

"What?" I asked this time.

"Squishy," she said proudly, dropping my hand and doing a little shimmy that was fucking adorable. "That's perfect." She grinned. "And so much better than *Air*."

"Um," I said, "care to clue in the big, dumb hockey player?"

"First"—she paused mid happy dance—"that's rude. You're a big, dumb, *sexy* hockey player." And damn, the burns from this one had me bursting out laughing. She never gave an inch and never failed to surprise me. "Second, Squishy." A nod. "*That's* your new nickname."

I groaned, dropped my head back. "Woman. Seriously?"

"Seriously." She laughed, presumably at my outraged expression, and tapped me on the butt just as Smitty turned the corner, spotted us, and grinned.

"Nothing going on, huh?" my teammate called, voice booming down the hallway.

Eva smirked. "I'll let you deal with that one."

Then she turned away.

Paused. "Theo?"

I was watching her ass and I wasn't going to apologize for it. "Yeah, Stubbs?" I asked, looking up.

Seeing she was glancing over her shoulder.

Her mouth twitched, but then her face went serious, and I braced.

*Breathed.*

"You're not dumb," she told me quietly.

Then she was gone, disappearing down the hall.

Leaving me.

With her bracelet snug on my wrist.

So not leaving me. Not really.

Because she'd shoved herself into my heart.

And I had the feeling the space she'd made for me wasn't going away, not any time soon.

Not ever.

# TWENTY-FIVE

Eva

DESPITE HAVING to rush up the stairs and bursting into the booth with sweat on my top lip and wheezing from my sudden —and unwelcome—burst of exercise (those fucking stairs), I managed to get myself composed and sweat-free before the broadcast began.

And watching the way that Theo had recovered, was jumping in on the plays, skating hard and using that big hockey brain of his, buoyed me.

The tightness in my belly dissipated.

I could watch the game and participate in the conversation and be witty and smart and kill it doing my dream job.

Because that hug had helped me too.

That conversation, the way Theo had trusted me...it had healed a wound deep in my heart.

He trusted me.

*He* trusted me.

Knowing I was smiling like an idiot and that my coworkers

probably thought it was from Mark telling me what a great job I'd done—in front of everyone!—I pushed up from my chair, waited as they removed my mic. My smile wasn't just from Mark's accolades. It also wasn't just being satisfied with my own performance, with trusting my own instincts, or even with the Breakers putting in a decisive win down on the rink below.

It was also…Theo.

My heart did a little flippy-flop, and my belly fluttered.

I liked him—liked him more and more as I got to know him.

"Thanks, everyone!" I called once my mic was off and I'd retrieved my purse and cell. I pushed out of the door, headed for the back staircase that would lead down to ice level and the underground parking garage, showing my badge to the security guard at the top and moving down at a much slower pace than four hours before.

I'd just reached the bottom when my cell rang.

I stepped to the side, avoiding the flow of people—staff and equipment guys, cleaners and trainers, security and players and coaches from both teams. It was always busy down here after a game, and I didn't want to get accidentally checked into a concrete wall.

Snorting to myself—knowing I was a dork and would also be happy to be checked in any way by a certain hot hockey player—I managed to drag my cell from the depths of my purse and saw that Dommie was calling.

My sis was a pain in the ass.

But she was also the best.

Calling me after every game to hype me up.

Grinning, I swiped, put it up to my ear, and said, "Hey, babe, I'm not ready for my postgame compliments yet. I need to get to my car—"

And maybe to the locker room for "content."

Yup, I was saying that with quotes, because I would use it for content, but also...a certain hot hockey player.

"Evie—"

I froze, the nickname not one that Dommie had used in years, the tone one that I hadn't heard since—

"What is it?" I asked, worry sitting like a ten-ton brick in my stomach.

"Mom—"

That ten-ton brick doubled in size. No quadrupled.

My knees went wobbly, and I leaned heavily against the wall. "What?" I asked again when Dommie didn't go on.

"I came home, and sh-she was on the floor—" A hitching breath that had me striving for patience, forcing down the urge to demand Dommie tell me what the fuck was going on. "I came home, and she was on the fl-floor and I-I couldn't wake her up and—"

Fuck.

My legs buckled and I went down, barely catching myself in a squat, barely saving my knees from connecting with the concrete floor. Not caring. Because—

"You couldn't wake her up and what?" I asked, throat tight, heart pounding against my ribs.

Dommie just kept crying.

"You couldn't wake her up and what, Dommie?" I rasped.

"Mom—her lips were blue and her heart—"

"*What?*" I pressed when Dommie broke off again. My nails scrabbled against the concrete wall, and my other hand gripped my phone tightly enough that I worried it might break. "What about Mom's heart, Dommie?" I asked, struggling to not yell, to keep my tone even, to not reach through the phone and get my sister to finish a fucking sentence.

But Dommie didn't answer.

And she didn't finish a sentence.

She just kept crying.

All while I clutched at a wall that had no handholds. That wouldn't collapse but couldn't hold me up. That was strong and completely useless.

A palm settled on my back, warm and gentle, before a body came close.

I'd jumped, head jerking to the side, gasp rising in my throat, but that faded away, the panic, the gasp, because I'd known who it was almost at the same moment.

Theo.

Because *Theo* had came close.

Of course he would be there.

His skin damp from a shower, the spicy scent of his shampoo and soap in the air, his warm palm sliding up to cup the back of my neck, squeezing lightly. "Give me the phone, sweetheart," he murmured, that hand still moving, shifting over, grasping my cell, tugging it from my fingers. "Hello?" he said a moment later.

A long pause.

"Okay, honey, this is one of Eva's friends, breathe for me," he said gently. "Breathe for me and tell me what's going on."

A pause. Longer this time.

"I can't understand you, honey. Take a deep breath with me, okay?" He inhaled. Exhaled. "Now let it go." A beat. "Good. Now, this is Theo. Who am I talking to?"

I had found myself following the quiet instructions.

Breathing in. Holding it for a moment. Letting it out.

"Okay, Dommie," he went on. "I'm right here with your sister"—my heart squeezed by that proof he remembered what I'd told him—"and she's okay, but she needs to know what's going on, all right?"

As he was talking, he was shifting, wrapping his free arm

around my shoulders, drawing me up to my feet, but keeping me close, tucking me into his side, into his warmth.

"Your mom is in the hospital?"

I released another breath, and my legs threatened to buckle again.

My mom was alive.

She wasn't dead on the floor somewhere, wasn't in a black body bag or covered in a sheet or in a morgue.

I wouldn't have to go and identify her.

Wouldn't have to see her lifeless, her skin pale and waxy.

Wouldn't have nightmares for months—like I'd had after my dad had passed.

"Okay," Theo said after a beat. "Which one?" Another blip of quiet. "Okay," he said again. "We'll be there in half an hour. Try to hold it together, honey. You won't be on your own much longer. Right," he added. "We'll be there really soon. Bye, Dommie."

He hung up.

I was...frozen, broken and pieced back together again.

Just breathing.

Then his hand came to my jaw, tilting my head up so that our eyes met, and I realized I'd been staring off into space.

Realized I needed to get it together.

My mom needed me. My family needed me.

I had to be strong—even if my heart was thudding and my palms were sweaty and I felt like my legs would give way at any moment.

"I need to go," I whispered.

"Yeah," he whispered back.

But he didn't release me, just took my purse from where it was somehow hanging from my arm and drew me forward.

"You need help?"

It wasn't a boom, but I recognized Smitty's voice anyway,

my stare darting to the side, seeing him standing there with Walker, seeing both of Theo's teammates looking concerned.

"I'm fine," I whispered.

Something that Smitty didn't seem to buy.

"We'll follow you over," he said. Then glanced at Theo. "What hospital?"

Theo told him.

"You don't have—" I started to protest, but all three of the hockey players in the hall ignored me.

"We'll be over," Walker repeated, his voice firm.

"I'm fine," I whispered.

"Yeah, sweetheart," Theo whispered back. "I know you are."

But he didn't drop his arm as he bustled me out of the arena, as he led me to his car.

I only lost his warmth when he tucked me in the passenger's seat, buckled me in, and rounded the hood of his car.

And got it right back when he picked up my hand, lacing our fingers together.

He pressed a kiss to the back of it.

Then drove me to the hospital.

# TWENTY-SIX

Theo

CONSIDERING the state I'd found her in, I had expected to have to take the reins in the hospital.

But I should have known better.

Eva had used the drive to pull out some Eva Magic, and she was completely composed when we strode into the waiting room and Dommie swept toward her in a cloud of sobs, knocking Eva back a step when she wrapped her arms around Eva's waist and collapsed against her.

I had steadied the pair with a hand on Eva's back and prepared myself.

But, again, I should have known better.

Eva had been...Eva.

Confident. Assured. Capable.

Dommie had been soothed and tucked into a chair, me beside her, before Eva had gone over to reception and spoken with the woman manning the desk. Then, escorted by a nurse, Eva had disappeared behind the wooden doors—with a glance at me first, ensuring I had Dommie (which I did and nodded at her to tell her as much).

She hadn't come out for a long time, and by then, Walker and Smitty had taken seats on one side of Dommie, while I was still on the other.

Walker—and this shocked the shit out of me—had picked up Dommie's hand and held it.

Not that Walker was an asshole (nope, that was my job), but he didn't do entanglements, was an even bigger manwhore than I was.

Than I *had been.*

I didn't know the story behind that. I just knew that Walker was pretty much the last person I would have ever expected to show up in the ER and provide comfort to a woman he didn't know, least of all to hold her hand and wipe her tears away and stroke back her hair, all while she continued to cry.

But Walker was doing just that.

I had just pulled my arm back, exchanged a raised-brow look with Smitty, and waited for Eva to come back out.

Now, as she walked through the automatic doors and moved toward us, I felt it.

*It.*

What I'd been scrambling to avoid for so long. Love. Not just falling—or even diving—into it, but deep, intrinsic, devoted *love.*

This woman was it for me.

This woman was everything I'd avoided and all that I needed and...

A well of panic threatened to take over, threatened to send me running. But just as quickly, I squashed that shit down. I wasn't my dad. And Eva wasn't like any of the women whose lives had been ruined by my sperm donor.

She was strong. And capable, confident, assured.

She handled her shit and had carried far more weight than she should have to.

And I wasn't going to freak the fuck out and add to it.

I could puzzle out the rest of the crap in my mind later, could come to terms with the past and all the bullshit that had been left behind because my fucking father was a dirtbag, but right now Eva needed me.

And I was going to be there for her.

I stood as the doors closed, as she came over to us, wrapping my arm around her shoulders again and tugging her close, thankful when she didn't fight the hold, when she gave me a little of her weight.

Her voice was tired. "She's going to be okay."

Dommie's breath hitched. "She is?"

Eva nodded.

"But her lips were blue," Dommie whispered. "And she wouldn't wake up."

Walker released her hand, put his arm around her and drew her as close as the chairs would allow.

"I know, sissy," Eva said, kneeling in front of her, taking Dommie's hand. "She passed out, hit her head, and her heart doesn't work well on a normal day, you know? Things were dicey there for a minute, but you did the right thing by calling the ambulance."

"But ambulances are expensive, and Mom—"

Eva froze, just for a second, but then she squeezed Dommie's knee, stood again. "That's what Mom needed, yeah? You did what you had to, and Mom will be okay. That's what's important."

"But—"

"I'll make sure we're all good," Eva said firmly.

Then she turned from her sister, glancing at me, at Walker and Smitty. "You guys should get going. It's late and you're tired and you have that road trip coming up and the playoffs in just—"

"I'm staying."

My words were probably a bit too sharp, a bit too intense, but that Eva would think I would leave her now—after all that had happened between us, with all that she was dealing with, not to mention all that was in my heart—yeah, no, that wasn't fucking happening.

I was staying.

"They're going to transfer Mom upstairs," she said. "That'll take a while."

"I'm staying," I repeated.

Her lips parted, the protest welling up in her eyes.

"Don't argue, Evie," Smitty said, which was a much better nickname than Stubbs and reminded me that I needed to get on doing better on that front.

But also, not the point.

Smitty was being serious.

And he could be more stubborn than Eva.

Which was probably why Eva sighed, leaned a little more heavily against me, and said, "It's late and Dommie needs to go to bed—"

"I'm not leaving," Dommie began.

Eva bent and squeezed her knees again. "I know you want to stay, honey, but it's really late and you didn't sleep, and you have to work tomorrow—"

Walker frowned. "She's not working tomorrow. Not after—"

"No," Dommie said, "she's right. They're finally trusting me to open the bakery. If I flake out on that—" She shook her head. "And I have class at night."

"Mom is sleeping anyway," Eva said softly. "And you can

come right when you get off, see for yourself that she's okay. I'm sure she'll be awake then."

Dommie nodded. "And Jer needs to know so he doesn't wake up t-to—" Her voice broke.

Eva leaned in, wrapped her arms around her sister, dislodging Walker.

She whispered something that I couldn't hear, but I wouldn't have been able to anyway because my teammate was standing and moving to me. "I'll take her home," Walker muttered. "But there is no fucking way that she's working tomorrow."

That made me want to laugh.

Because arguing with a Moreno...

Yeah, that wasn't going to go well.

"Just get her home, yeah?" I muttered, turning back to see Smitty standing and wrapping both Moreno women in a hug, bending to murmur in their ears.

A bolt of jealousy slid through me.

Not that I had time to process that, to worry about what it would mean for my future—that I wanted to destroy my happily-committed-and-very-much-in-love teammate and friend. Not with Walker scowling (his expression looking like it was trending toward the same destruction I was feeling), moving over to the women and picking up Dommie's purse as Smitty released the sisters. My nosy, matchmaking teammate gave me an arch look (though I couldn't tell if it was in regard to me or Walker) then strode out the emergency room's doors.

And I didn't have time to process *that* because Eva was coming to *me*, wrapping her arm around my middle, and leaning against me.

Dommie murmured a goodbye and turned, following Smitty out, Walker right at her side, his head bent, his body close, every cell in my teammate's body screaming protective.

Eva sighed, rubbed a hand to her forehead, and pulled away.

Immediately, I hated the loss of her body pressed to mine, but my watch buzzed at the exact same moment, drawing my focus for long enough to see it was a text from Smitty.

> If you let her push you away now, you will never forgive yourself.

Smitty might be a pain in the ass.
But he was right.
Not that I intended to let her push me away.
Not that I intended to be anywhere but at her side.
Now. *Forever*.
Eva looked up at me, eyes tired, skin pale, lips parting—
"I'm staying," I said.
And then I took my turn arguing with a Moreno.
It went about as well as I'd expected.
But I stayed anyway.

# TWENTY-SEVEN

Eva

I STRETCHED MY SORE MUSCLES, every part of me hurting from sitting next to my mom's bed for hours.

And Theo had sat next to me the entire time, a strong, steady shoulder to rest my head on when the fatigue had overwhelmed me. He'd lifted a hand, tugged me down to that shoulder of his, and run his fingers through my hair, keeping me steady in the uncomfortable chair, allowing me to drift off.

Such a simple touch.

A small connection.

But, for the first time since my mom had gotten sick—hell, for the first time since my dad had passed and the extra stress of keeping our family together had fallen on *my* shoulders, I didn't feel alone.

And...it was nice.

It was fucking earth-shattering.

Even while sitting in a hospital room, waiting for my mom to wake up.

Dommie had come just before noon after she'd opened the bakery and finished her cakes for the day, and I had let Theo bustle me back to my apartment.

To my bed.

Sighing, I rolled over, lids peeling open, and I winced against the brightness.

Not enough sleep, but I didn't dare to close my eyes, to allow myself to slip back under. Not when it would mess up my sleep schedule even more than it already was.

I tossed the blankets back, stood, and all of a sudden realized that Theo had gone to bed with me.

Whirling, I spun toward the bed, wincing because all of my flopping and stretching and blanket-tossing hadn't exactly been gentle, nor conducive to allowing someone who was sharing my bed to continue sleeping.

But...my bed was empty.

And disappointment was coiling in my belly.

Then I saw the note, lurching toward it in a way that wasn't the least bit graceful.

*Had to go to practice. My car is in your spot, keys on the counter if you need to go anywhere. Took your keys and will get Smitty or Walker to help me get your car home from the arena.*

*—Theo*

He'd left a note.

He'd left a note telling me where he'd gone.

He'd left a note telling me to take his car.

He'd left a note telling me that he was arranging to bring mine back home.

*He'd left a note* detailing all the thoughtful things he was doing for me *after* he'd done something nice and kind and spent the night with me in a hospital not sleeping, *after* getting me to said hospital because I'd been falling apart.

*After* being nice to my sister.

To me.

"Shit," I whispered, my eyes stinging.

I could get used to this, could crave this, could want *this* man in my life forever.

Dangerous thoughts.

But I still smiled all the way to the bathroom.

All the way through my shower.

Through shaving my legs and bikini line, through sudsing up and rinsing off and deep conditioning my hair.

Through lotion application and tweezing and putting on my makeup.

Even through drying my hair, something that I normally hated because it was thick and my blow-dryer wasn't all that powerful.

Today, I didn't care.

I grinned like an idiot the entire time.

And made plans.

Some razzle dazzle and secret recipes—brownies this time and a scheduled DoorDash order for tacos because I was tired and wanted to impress, but I wasn't up to making pasta from scratch so I could *really* impress him.

I was grinning as I tugged on a pair of jeans that made my ass look incredible and a slinky tee that Dommie wouldn't be caught dead in because I had bought it at a big box store and it was technically a pajama shirt, but it was cut perfectly and cradled all the right curves and felt like heaven on my skin.

Still grinning as I pulled on socks, snagged a hoodie from my drawer.

But that all changed as I started to leave my bedroom, focus on chocolate chips and cocoa powder.

Because my cell rang.

For a minute, my heart seized, remembering the call from the night before, but I shoved that down, processing that it was my mom's assigned ring.

My mom was okay.

Okay enough to be calling.

I exhaled, strode across the room, and snagged my cell, unplugging it from the charger that Theo must have sorted out when we'd come back to my place just hours before.

Another thoughtful thing.

My phone rang again, jarring me back to focus.

"Right," I whispered, swiping and bringing it up to my ear. "Hey, Mom."

"Dommie just left," came the sharp voice. "Where are you?"

"At home," I said. "I just woke up. How are you feeling?"

"Terrible."

"I'm sorry to hear that," I replied, knowing that my mom hadn't always been like this, hadn't been sharp and brusque and mean, that life had sharpened the edges of her personality, buffed up the bad parts so they shone more brightly. Once upon a time, my mother had been my best friend, a playmate and confidante, a soothing presence. Now, it was sandpaper on bare skin and being burned like an ant beneath a magnifying glass positioned under the sun. "Did the doctors come in and see you?" I asked instead of focusing on that loss.

"Yes. They gave me some medicine, baby, but it's not helping."

My head began to pound. "I'll reach out to them and see what we can make happen, okay? They want you comfortable so they can try a new combination of medicine to help your heart."

A sniff. "None of them know what they're doing. Stupid. Just like you," my mom muttered, the words lashing through me. "None of it helps."

"They're trying to help," I told her, burying the hurt, knowing it was the illness, the pain, the fear. "If you can be open to the new medicine and follow your doctor's instructions that would help."

Something my mother *hadn't* done. Skipping meds. Well, okay, *forgetting* them and then taking them all at once and causing the scary reaction Dommie had walked in on last night —something that wouldn't leave my sister's mind, I knew.

Because I'd lived that firsthand—walking in on a parent on the floor.

Only my father hadn't survived.

And I had been left with far too many of traumatizing moments burned into my memories.

"It's too many instructions," my mom muttered. "And too many pills."

I sighed, strived for patience. "So, what do you want me to do, Mom? You put off the treatment for months and it's more complicated now. You're *this close* to going into congestive heart failure and your MS is out of control. You're miserable and hurting and—"

"It's not my fault!" my mom cried, breaths coming far too fast.

Dangerously fast.

"I know," I soothed quickly. "I know it's not your fault and that you're feeling terrible." Bullshit, but my mother didn't need to get even more worked up. "I'm sorry. I'll call the doctors and we'll figure it out, okay?"

"O-okay," my mom wheezed. "I'm s-sorry, baby."

I sighed again. "I know. I'm sorry too, and I'm sorry I'm not there right now."

"Y-you h-have a l-life."

Why did that sound like an accusation?

Rubbing my forehead, I made sure my voice was gentle. "I'm going to let you rest, so I can talk to the doctors, okay?"

"O-okay."

We said our goodbyes then hung up.

My headache intensified.

One that got even worse by the time I spoke to the bevy of doctors in charge of my mother's care.

One that became splitting when an administrator called me and needed a deposit for my mother's stay.

A *large* deposit.

One that then turned into a pounding migraine that had my vision going slightly dimmed at the edges as I pulled out my ring light, my camera, as I changed into something more suitable and thanked God that I'd decided to shave so I didn't have to do it with blurry eyes.

Then I raided my fridge.

Improvised.

Because Dommie hadn't been at the bakery long enough to bring me the day's rejects.

And, even as my headache raged, I filmed.

Posted the video.

Continued doing something I hated, something I kept promising myself that I would stop because it made me feel like shit.

Something I had to keep doing because...

Medical bills and ambulance rides and art school and ruined silk blouses.

# TWENTY-EIGHT

Theo

I KNOCKED at Eva's door, intending to drop her car, see if she needed anything, and then head home.

I was exhausted, and practice hadn't made it any better.

We were less than a week away from the playoffs, had four games left in the season and two of them on the road beginning the day after the next—which I had to report for at five in the morning.

Ten hours from then.

I needed to make sure Eva was good.

Then I needed to pack, sleep, and haul my ass to the bus.

My stomach rumbled.

Right. I also needed to eat at some point during the next ten hours.

The door swung open, Eva standing in the opening looking fucking gorgeous with her hair pulled up into a ponytail, her eyelids sparkling with some kind of shimmery glitter shit, and her body—

Fuck, but her body was a lesson in sin.

Curves that pushed at the material of jeans and a plain, gray T-shirt.

And—*fuck*—plain and gray wasn't a good description, not in the freaking least. It dishonored the fucking beauty of her standing in front of me in those sinful jeans and that T-shirt, her smile wide, her eyes warm.

"Hey, honey," she murmured, stepping toward me, her hand dropping to my chest.

Pressing to the spot over my heart.

Which skipped a beat beneath my rib cage.

Then sped like a fucking jackrabbit when she rose on tiptoe and kissed my cheek.

"Come in," she ordered softly. "I'll feed you before you need to head home and pack for your trip, Squishy."

I blinked for a moment, confused that she'd seemed to pull that list of tasks from my mind, but then she was taking my hand, drawing me in through the door.

"Sit."

Another order, and I was bewildered enough, tired enough that I trailed behind her to the couch, perched on the cushions as commanded.

"I'll be right back," she whispered.

And turned to leave, but I got it together enough to catch her hand, draw her to a halt. "Are you okay?"

A nod. "Still a bit tired, but I'm fine."

"Your mom?"

Her palm came back, resting on my chest again before sliding up to the side of my neck. "She should be okay as long as she follows the doctors' orders and takes her medicine." Eva sighed, sad creeping into her pretty brown eyes. "Whether she actually does that or not is yet to be seen."

"And her pain?"

Because she'd been out of it—*really* out of it in a way that had wanted to send me from the room, that probably *would* have sent me from the room if not for Eva needing me, for *me* needing to be there for her.

Proving to her that I wasn't like my father.

Proving the same to myself.

Eva winced. "She's still hurting, but I spoke to her and the doctors this afternoon. They're trying a new cocktail of drugs and are going to get her into some PT." She rubbed her forehead like it hurt. "Of course, whether or not I can actually get her to go or practice at home is a whole other beast."

Yeah, I imagined it would be.

"She's lucky to have you."

"Yeah," Eva muttered, but I knew that she didn't fully believe me. Felt it when she whispered, "I made her cry today."

A tug drew her down onto my lap, and I took the opportunity to tuck her against me, to hold her tight. "Tell me," I demanded, albeit gently.

Eva dropped her forehead to my collarbone. "She doesn't listen. To me. To her doctors. And she hides things, like whether or not she takes her medication or goes to her appointments or how she's feeling." She sighed, voice dropping. "And then it gets really bad and I have to babysit her and take her to every appointment and count the pills in her medicine bottles."

"Gets bad how?" I asked. "Like last night?"

"Like last night," she agreed and sighed again. "And now Dommie has to have finding our mom on the floor like that burned into her brain forever. And the added stress of worrying about paying for the ambulance ride and the ER visit and all the new medications." I froze, but she didn't notice, just pressed her forehead against me a little harder. "It's a stretch on a normal month, though things have gotten easier as my blog has taken off and with the Breakers games, and I'll manage, mostly because I always do. But now my little sister is going to worry too." Eva lifted her head, smile heavy in a way I hated. "I want her worrying about buying clothes, not paying my mom's medical bills."

"So, *you'll* worry about them instead?"

She stilled then shrugged. "I'm the oldest." Another shrug. "It's my job."

"It shouldn't be."

"Maybe not," she said. "But this is America and that's the way it is, especially when you come from a family that has to live paycheck to paycheck and has already been burned badly by medical debt." She pushed lightly against my hold. "I got us out of it before and look where I am now." Her expression became determined. "I'll get us out of it again."

"I know you will."

She softened, leaned in, and brushed her lips over mine. "Enough heavy," she murmured. "I've got brownies that just came out of the oven that I'm going to douse with ice cream and chocolate syrup, and we're going to eat our dessert while we wait"—she reached into her pocket, tugged out her cell and tapped at the screen a few times—"for our tacos to be delivered. There," she said, "all ordered." Grinning, she dropped her cell onto the coffee table, turned for the kitchen again. "I'll just—"

"New plan," I said, all of the respect and love and *need* I had for this woman welling up and taking over.

Definitely taking my mind off brownies.

Although, not off tacos.

Smirking to myself, I leaned back onto the couch, kicking off my shoes and swinging to the side so I was lying lengthwise out on the cushions. And I did that while snagging Eva's wrist again, tugging sharply so that she went off balance...

And landed on top of me.

"New plan," I said again, dropping her wrist and sliding my hand beneath the fabric of that damned tempting T-shirt.

"What's the new plan?" she asked and if it was breathless, I was counting it as a result of my closeness rather than the fact that I'd just—literally—knocked her off her feet.

"I play with your taco"—I slid my hand down, dipped my fingers beneath the waistband of her jeans—"and then *eat* your taco"—a squeeze of one lush cheek—"and *then* we eat the ordered-in tacos and your brownies with ice cream and chocolate syrup."

"Okay," she murmured, hips pressing to mine, taking my cock from chub to fully hard in just one movement. "I like this plan."

I flipped us, dropped my forehead to hers.

Flicked open the button on her jeans.

Tugged down her zipper.

Black lace over blond curls.

*Fuck.*

I needed to taste, to touch, to fuck.

So...I did that.

Dragging off her jeans, tugging off her shirt, worshipping all those parts that were covered by tempting black lace.

Tasting her.

*Eating* her.

Fucking her.

We were both still breathing heavy—and I wasn't sure I could still feel my legs—when the doorbell rang.

"Tacos," she gasped.

And I didn't miss the longing in her voice, even as she was sprawled naked on the couch, her glorious body on display, her eyes still closed as she panted lightly.

Laughter bubbled up in my chest and I tugged the blanket off the back of the cushions, tossed it over her.

Then snagged my jeans, pulling them up as I hopped my way to the door.

She sighed.

Worried, I turned back.

Her lips were curved, eyes at half-mast. "Just saying," she murmured, "hockey players have the best asses."

# TWENTY-NINE

Eva

I REMEMBERED the look he'd given me at random points throughout the next two weeks.

The heat in his eyes.

The wicked smile.

The way the bag of tacos had ended up on the coffee table.

Eating the cold food naked much later with an action movie playing in the background and his body the only thing keeping me warm—well, his body after his mouth and tongue and fingers and cock had all worked together to ensure my temperature didn't drop.

And *then* we'd had brownies.

And then he'd held me while we slept, getting up an hour early to go back to his place to shower and pack and head off to the final two road games of the season. I had watched them on TV from my mom's place, getting everything settled after she was discharged, babying her so that she would be on board—as much as my mom was on board with anything—with her new routine.

Then had spent the subsequent days driving and arranging transport for when I—or Dommie or Gabe—couldn't take our mom to her appointments, setting up pill bottles on the counter and alarms on my mom's phone so she would take them on time. Making sure Jer was okay, because he was the baby and because I knew how hard it was to be in high school while everyone was going on with their lives, totally unaffected as big shit went down at home.

He was doing all right, still shaken up.

But so was Dommie. Because even though our mom had done a lot of damage over the last years, had taken out our shitty circumstances on all of us, Dommie and I had the benefit of remembering the good times before everything had changed.

Jer and Gabe...not so much.

So Jer was more worried about me and Dommie.

And Gabe was...well, Gabe held things closer to his chest. He'd learned to distance himself, and I knew he wouldn't talk with anyone about what he was feeling. He'd throw himself into work, into canvas and paint, maybe make a few bracelets I'd gladly take because I knew that was how he processed.

Still, regardless of the chaos at home, I'd managed to color commentate the second to last home game, as scheduled, and had returned to sports blogger and influencer since then.

Because the broadcast of the playoffs wasn't run by the local teams.

They were national productions and expensive, with big-ticket names.

I wasn't there yet. But watching it on TV...I vowed that someday I would be.

I had to give those guys a run for their money.

I *would* give them a run for their money.

Now, though, I was getting ready to leave for the arena. Theo had actually gotten me tickets, but then I'd been invited to create some crossover content for the team's socials and my own and then to watch the game from the owner's box.

The *owner's* box.

Not crammed like sardines into the media box.

Not in the stands with a bunch of other fans screaming "Shoot!" at regular intervals.

But in the *owner's* box.

I did a little shimmy, finished smoothing on my lipstick then flicked off the lights, all but bouncing down the hall as I slipped into my coat and grabbed my purse, my keys. I tugged open my door, stepped out, locked up, and turned for the stairs.

"Oof!" I exclaimed, arms shooting out to catch the person I'd just run into. "Shoot, I'm sorry," I sputtered, dropping my hands so I could fix my purse, could drag it back up to my shoulder. "Are you okay?" I asked, genuinely concerned. The man I'd run into wasn't much taller than me, and he seemed... almost familiar somehow.

"I'm fine," he said gruffly, turning away from me, bags hanging from both wrists.

"Can I help you with those?" I offered along with a sheepish smile. "Considering I just barreled into you?"

"No," he snapped. "I said, I'm fine."

"Okay." I stepped back and to the side. "I'll let you get on with it then."

A grunt.

The man walked past me, down the concrete corridors between the apartments, and I sighed, whispered, "Focus, Eva."

Then shook off the embarrassment of my klutzy inattention.

I had a hockey game to get to.

<hr>

"IT'S A DIFFERENT BEAST, HUH?" Luc Masterson, the GM of the Breakers, said, coming up beside me, mirroring my position of forearms on the railing, gaze on the ice below.

Something I knew because I'd peeked...before looking back at the rink and the man who was slowly becoming my obsession. He'd sent me flowers four times over the last two weeks. Four times! And had taken me out to dinner and back to his place twice (for the entire night, I thought with a snort). The rest of the nights he'd been at my apartment when our schedules aligned.

Two weeks of the Theo Young I'd dreamed of.

And now I was going to get to watch some playoff hockey.

"It's going to be great," I said aloud, glancing at Luc again, knowing that part of the reason the team *was* great was because of the man standing next to me.

A former player.

A solid GM, seeking balance and family and competitiveness.

The guys weren't just cogs in a system. They were important.

And if they were toxic, he wasn't afraid to send them packing.

They'd won the Cup twice under Luc's tenure but they were just as hungry for another one. That made it exciting to be a fan, especially when the second one had come after Oliver James's career-ending injury. I'd cried like a baby that night— and it had been on my live stream, and it was part of why I was here tonight.

My first viral.

Crying while talking about hockey.

Ridiculous.

Luckily, I'd managed better since then, but I would never forget that moment. The joy. Feeling like I was part of something (even while being aware I hadn't actually done anything). So proud of them.

Epic, for sure.

"We've got a good squad this year," Luc said. "Despite the California teams coming for us."

"The Sierra have a strong squad, but even with Lake Jordan, I don't think they have the maturity to take it all the way."

Luc nodded. "The team culture sucks."

"According to my sources"—I gave him a half-smile while tapping my fingers together, evil genius style—"they're going to be making some major moves in the off-season."

"They do, and clean up that locker room, and we're *really* in trouble."

I glanced over at him.

He shrugged. "They're a tough match-up for us *with* the dysfunction. They sort that out, and they'll be a force to be reckoned with." His mouth curved and he pointed a finger at me. "But don't let that end up on your blog, yeah?"

I grinned back. "I make no promises." A beat. "Which is why you guys hired me in the first place."

"Real." He sighed, shook his head, but he was smiling. "You're real."

"I try."

He nudged my elbow with his. "We're lucky to have you."

That had my lungs freezing, belly full of bubbling happiness. "I'm just happy to be here."

"Speaking of that," he said. "When Theo—" A questioning look that told me that my newfound peace accord with Theo (and fucking with frosting, chocolate syrup, and watching movies while naked) must be a hot topic of conversation via the Breakers gossip phone tree.

Then again, he *had* slammed a door into my face then carried me like a caveman through the halls where anyone could see me.

And, of course, had bundled me out after I'd gotten the call from Dommie about my mom.

"When Theo...?" I prompted, not biting.

Luc smiled, clearly seeing he wasn't going to get more fodder for that gossip phone tree, and went on, "When Theo made the request for tickets, I figured I'd take the opportunity."

For what?

But I didn't get the chance to ask that because he was turning away, walking toward a table, coming back with a manila folder in hand.

"I asked Lexi to draw this up for you," he said, passing it over.

"Are you serving me with a lawsuit?" I asked with forced lightness, since my heart was pounding and his wife, Lexi, was one of the team's attorneys.

Luc chuckled. "That's a contract for a permanent broadcast position next season. Hopefully, you'll give the team a couple of good years before the national coverage bigwigs snap you up."

"I—"

He clapped me on the shoulder. "Review the contract. Negotiate for better terms"—his mouth curved—"but not *too* good, considering I have a business to run. Then sign, yeah? We want you in the family."

All the air hissed out of me, and I legitimately worried for a moment that I was going to pass out.

Was this actually happening?

A permanent broadcasting gig?

A whistle blew down below and he squeezed lightly before moving back to the railing. "Come on, Evie," he called. "We've got hockey to watch."

THIRTY

Theo

*FUCK.*

"Fuck!" I heard Walker say at the same time the word crossed my mind.

The puck had just taken a bad bounce.

Like a really fucking bad bounce.

I was already moving, seeing Walker doing the same out of my periphery, but the other team—recipient of said bad bounce, albeit it was a good bounce from their perspective—was already hustling toward the other end of the ice.

And Walker and I were both about as useful as—

Well, *not* useful things, I thought, digging in, skating hard, and knowing that I was going to get to back in time to be no help for the first shot.

And maybe no help for the rebound.

Playoff hockey was unforgiving.

But in overtime, after a long season, being caught out of position it was even more so.

I didn't stop skating, though, not even as I watched the four on two develop, the puck sail across the ice, leaving Smitty and our other defenseman, Cas, scrambling to stay in position and not overcommit, giving the other team an even easier run at the Breakers' goal.

Pass. Skate.

Drop the puck to our teammate.

Swing it to the other side.

I crossed the red line.

One of the guys on the other team floated the puck across the middle—

*Crack.*

Smitty had extended his stick—extra-long because he was a big fucker—and intercepted the puck. He didn't gain control but redirected it enough that it bounced over a series of sticks—Smitty's, two of the opposing players, Raph's.

Walker, though, got control of it, and I was already throwing on the brakes, starting to hurry back the other direction.

Because I knew the pass was coming.

And it did, flying up the ice, landing on my stick.

I skated hard, carrying it over the blue line, careening for the goal, knowing the other team wouldn't give up, knowing they would backcheck like motherfuckers, would take me down in an instant if they got the chance.

So...I didn't have much time.

So...I *hustled.*

To the net. Toward the goalie—searching for openings and when I didn't find any, cutting sharply to one side, drawing the 'tender out, gaining some space—

*There.*

A deke to the opposite side, but, at the same time, I extended my stick, used it to flick the puck up and over the goalie's shoulder, sending it sailing into the top corner of the net.

Holding my breath until I watched the white mesh move, until the puck dropped to the ice inside the goal.

*Behind* the goalie.

Until the red light flashed on.

---

"Fuck, yeah, man," Walker said as we dropped onto the bench, huffing like we didn't play hockey for a living.

Because, *fuck*, that shift had been a doozy.

Up. Back. Up again.

At least it had ended up with a point on the proper side of the scoresheet.

And I didn't mind being the one to get the goal.

*Hello Ego, my old friend.* (And yes, I sang that to the tune of *The Sounds of Silence*.)

Raph flopped down next to me, grinned and bumped his shoulder against mine. "Just saying, I'm gonna get CakeGirl28 to make you a special video."

I glanced over at Walker, rolled my eyes. "What the fuck is this idiot talking about?"

"This idiot is going to treat you," Raph said with a smirk, yanking the water bottle I had just picked up from my hand and drinking deeply.

Walker sighed, snagged a bottle from the rack, squirted some in his mouth, then offered it to me, and I chugged it down because I'd just skated my ass off. "That OnlyFans chick the rookies are obsessed with. Apparently, she'll take special requests for a price."

"They need to get laid," I muttered. "In the real fucking world."

"Word." Walker took the bottle back, dropped it into the rack.

"I don't know," Raph said, sliding down the bench as more players hopped off and on the ice. "You saw them after the game in North Carolina. They seem to be doing fine."

I *had* seen them, surrounded by women in the lobby and enjoying every minute of it—somewhere I myself would have been, if I hadn't wanted to get up to my room to call Eva. "I still think if they were doing as *fine* as you say, they'd be less obsessed with some girl smashing cake with her ass on video and more with actually *touching* a girl's ass."

Raph chuckled. "Man makes a point." A beat. "Though, I hear she's got a great ass."

Walker huffed out a breath and rolled his eyes. "You so know that Beth is going to hear about this conversation, right?"

"Beth and I have a very open relationship." He glanced out at the rink, at the play that was developing near the boards in front of us. "We can talk about anything."

"Including cake smashing?"

"Yup."

"Sure, man," I said. "I've seen your little redhead lose her temper. There's no way that she'd be cool with you paying for an OnlyFans."

Raph tossed us a smirk as he stood up, one leg lifting over the boards. "Who says she doesn't do some cake-smashing of her own?"

Then, waggling his brows at us, he hopped over the boards.

Leaving us staring for a beat, mouths hanging open.

Before we processed that we needed to follow him.

That we needed to go play hockey.

That I needed to stop thinking about Eva giving me a private show by doing some cake smashing of her own.

Damn.

Maybe the rookies really *were* on to something.

———

"TELL me where you got that energy at the end of your shifts tonight," the reporter said. "How did you find the strength to keep pushing?"

Ugh.

I hated questions like this.

I pushed because it was my job and I wanted to win tonight because it would bring us one step closer to the Cup.

I pushed because I liked scoring goals...and I repeated, it was part of my job.

But no one wanted to hear that shit, wanted to hear another boring soundbite.

So, I decided to change it up.

Because my woman was bouncing with joy as she talked to almost every one of my teammates.

Except for me.

She hadn't come over and peppered me with questions. She'd just flashed me a smile—beautiful and wide and bright—when we'd let media into the room, and then gone and talked to Smitty.

Smitty!

Christ.

So, when the reporter asked the question that I found really dumb—and something I'd answered a hundred times in a hundred different ways over my career—I did something that was completely out of character for me—

I drew more attention to myself.

"I found the strength to keep pushing"—I let my voice rise over the din of the room and voices and people—"because a certain sports reporter gave me her lucky charm." I held up my wrist, the bracelet she'd tied on weeks ago sparkling in the overhead lights.

The room went quiet.

Really quiet.

And then Eva slowly spun to face me, her eyes wide.

"Come here, sweetheart," I ordered softly.

And, fuck, I really needed to come up with a better nickname for her.

Her brows lifted.

The room went even quieter—probably waiting for her to explode.

Then—thank fuck—she crossed the room, avoiding the team logo on the carpet because she knew how locker rooms worked and wouldn't dare to bring us bad luck by stepping on it (hockey superstition at work there).

"You rang?" she asked dryly, the room still quiet enough that I knew everyone could hear every word.

"Yeah, sweetheart, I did." I wrapped an arm around her waist, tugged her onto my lap then grinned at her shocked expression and looked up at the cameras. "She's the reason I'm pushing, why I'm skating my ass off." My lips twitched. "Can't end up as another story on her blog."

And...silence.

Silence and people watching us with their mouths agape, questions not coming as I'd expected.

"Okay, so this was a dumb idea," I muttered after several long moments, discomfort creeping in.

Everyone was watching. Cameras were rolling. This would definitely end up on social media.

And even though I orchestrated it, I hated all of it.

Well, all of it except for Eva being in my lap.

*That* was perfect.

"You know what's *not* dumb?" she whispered, leaning close so the words brushed my earlobe.

"No," I murmured back.

Her lips were soft and warm and tempting and almost distracted me from my words. "Luc gave me an offer tonight for a permanent position in the booth."

"What?" I asked, pulling her back enough to see her face. "Really?"

She nodded.

I yanked her close again, hugging her tight. "That is fucking amazing, sweetheart."

"I know," she whispered. Then, after a long moment, leaned away from me. "Just saying, though, they're still watching us."

"I know," I whispered back. "I'd say mistakes were made here, except"—I gently cupped her cheek—"you're not a mistake. You're Eva, and you're the best thing to ever happen to me. Even when you don't give me good luck bracelets," I added as her face softened.

As her eyes went damp.

As Smitty sniffed loudly in the corner. "Romance, man," he blubbered. "It gets me every time."

"The romance gets *me* every time too, Squishy," Eva said lightly, and leaned in, kissed me squarely on the mouth—and did it long enough that I knew this would also end up on the team's social channels.

I couldn't find the strength to care.

Not with Eva looking at me like that.

Not with her hand dropping to my chest, to the spot above where my heart was pounding.

Pounding so hard it took me a minute to really hear what she'd said.

To process it.

And the fact that Smitty was grinning.
*Squishy.*
He'd heard.
My whole team had.
The entire *locker room* had—players and press alike.
Fucking hell.

# THIRTY-ONE

Eva

IN RETROSPECT, calling Theo Squishy in a locker room full of cameras, teammates, and tape recorders hadn't been the smartest.

Case in point?

His stall currently filled with Squishmallows and those rubbery squishy toys all the kids had these days.

He hated it.

His smirking teammates, however, were already in love.

I winced into my phone's camera, mouthing, "Sorry," before I turned it around, catching the full stall and now my extended hand, holding yet another squishy, this one with an adorable little face I wanted to...well, *squish*. I walked forward, placed it on the already overflowing pile, gently patting its head for good measure.

Then I flipped the camera back to face myself, grinned, winked, and clicked off, pocketing my cell.

And rotated to face Theo, who'd already showered, hair darkened from the water and haphazardly pushed back.

"Hi," I said, lips curved as I moved over to him, winding my arms around his middle.

He was hard and hot from the shower, his skin a little damp.

Just the way I liked him.

Mostly because it reminded me of the other times I'd been pressed to him and his skin was damp.

And naked.

And...my inner dirty-minded woman cackled.

More naked time please!

I smiled up at him, knew that—considering they'd just gone up three games to one in the first round of the playoffs with the win tonight—sexy, naked time was on my agenda.

The only question was his house or mine.

"You're lucky you're beautiful," he grumbled, even as his hand came up, gently pushed back a few strands of hair that were getting in my eyes. "You know that, right?"

Gentle, even while I was teasing him.

And helping his teammates burn him.

By filling his stall with squishies...and posting that fact online.

And he wasn't freaking out about it—not about that or about our story being fodder for *all* the TikToks. Hell, *I* was feeling a little weird about our sudden blip of fame, even knowing that we'd fade right back into oblivion once all the hockey daddy and STFUATTDLAGG memes went away.

However long *that* took.

Because I had to admit I'd watched him crooking his finger at me, his soft, "Come here, sweetheart," echoing through the speakers of my phone and sending a chill down my spine more than a few times.

It was fucking *hot*.

And I had lived it.

Maybe I'd get him to order me around when we went back to his place.

Just to feel the commands shiver down my spine.

His place because his bed was bigger and neither of us had to work tomorrow—and neither did Dommie, who was on Mom Duty—so we had all day.

*All* day to play.

Smiling, I leaned back and pressed a kiss to his jaw, the bristles of his beard (that he wouldn't shave because he was a superstitious hockey player and during the playoffs, those superstitions grew for all of the players—along with their playoff beards). "I *am* lucky," I told him—half joking, half seriously—"that you hit me with that door."

He'd been reaching for my misbehaving hair again, probably intending to do more of that gentle smoothing back.

But my words had him freezing and slanting a look in my direction.

He didn't even have to say, "Really?" out loud.

Grinning, I rose on tiptoe, kissed him long enough that Smitty boomed, "Break it up, kids, and find a private room!"

To which I dropped back onto the soles of my feet, my cheeks flaming hot.

Smitty tugged lightly at my ponytail as he moved by us to his stall, grinning as he took in the pile. "Though," he said, still booming, "I have to say I am impressed with your *Squishy* stacking skills."

He bent, started to put on his shoes.

Perfect timing.

I reached into my backpack, tugged out one last squishy— and waggled my brows at Theo, showing him the stuffed toy I'd brought especially for Smitty and all his troublemaking, shit-giving glory.

He was still talking, teasing Theo as he tied his shoes. Whistling softly, I quickly tossed the stuffed toy to Walker, who was on Smitty's other side.

Squishy pile. Smitty. Walker.

My partner in crime.

He caught the toy, and I bit my lip to hold back my giggles as he stealthily placed it on the bench, all of an inch from Smitty's thigh.

"And if you're really going to keep your woman happy, you really should—*eek!*"

Smitty was tall, the tallest guy on the team, and huge, with shoulders that rivaled the breadth of a Mack truck, but the sound that came out of his mouth was...inconceivable.

High-pitched.

Loud—well, okay, *that* was Smitty to a T.

The big man lurched up to his feet, hopping away from the toy at his side and knocking into the pile of squishies that had taken over Theo's stall.

Theo, who had thought far enough ahead to pull out his phone and start recording Smitty.

"Please tell me you got that all on video," I whispered.

"Every glorious syllable of it," he told me.

I giggled.

"I didn't know a human could make that sound," Walker said, chuckling as he moved to stand by us, where we were watching the show of Smitty trying to crawl out of the pile of squishies without getting close to the offending toy.

A wombat.

I didn't get it. Wombats were adorable and fluffy and cuddly and—

Somehow Smitty had gotten a stick because *my* wombat

went sailing across the locker room, colliding with the other wall.

Smitty clenched the stick, hung his head, breathing heavily.

Then he was glaring up at me and Theo and Walker, along with most of the rest of the team. All of whom were busting up.

"Evil," Smitty said, pointing the stick at us. "All of you are evil!"

I smiled at him beatifically. "You know we love you."

"Evil," he repeated, setting the stick next to the pile of scattered squishies. "And because of that, I'm not cleaning this"—he waved a hand at the stuffies—"up. Well"—he crouched down, picked up an adorable bunny and carefully set it on the bench—"I'm not cleaning them up except for that one," he muttered, snagging his messenger bag from the shelf overhead, slanting a glare at all of them one more time. "I'm going to sic Kailey on you fuckers."

"Love you!" I called as he beelined for the door.

Theo wove an arm around my middle, hauled my back against his chest. "You trying to make me jealous, Stubbs?"

I dropped my head back onto his collarbone, smiled up at him—

And felt every part of me freeze.

Because it was like all the puzzle pieces of this man had just slotted into place.

Because I'd almost said, "You know I love you too."

But...it was too soon, and I'd only had nice Theo for such a short amount of time, and...

It was too soon.

So, I shoved that down even as the truth of it settled in my belly, my heart, my mind.

Too soon.

Too much.

I just needed to ride this wave, enjoy this moment. I knew

how quickly things could go bad, could turn toxic, how quickly my future could be derailed.

*This is different.*

*He's different.*

Those statements were written across my brain in big, fat Sharpie.

And I wanted to believe them.

It was just...too soon.

"It's working," he rumbled, nipping lightly at the spot behind my ear. "Let's go home, yeah?"

Too soon. Too soon. Too *fucking* soon.

*Breathe.*

I exhaled.

We had now. We had this moment, this laughter and togetherness and bright, shiny blip in time.

That had to be enough.

Because, someday, it might all go away.

"Yeah," I said, pressing my hand to Theo's chest, feeling the steady pulse of his heart below. "Let's go home."

Because I was going to soak up every moment.

For as long as I had it.

# THIRTY-TWO

Theo

"FUCK," I groaned as she moved on top of me, tits bouncing as she worked my dick, drawing herself up and down the throbbing, hard length of my cock, each bounce and stroke catapulting me closer and closer to a fucking explosion.

Her cheeks were flushed, hair a mess and all in her face, but she didn't seem to mind as she arched back, resting her hands on my thighs as she lifted up and ground down.

"Theo," she moaned, her pussy convulsing, fluttering around me.

Telling me she was close.

But not close enough.

Because I was closer.

Snaking a hand down between us, I pressed my thumb to her clit, circled it exactly as she liked it, got to feel her clench around me, the rhythm of her strokes faltering.

I had her, though, steadying her with a hand on her hip,

sliding her up and down while still working her clit, driving her to the edge with a frenetic type of focus.

Because *I* was close.

Too close.

Bucking up, I latched onto her breast, using my free hand to drive her down on me as I thrust deeper, faster.

*Harder.*

She shuddered. "Theo—" Her head flew back again as she ground against my hand and came, squeezing my cock like a vise and sending me right over the edge behind her.

We rocked through the subsiding waves of pleasure, moving together slowly.

Until she collapsed against me, breath hot and damp on my throat, her body limp and still aside from the occasional shuddering breath as she slumped against my chest.

"Why?" she murmured.

"Why what, sweetheart?" I murmured back.

"Why is it always so good?"

I chuckled and carefully set her on the couch. "The universe needed to find a way so we wouldn't completely fuck this up." She blinked up at me. "Make it so we couldn't ignore the attraction...thus, eventually, we couldn't ignore all the good there is between us."

Expression softening, she placed her hand over my heart. "I think you may be right."

And just like always, the organ beneath her palm skipped a beat, knowing it belonged to her.

"I *know* I'm right." Smiling at her frown, I covered her with a blanket then closed the drawer of the side table.

A yawn vibrated through her as her eyes slid closed then back open slowly before she muttered, "I still don't know why you have condoms in every room of your house." Those lids dropped to half-mast, sleep making her irises soft. We'd both been tested, given clear bills of heath, but had opted to use protection because it was responsible. "I'm not saying I don't like it for convenience's sake." Another yawn. "Just that it seems like overkill."

Chuckling softly, I tucked the blanket around her. "I'll tell you another time, yeah?"

She nodded jerkily, sleep clearly already intruding, so I left her there and went and took care of the condom. She was snoring softly by the time I made it back, so I just carefully scooped her up and held her securely to my chest before climbing the stairs and tucking her into bed.

I didn't feel the least bit tired—not with the adrenaline from the game coursing through me—but when I got into bed next to her and held her close, my eyes slid closed.

And I fell asleep, more content than I'd been...

Perhaps ever.

---

"You really don't have to be here," Eva said a couple of days later. For at least the tenth time since I'd swung by her apartment and picked her up that morning.

"I *want* to be here," I said—also for at least the tenth time.

Charged silence from her side of the car.

Teeth nibbling into a plump bottom lip.

"Sweetheart," I murmured, reaching over and taking her hand, heart squeezing when she gripped onto mine tightly enough to make my bones protest. "I *want* to be here."

"But you have to fly out tomorrow, and you should be using this time to rest and prepare. If you guys win the next game, the series will be over and you'll have extra rest before the next round."

"First," I said, drawing her hand over the console and

placing it on my thigh, smoothing my fingers over hers when she would have pulled back. "Hockey is my job, but it's not my life. If I want to help my girlfriend"—she sucked in a breath here, nails biting through my jeans—"yes, my *girlfriend*"—I slanted a look at her as I stopped at a signal—"if I want to help my girlfriend check some items off her to-do list, then I'm going to do that. Especially if it's on my day off and I want to spend time with her instead of sitting on my ass and playing video games by myself."

Her brows drew together. "But you don't play video games."

"I don't play them around you because I'd rather do other things." I sent her a look that told her exactly what *other things* I'd rather do.

Another pause. Then, "I don't want you to change for me."

I huffed out a laugh as the light turned green. "*I* wanted to change—or wanted to stop being an asshole, anyway."

"That wasn't you," she said softly.

Standing up for me.

When *I'd* been the asshole to *her.*

"It *was* me," I told her. "Bullshit in my head, yeah, but it was still me."

"That wasn't you," she said again.

"How about I stop arguing about that when you stop arguing about me being happy to help you out?"

She inhaled.

"Mostly because people who care about each other should lighten their partner's load, but also because the sooner we get your mom sorted, the sooner we'll get back to spending the day together—preferably naked and horizontal." A beat. "Though, I'd take a repeat of the shower like last night."

Her hand tightened again, for a whole other reason.

The same one that had my dick twitching in my underwear.

"I'm not used to this."

*This*, I assumed, being someone having her back. I knew that Dommie was there and did her best, but it would be like Lana or Rose trying to take over for me. There were just some things that came with being the older sibling.

Eva wouldn't relax until she'd done it herself, and this had been doubly influenced because of the bigger role she'd taken when her dad had gotten sick and, more so, after he'd died.

So, I'd help her.

I'd be there for her today because tomorrow I was flying out on a fucking airplane and would be gone for two days, and she would be on her own.

And that would be our future for the next chunk of time during my—hopefully—long playing career.

Me here.

Gone. Training. On the road. Potentially traded.

This professional hockey thing wasn't for the faint of heart.

So, I would be here for her when I could. Would drive us over to Eva's mom's house and make sure she felt like her mom was secure and settled and feeling okay.

Because I wasn't always here to help.

"I know you're not used it," I told her, turning onto her mom's street, scanning the houses, looking for the tan and blue one that I'd driven to one time before, when I'd dropped some clothes and food off for Eva and her family.

I hadn't met the Moreno clan then—had just left the stuff on the porch, not wanting to intrude.

But I was going to meet them today.

Or at least, I was going to meet Eva's brothers and Dommie when she wasn't upset and crying at the hospital and Eva's mom when she was feeling a bit better and not in a medically aided rest.

I was nervous, no doubt.

But determined to be there for Eva.

I pulled up to the curb, turned off the engine. "I know you're not used to it," I said again. "But I'm here and not going anywhere."

What I didn't know was how hard that promise would be to keep.

# THIRTY-THREE

Eva

"YOU'RE STUPID, BABY," my mom said, like the endearment would soften the insult.

Like the *baby* would mean that calling me stupid didn't slice deep.

The only thing that made it somewhat bearable was that I'd heard it all before—that and worse—and I could just let it roll down my back, ignore the slight sting of the words and get on tackling the to-do list that seemed to grow longer every time I visited.

*"I need help with grocery shopping, baby."*

*"Why'd you pick such crappy fruit? Do you not know anything?"*

*"Vacuum the carpet in my bedroom."*

*"No, stupid. Not like that. You need to go in all the same direction, baby."*

*"The milk doesn't go in the door, stupid."*

*"That shirt isn't a light, stupid."*

*"Ugh, stupid. Don't chop the lettuce like that."*

Okay, so maybe there were more *stupids* than *babies*, and that was why it always hurt.

Though, I supposed, that being called stupid by one's mother would always hurt.

What was unconditional love?

Not what was found between parents and children in the Moreno household.

And yet, I was here. When I could be spending Theo's day off doing anything else, spending it together in peaceful isolation like we had a few days before. Spend it doing *anything* else —sex, video games apparently, eating, sex, making TikToks, sex, shopping, sex, relaxing while watching crappy TV, *sex...*

I smiled.

Despite my mother still blabbering in my ear about improper vacuum lines in the carpet.

I just needed to cook a couple of meals to put in the fridge, make sure Jer had enough spending money for school, leave a check for Gabe's tuition for him to drop off at the school's office, and follow up on the medicine delivery I'd arranged—as one of my mom's new medications needed to be refrigerated, so someone would need to be home to receive it.

And...my mom had gone back to work a few days before.

Yup. My mom could go to work, but she couldn't arrange for her medication or make sure Jer had food to eat in the house —food that wasn't complete junk my mom wasn't supposed to be eating.

Gabe's tuition wasn't even a question.

My mom couldn't pay for art school. She could barely afford her medicine and mortgage and bills, even with me paying for a huge chunk of it and Jer kicking in some from his after-school job.

Something I had put a stop to the moment I'd found out.

Jer was saving up for a car for himself and he had prom and a girlfriend, and he needed to be a kid, not to be paying for heart medicine or water or...the Netflix account.

So, yeah, my mom could work and tell me I was vacuuming incorrectly and order Theo to pull weeds in the back yard, but she couldn't...parent. Not for me, not for Dommie or Gabe or Jer.

At least she'd saved most of the *stupids* for after Theo had been dispatched to weed duty.

Something I was going to relieve him of as soon as those meals were cooked and the medicine delivery followed up on and Jer had been checked in on and I left the money for Gabe.

Thankfully, I knew how to work fast and could multitask.

Ignoring my mom still sputtering about vacuum lines, I turned it off and started winding the cord, noting that the windows in my mom's bedroom looked a little dingy as I rolled it down the hall and tucked it into a closet. Theo's weeding form was tinged a bit brown, and the same dusty tint was present in the kitchen and living room. So, apparently, all the glass needed a clean.

Something that was going to wait for a future visit.

I had a hot, hockey *boyfriend*—eek!—to hang out with.

Closing the door to the hall closet, I turned for the kitchen, ignoring my mom sputtering after me, ignoring the anger and sharp words and trying to hold on to the fun memories, the times before it had all gone to shit, knowing I was lucky to have them because Jer had grown up without anything similar to hold close.

So had Gabe.

Dommie hadn't, which was why she helped out as much as she did.

I, though, was the oldest. I'd had the most for the longest, so I needed to do right by my siblings, and I even needed to do right by my mom—the one who had laughed and hugged and wouldn't have dreamed of calling me stupid.

Though I couldn't deny that I'd been crunching the numbers on paying for a home aid for my mom.

Anything to save me from vacuum micromanaging.

Plus, my mom would love to have someone new to boss around.

Inwardly shaking my head, I went to the fridge and started pulling out ingredients, lining them up on the counter as I dialed the number for the pharmacy and began the process of being on hold for long minutes. Chopping veggies, stirring them into some heated olive oil on the stove, adding some chicken and seasonings and broth and letting them come together in a soup that would be easy on my mom's heart.

Then whipping together some biscuit dough and cutting them out, sliding them into the preheated oven.

By the time I was pulling the golden brown discs of dough out and setting them on the counter to cool, I'd rescheduled the delivery to a time Jer would be home to put it in the fridge, had finished the rice and veggie stir fry, and was working on chopping ingredients for fruit salad.

Thankfully, my mom had retired to her bedroom, leaving me safe from micromanaging as I cooked.

Soon, I could blow this popsicle joint.

Soon, I could get back to my plans of all the things... and sex.

That had me smiling as Theo came in through the back door, looking a little sweaty and a whole lot yummy and making me realize that *all the things* would be just fucking.

No shopping. No video games.

Just that man naked and pounding into me.

He winked at me, moved to the sink, and started washing up.

Which felt domestic and right and—

The front door opened, Dommie, Jer, and Gabe coming in, talking a mile a minute, the sudden influx of noise drawing my attention to my siblings.

Fuck, I loved the little bastards.

"Hey, sissy," I said, moving toward my sister and squeezing her tight.

Only Dommie didn't hug me back.

In fact, she slipped out of my hold and glared darkly at me.

"What?"

"Did I tell you yesterday that I had this?"

I rocked back on my heels. "Um, yes? But you're busy and already took a day this week. Plus, Jer really likes the stir fry I make and Mom's room really needed a vac—"

Dommie plunked her hands on her hips, disapproval on her face.

Gabe leaned against the doorframe, mouth tipping up at the edges.

Jer, sweet boy that he was, came over and hugged me, murmuring, "Thanks for the stir fry, big sis."

I hugged him back, glaring at Dommie, whispered, "There's money for you in your sock drawer."

"Eva," he said, expression darkening as he joined in with Dommie's disapproval.

"What?" I asked.

He pulled away, joined Dommie, even going so far as to cross his arms.

Traitor.

"Let me guess," Gabe said, pushing off the wall and narrowing his eyes at me, "you came by to leave me a check even though I told you that I had next semester covered."

I narrowed *my* eyes. At all of them.

"Art school is expensive and supplies—"

"I have it covered," he said, more firmly this time.

My lungs seized, worry brewing. "But—" I began.

"And you shouldn't even be here, considering it's *my* day," Dommie said.

Okay, that was a good point, but—

"I had to call the pharmacy and—"

Gabe moved to me, pressing a kiss to my cheek before gently nudging me away from the fruit I'd been cutting up.

"—and I had to run the vacuum—"

Dommie joined in on the nudging me—a little less gently than Gabe had, but not hard either. "Here," she grumbled, glancing over my shoulder. "Wrangle this one so I don't have to."

And I found myself pressed back against Theo's chest, his arm winding around my middle. "You okay?" he murmured in my ear.

*No*, I was not okay.

I was—my siblings were—

I sighed. "You work too hard to come here, sissy, and—"

Dommie snorted. "Pot meet kettle." Then she looked over my shoulder again. "Take that one home. Do something fun that's not taking care of someone else for a change."

"Dommie—"

But my siblings were ignoring me. Gabe taking over chopping. Jer raiding the fridge. Dommie moving down the hall to presumably check on our mom.

"Breathe, sweetheart," Theo ordered softly.

But he wasn't letting me go.

In fact, he was steering me toward the front door.

*Traitor!*

"I'm Theo, by the way," he called as we hit the hall.

Halfway down the hall, Dommie grinned. "I'm Dommie, as you probably remember." A blip of sad in her eyes that had my heart squeezing, but my sister pushed it away. "The annoying one is Gabe."

"Hey!" Gabe snapped.

"And the baby's name is Jer."

Jer scowled as he trailed Theo and I into the hall but he didn't let *the baby* comment distract him. "Nice to meet you, Theo." He leaned back against the wall. "You take care of my sister and keep making her happy and no proper introductions are needed."

Theo's arm squeezed, and he chuckled (probably for the same reason a blip of amusement slid through me—*proper introductions?* Where did the kid get this stuff?). But when my man spoke, his voice was completely serious. And it sent a different feeling through me—pleasure and more of that rightness and...well, my belly was full of fluttering butterflies. "I'll take care of her," Theo said solemnly. "I promise."

Jer nodded approvingly.

Dommie called her goodbye.

Theo, arm still around me, tugged the front door, pulling it wide—

To reveal Walker, hand raised like he'd been about to knock.

I froze, felt Theo still behind me.

Then I was looking up, and he was looking down, matching my expression—eyes wide, brows up—before he glanced forward again.

At his teammate.

Who had growing patches of pink on his cheeks.

But who also didn't retreat or slink away or do anything except say, "Theo." A glance at me. "Eva."

Then he turned sideways and maneuvered past us...

Into my mother's house.

# THIRTY-FOUR

Theo

I TOOK A SIP OF WATER, leaned back in the booth, and watched my stepdad down a beer.

Was I jealous?

Yup.

But was I going to drink a beer four hours before a playoff game that could determine us moving on to the next round?

Nope.

It wasn't fun skating around bloated, and I wasn't going to do anything to fuck up my team's chances, wasn't going to be the player on the roster who didn't pull my weight. Nope. Been there, done that, and even if it hadn't been intentional—hello, midseason asshole slump—I'd hated it so much I was never going to allow myself to get to that point again.

Maybe I wouldn't always be on the scoresheet.

But I sure as hell could be ready and willing to skate my ass off every game.

Including in playoff matches that winning would take the team into the next round.

So, as tasty as that beer looked, I was sticking to water.

And eating my typical chicken and brown rice and broccoli. I'd already had my nap, now I would eat with Roger—the fucker was getting a hamburger—and then head to the rink to get ready for the game.

Still, it was cool that Roger was here. He was on a business trip and had flown in especially for this game.

He'd also bought a ridiculously overpriced ticket to the game itself, even though I could have arranged to get one for him. Because Roger was a good guy and never wanted to take advantage.

Not like my dad.

Not like Eva's mom.

Roger was like Eva's siblings. Like my mom. Like *my* siblings.

Good people.

"You know that you only have a couple more days before your mom pounces, right?"

I glanced up from where I'd been tracing random patterns in the side of my water glass. "What?"

"I believe you remember that Lana and Rose adore Eva Moreno." Lifted brows as he added, "And you know the Terrible Trio shares everything." A beat. "Including certain viral TikToks."

"Shit," I muttered.

I'd been too wrapped up in the fact that I was in love with a woman for the first time in my life, that things with Eva had been going great, in the sex—cough—to actually process that.

"And your mom asked me last night if she thinks you need more condoms to replace the stashes she put around your house."

"*Shit*," I muttered again.

Though, I probably *did* need to restock. Eva and I had been blowing through the caches at a rapid clip. Not that I was going to let my mom know—her squirreling them away was convenient, but...

Awkward.

"Yup," Roger said, mouth twitching at the corners. "I've managed to hold her off a bit with this visit, but you broadcasting your new girlfriend on socials and not sharing it with your mother, who you're extremely close to, isn't..." He lifted his brows as he trailed off.

And I filled in the rest for him. "Smart."

"That." Roger tapped his nose.

I sighed. "Do me a favor and let Mom know that I'll fill her in on my love life next time I talk with her."

Roger's mouth turned up. "Consider the message passed along."

The server came then, dropping our respective dishes in front of us and topping off my water before slipping away again.

I loaded up my fork with rice and broccoli and brought it to my mouth—

"So, is it serious?"

I froze, broccoli and rice dropping off the tines of my fork, landing on my plate with a soft *plop*. I looked from the fallen food—that wasn't in my mouth where it *should* be—up to my stepdad. "Seriously?" I asked dryly.

More mouth-twitching. "Part of your mom not flying out to join me on this trip was a promise that I would interrogate you properly." Roger took a huge bite of his burger, spoke through the food. "Don't make me regret saving you from the Terrible Trio's cross-examination."

"You know," I said, "I could easily solve this problem for myself by telling them you call them the Terrible Trio."

Roger swallowed, took another bite. "They already know." A beat. "That *both* of us call them that."

Shit.

I scowled.

"I covered your ass on that too," my stepdad said with a swig of his beer.

"Bullshit," I grumbled even as laughter bubbled in my chest. "Mom probably let you off the hook because it was *our*" —I waved my fork between us—"thing."

"Maybe." Roger grinned.

I sighed, ate a bite. Another. Then gave in. Because I knew that Roger wouldn't push further, even if my mom would turn the interrogation to him or give him a hard time about not getting *all* the answers to *all* her questions. If I didn't want to talk, that would be cool with Roger.

But it wasn't that I didn't want to talk.

I just...didn't really know what to say.

The big feelings in my heart, the love for Eva in every cell of my body, the worry that sat beneath that affection, the all-encompassing desire to make Eva mine...they were real and intense and I was scared shitless that I'd avoided commitment for all these years only to fall for someone who meant more than any woman ever had.

Who I didn't want to hurt.

Who I was afraid I would anyway.

"Shit."

I blinked, glancing up from my plate to see that Roger had set his burger down, was looking very serious.

"This is it for you, isn't it?"

My stomach convulsed—less *Squishy* and more tumultuous

storm on the open ocean, but I didn't bother to hide the truth. "Yes."

He nodded, falling silent for long enough that the tumultuous storm on the open ocean became a full-on hurricane barreling toward shore, that all of those worries I'd been working at burying—that I wouldn't be able to commit to one woman, that I'd end up just like my dad, blowing into lives, setting them alight, and then blowing right back out of them, that I'd hurt Eva, hurt the one woman I'd ever loved and fuck up her life and—

The cushion of the booth I was sitting on shifted and I glanced to the side, realized that I'd been so in my head that I'd missed Roger getting up, crossing around the table, and was now sitting next to me.

"I—" I didn't know what the fuck he was going to say, but I didn't get the chance to.

Because he shoved my arm.

Hard.

"What the fuck?" I snapped.

He leaned in, his face only a couple of inches from mine. "You stop that shit right now."

I blinked.

But he wasn't done. "You are *not* your father. You are a good man, and this Eva is lucky to have you in her life."

"I almost fucked it up with her."

"So?" he snapped. "I've almost fucked it up too many times to count. The important thing is that I get my shit together, learn from my idiocy, and don't make the same mistakes again."

"You've fucked up?" But he and my mom seemed so... perfect?

My stepdad lifted a brow. "Is that the pissed-off son wanting to protect his mom or the worried man who's afraid that he'll mess things up with the woman he loves asking?"

I exhaled, the mix of lightness and seriousness breaking through my panic. "Both." I narrowed my eyes. "How many times have you fucked up?"

He grinned, shoved my shoulder again, much lighter this time. "Enough."

That settled the storm in my stomach, the worry swirling through my insides.

But I still didn't like it.

"Mom hold your feet to the fire?"

That grin widened and he slid out of the booth, settled back on his own side. "Oh yeah, and I learned from that shit, learned what was important and that was your mom and you and the girls. And your mom learned that while I might fuck up, I wouldn't ever intentionally hurt any of you and that I would do my best to fix it."

I inhaled, fingers tightening on my fork.

"But, more importantly," he said, picking up his burger, bringing it toward his mouth, "I've gotten to know you, bud. The man you are inside, the person you strive to be, and that's why I know that while you will definitely fuck up—because we all do—you'll also bust your ass to make it right. And"—he took a bite of his burger, chewed and swallowed—"you're smart, considering all those fancy degrees you have, so I know you'll learn from your fuckups. I know you might make mistakes, but you won't make the same one twice. Now"—he gestured at my plate—"stop with this bullshit, put it out of your head and focus on the future. You've got hockey to play, a game to win, and a girl to impress."

A beat.

Then he added, "Something that's a fuck ton harder to do when you're not in the same city, yeah?"

It seemed impossible that it was this easy. To keep the woman I loved. To not be what my past, my father dictated.

That I just accept I'd do my best and still fuck up.

That then I'd make things right.

And through all of that I'd keep Eva.

But Roger was the best man I knew, and my mom was happy, and...

Maybe I could be that too.

# THIRTY-FIVE

Eva

GABE SAID he didn't need the money.

So, why was I doing this?

Why was I reaching into the depths of my closet for clothes I didn't like wearing? Why had I made sure that Dommie had brought me an extra cake? Why had I used a tube of icing to write the requested message on top of it?

Why was I even *considering* taking this special request?

For the money.

Except...I didn't *need* the money.

And Gabe didn't need it. And neither did Dommie or Jer or—

My mom.

Medicine was paid for. There was money in savings. My mom was working again—not full-time, but enough to take the pressure off. Jer had his job to pay for prom and dates with his girlfriend and to keep adding to his car fund. And I had just signed a big contract that would ensure I would have consistent money coming in even if the income from my blog and socials went away.

So...*why* was I doing *this?*

"It's the last time," I whispered, not answering that question, not diving too deep into the swirling mess in my head. I just...lied to myself, pulled out an extremely skimpy bikini, and carried it into the bathroom. Pretending that it wasn't a lie, of course, that this was definitely the last time, that it really *was* just for the money and as soon as I was stable, I'd stop. But after I'd set it on the counter, I just stood there like a statue, staring at myself in the mirror, studying my eyes.

And...I couldn't hide from the truth.

This would always be in the back of my mind. A specter that clung to my future.

A temptation that made me feel—

"No," I said. This *would* be the last time. It was a lot of money, and it would give me a cushion if things went wrong. Because things always did. And...it would be the *last time.* "This is the last time," I said more firmly, my expression filling with determination.

Only...would it?

Because beneath the determination was...reality.

Things went wrong. Life liked to slap me around.

My siblings might need me.

And I'd hustled for so long and done *this* for so long and I didn't—and probably wouldn't ever—have enough money for the offer I'd gotten to *not* be tempting. So, what was it to say that I wouldn't promise myself in the mirror that this would be the last time and then do it again the next time my mom needed help with a bill or Jer went off to college or, hell, I wanted to buy a house.

I'd like to afford that in the next century.

And seriously, was this so wrong?

Of course not. It was my body. My fucking choice.

It was just...before it *hadn't* been my choice.

I'd been in school and money had been short and...well, I'd been desperate. When a friend had jokingly suggested I start an OnlyFans, I had thought...fuck it. I'd needed to make money to finish my degree and help my siblings and make sure my mom didn't lose the house and make myself and Jer homeless and...

I'd liked the money.

For the first time since my dad had died, I'd been able to *breathe.*

And it had been fucking amazing.

Except for the whole being backed into a corner and forced to make a decision that meant I'd had to sell myself.

It was cool if someone wanted to do that, had made the choice to make a living this way—but for me...it didn't feel good. Because I *wouldn't* have chosen this.

Because every time I made a video, took a request...

Something deep inside me broke a little more.

"So," I said on a sigh, gripping the counter tightly, "why are you *still* doing it?"

Money.

Fear.

*Fear.*

That it would all go away, and if I let go of this secret, shameful baby blanket, my entire life could fall apart.

I'd lose everything.

But I didn't *need* it.

And—I sighed again—what was eating away at me was not just the shame I knew I shouldn't feel, and maybe *wouldn't* feel if my circumstances were different and this all had been my decision, but the guilt and the worry about what might happen if people found out.

What it might do to Theo.

His career.

*Mine.*

That had a knot tightening in my belly, worry wrapping around my lungs and threatening to steal my breath.

Because it was *my* decision now to keep going.

I didn't have to.

But that fact didn't stop me from putting up the portable background I'd bought years ago—a generic white wall that hid anything personal from the people who might watch the video.

And it didn't stop me from putting the tarp down on the floor.

Or positioning my ring light, my camera.

Or grabbing the cake from the kitchen.

It didn't stop me from getting that money.

So, what the hell did that say about me?

# THIRTY-SIX

Theo

"LANA SHOWED ME THE TIKTOKS," my mom said, her voice coming through the speakers of my car.

Eva, who was sitting in the passenger's seat next to me, giggled softly.

"Everyone has seen the TikToks," I muttered, shooting her a look—to which she just smiled back at me, totally unaffected—then glanced back at the road.

The attention wasn't going away.

But neither was Eva.

So...I was going with it. And anyway, it didn't bother me all that much that people knew Eva belonged to me.

Cue caveman.

"Your sisters are also now even more desperate than ever to meet Eva," she said before adding a moment later, "And so are Roger and I."

Eva wasn't giggling now.

In fact, she'd gone really quiet.

*Really* still.

And I didn't miss the panic in her eyes.

I reached out, dropped my hand on her thigh, squeezed lightly and forced myself to focus on the road when all I really wanted to do was haul her close and hold her tight.

"It's new, Mom," I said instead of causing an accident. "We can talk about that later, yeah?"

"When we come out next week?"

Eva inhaled sharply, thigh going hard beneath my palm.

"We'll see," I told her instead of committing to that.

Not because I didn't want them to meet Eva—I did. For the first time in my adult life, I wanted my parents' approval of a woman. But maybe less approval and more...slotting her into my family.

Because I wanted to keep this woman forever.

Even with the social media. Even with her blog full of posts that held my feet to the fire. Even with the specter of my father and all the insecurities that wrought in the back of my mind.

Eva was different.

Eva was *it* for me.

If I was being honest, she'd probably been *it* for me from the first time she'd asked me a tough question.

I'd just been too fucking scared and closed down to see it.

To see *her*.

Smart. Sexy. Working her ass off. Beautiful. Generous. Somehow forgiving my dumb ass.

I wasn't going to fuck it up with her again.

I *wasn't*.

Or when I did—per Roger's advice—I was going to fix it.

"Okay, honey," my mom said, giving in because I knew *she* knew this thing with Eva was a big deal—not only because of the TikToks, but because I'd never claimed a woman as mine. Not on social media. Not in the locker room.

Sure as shit, not in front of a bunch of reporters to broadcast on live TV.

That I had told her enough.

"See you next week," I said.

"Bye, honey."

I clicked off and carefully changed lanes, pulling into the parking lot of CeCe's, where we were supposed to be meeting the girls for a Cheese Night Extravaganza, finding an empty stall and turning off the engine. Beth had invited Eva to partake in the festivities, but we all knew what the invite was about—pulling Eva into the fold and getting *all* the gossip...on their favorite Squishy.

Yup.

That was pretty much what Beth's text to Eva had said.

At least the woman was honest.

But I didn't think an inquisition at Cheese Night Extravaganza would go well with Eva's current state of mind.

Her panic and worry were palpable.

"Hey," I said gently. "Talk to me, sweetheart."

A shake of her head. One abrupt jerk that sent her hair sailing into her face.

I pushed it back, realized that I'd be the one who needed to talk. To give and put my cards on the table.

"You know a little about my dad and his multiple marriages and making and then leaving new families." I cleared my throat as her expression cleared. "What you don't know is that he's so good at it that it was actually a news story."

Eva's eyes went wide, lips parting, as though to speak.

But I kept going before she could say anything. I'd started this, and now I needed to get it off my chest, needed her to know the last pieces of my past that I'd used to drive us apart.

"He had ten families. *Ten*," I repeated when her eyes went wider. "And thirty-six kids."

She sucked in a breath, released it slowly then reached up and took my hand. "Honey."

One word...and it told me everything.

Her panic was gone, and worry for me had taken over, and —fuck—how could I not love this woman.

"He couldn't even name all of us," I admitted. "And he sure as shit couldn't *support* all of us, and"—I sighed—"it was worse because my mom was his only official wife. She lost half of everything in the divorce—she couldn't afford to buy him out of the house, even though she'd put the down payment down on it, even though she was the one paying the mortgage and all the utilities. But he fought her on the divorce, and she had attorney bills to pay, and I think she was...just ready to be free of him, so she gave him half."

"Theo," Eva whispered.

"But before the divorce was final and because she was his wife on paper, it was easy to find us, easy for reporters to stake out our house and my school. Easy for local news and then the national news to pick up on the story. And exploit it." I braced because the rage was boiling in my belly, because the memories were burning through me. "It didn't help that my dad was happy to trade on his infamy, parading his kids and wives— though thankfully never me or my mom since the first thing she did was make sure she had full custody—on trashy television shows and infomercials and selling MLM and jumping head-first into any sort of scheme that would make him a quick buck. That is, until one of those schemes landed him in jail."

"Theo," she whispered again.

"I was relieved. I thought that would be the end of it. But it wasn't. His arrest and the trial brought everything back up, and we were inundated by reporters again. They didn't care that I was a kid, didn't care that my mom knew nothing about my dad's other lives—he traveled for work, so she didn't know about his other families or kids. And, honestly, she was thinking of leaving him since he didn't contribute." I ground my teeth together. "But she didn't want to upend my life."

Eva's fingers tightened.

"Then the story broke and both of our lives were upended anyway."

"I'm so sorry, honey," she whispered, sliding her hand up, placing it on my chest, above my heart. "That sounds awful."

"It was," I admitted. "For a long time. But then we moved out of state and changed our last names. I found hockey, got lucky I had a natural aptitude for it, and we moved on with our lives. She remarried—to a good guy this time—had my sisters and all is good."

"Yeah," she murmured. "Until your dad pops up."

I sighed, covered her hand with my own. "Yeah. He pops up occasionally, makes threats, asks for money, and then disappears back into the shadows."

"Shit, honey," she said softly. "No wonder you hated me." She shook her head again, hair scattering. "You should still hate me after what I wrote about you."

"No."

Her eyes locked with mine.

"I could *never* hate you, even when I really tried."

Her eyes glimmered and she released a shaky breath, her words barely above a whisper. "I hate that happened to you and to your mom."

I squeezed her fingers. "I know you do."

Because she had a big heart. Because she wasn't one of the vultures doing anything for a buck. Because she was Eva Moreno, and she was fucking *great.*

"Thank you for giving me a chance," she told me, and fuck if that didn't make my heart squeeze. "That must have been really hard."

It had been.

But—

"Don't thank me." I touched her cheek. "I need to thank *you* for seeing past my asshole and giving *me* a second chance—or third or ninth or—" I grinned. "Whatever."

Her lips turned up and the glimmer of mischief in her eyes told me her panic wasn't coming back, that we could both tuck the past away for the moment, could enjoy being right here. *Together.* "It was mostly because you impressed me with your frosting skills," she teased.

That had my grin widening, laughter blooming in my chest. "I know I did." I tapped a finger to my bottom lip. "Was your favorite when I licked it off your breasts?" I leaned in brushed my mouth over hers. "Or your cunt."

A blush spread on her cheeks, and she lightly swatted at me, pushing me back. "You know that's not what I meant."

"*You know* I love you."

Time froze.

And...nope.

That wasn't how I'd intended to say the words. Hell, I hadn't *intended* to say them for a while yet, and definitely not giving them to her by blurting them out in the car after dumping all of my family history on her.

I was supposed to be making her feel better.

Not saying something that had her pulling back, looking like she was going to tuck and roll out of the car.

Panic was back. Full force.

"It's okay," I told her quickly. "Just...forget I said it—" What? What the fuck was I saying? "*No.*"

Her head jerked up, eyes filled with dread.

"Don't forget I said it." I resisted the urge to drag her across the console and hold her prisoner against my chest. "Know it's there and I feel that for you, but don't let it pressure you to..."

I trailed off.

Because, fuck, that was just as bad.

Don't let it *pressure* her? Forget it but don't?

"Sweetheart," I said carefully, deciding to cut my losses and start with the basics. "Can you just...say something? *Anything.* It doesn't have to be about..." I waved a hand.

Silence. Long enough I was tempted to lock the doors in case she really *did* try to tuck and roll.

But then she spoke, her chest rising and falling in rapid succession. "I-I don't let people in." A breath. "And, I especially don't let *men* in." Her gaze came to mine, the panic still in her eyes. Twice in one car ride.

That had to be a fucking record.

And not one I wanted.

I leaned closer, cupping her cheeks. "I know, sweetheart. I *fucking* know. Believe me. The panic you're feeling right now is why I was an asshole for so long, why I spent so much effort pushing you away, trying to make you hate me."

Her hands came to mine, eyelids sliding closed.

"But you're more important than some bad press or reporters hounding me. You're more important than all my fucking hang-ups. You're more important than *everything* else."

## THIRTY-SEVEN

Eva

"YOU'RE MORE important than everything else."

Earnest words.

Beautiful words.

As beautiful as him casually telling me he loved me.

As beautiful as the love I had for *him*.

But this was...

A lot. Too much. Panic-inducing.

Having my fingertips itching to pull away, to yank at the door handle, to run screaming from the car into the cold Baltimore night.

To run from this feeling of vulnerability.

I might have if I hadn't seen the stark expression and the worry in his eyes.

That I would do just that.

Deny him.

Deny myself.

The happiness we both deserved.

"Nothing has ever been good enough for my parents," I admitted. "Not for my mom now and not for my dad when he was alive. With him, there was always something to be disappointed about, something to not live up to the standards of. And"—I sucked in another breath, released it slowly—"it got worse after he was gone. She...I don't know...*became* like him. Suddenly my best friend was gone and in her place was a woman who was..." A sigh. "I tried to fill the spot, tried to be what everyone needed, and it was never enough." I forced myself to hold Theo's gaze. "What if I'm not enough for you?"

"You are," he said quickly.

I sighed, leaned in, and dropped my forehead to his collarbone, settling when his fingers started drifting through my hair. Touching me. *Soothing* me. "You say that now. But what if that changes? What if you look at me and you don't love me anymore, or I do something so heinous that you—"

"You couldn't do something like that," he said. "And, more importantly"—a tug at a lock of my hair—"you wouldn't."

Believing in me.

*Loving* me.

When I knew.

Knew I'd already done something that could hurt him, *would* hurt him if he found out. And...might destroy him.

If the world found out.

Because it would be as much of a shit show as his father's exploits had been—maybe more.

Because of my online presence.

Because of the fucking TikToks I'd posted.

Because—

"I love you."

God, his voice. And those *words*...they settled on my heart, my mind like he was sprinkling my soul with glitter and filling my bloodstream with champagne and...insert all the romantic sentiments here. I lifted my head. "Theo, I—"

He pressed a finger to my lips. "You don't have to say it back," he added before I could swivel back into panic. "Not now. Not in the future. Not *ever*. But"—he held my cheek again—"know that's how I feel about you and it's not going to change."

Oh, how I wanted that to be true.

Oh, how I worried that it couldn't possibly be.

Oh, how I wanted it so much that I took his hand, peeled it from my lips, and held it tight as I said what was in my heart, "I love you too, Theo."

He exhaled, forehead dropping forward to settle on mine, his hot exhale drifting over my lips like a kiss. "That's the best thing I've heard in a long fucking time." He chuckled. "Maybe even *ever*."

"Even better than the headline on tonight's blog post?"

A shift back, dancing eyes on mine. He sighed, mouth edging up at the corners. "Sock it to me."

"*Young Pulls Out Heroics in Game Five.*"

He stilled, but only for a moment. Then his mouth was curving further, and he was leaning in again, slanting a kiss over my lips that had my heart pounding and body melting against his. His fingers slipping under my shirt, skating along my side, drifting up to the band of my bra—

Beneath it.

*Yes!* That was exactly what I need—

*Tap. Tap. Tap.*

"Quit feeling up your girl, Squishy, and get your ass inside!" Smitty's voice boomed through the window. "We have mozzarella sticks to eat!"

Theo and I broke apart, lungs working, breaths coming in rapid gusts.

"Fucker," Theo muttered.

I grinned. "Probably better that he interrupted us before you got your hand all the way in my bra."

"Fucker," Theo repeated, but it was lighter this time. Lighter and paired with a brush of his thumb over my cheek that had my heart skipping a beat. Then his expression sobered, and he cupped my jaw. "You good?"

I was good.

I was great.

I was...

"I'm freaking out a little," I admitted.

The corners of his mouth tipped up. "Good."

"*Good?*" I asked, aghast.

He tugged at the end of my ponytail, released me, then unbuckled both of our seat belts. "Yeah," he said. "*Good*. Gotta keep my girl on my toes." He popped his door, got out, and rounded the hood, opening my side of the car and helping me out.

"Good?" I asked again, brows up.

A shrug as he helped me into my coat.

He dropped a kiss to my lips. "I stand by my statement."

I swatted him lightly, sat in the love in his eyes, his words, his touch, in the way he carefully zipped my jacket so it wouldn't catch my hair, even though I was just walking inside and wouldn't normally bother to put my coat on, let alone zip it. "Okay, Squishy," I teased. "Stand by your statement, but at least buy me some cheese to make up for it."

A grin. Another kiss. A gentle touch straightening my coat.

Then he took my hand and led me inside.

THEO LOVED ME.

I loved him.

And I was sitting there freaking out because I *wanted* that.

He'd bared his soul, laid it all out there, all but given me his heart...and he didn't know everything about me, hadn't seen all the skeletons in my closet. If he did—

"Cheese stick for your thoughts?"

I jumped, jerking the chip I'd been holding and losing all of the delicious—and cheesy—toppings. Sadly, they fell to my plate. My eyes slid from those yummy toppings to the naked chip that was suddenly not very palatable, then up to Beth, who lifted her red eyebrows expectantly.

That was probably a very effective interrogation tool.

But it wasn't going to work on me.

Because yeah, no, I wasn't sharing any thoughts, cheese stick on offer or not.

"I think I'm cheese-sticked out," I said lightly, smiling at Beth—who didn't buy that for a second and made no compunction of showing that in her expression.

Though, Beth didn't fight me when I just smiled in the face of that no nonsense look and deliberately steered the conversation away from myself.

"How are the twins?" I asked.

Beth had carried them as a surrogate for Pru. They were well-loved, along with Hazel's baby, Dominic, and very cute—which meant that my question was a successful diversion as they—Beth, Pru, Julie, Kailey, and Hazel—spent the next little while talking about all things kid-related.

But I knew I hadn't avoided the laser focus of Beth completely.

At some point Beth would corner me...and I had the feeling I'd crumble like a house of cards.

Just...vomit up all of my secrets onto the table.

But not *that* night, mostly because the Cheese Night Extravaganza was already winding down, the guys coming over and crashing our table. Crashing because despite Theo escorting me inside (and helping me out of my coat), I hadn't seen much of him over the last hours. The guys had been banished to a table on the far side of the bar, where they had ordered their own cheese—Beth was very strict about her no cheese sharing policy—and made their way through a pitcher of beer. Slowly sipping down their cups as we got increasingly tipsy.

Hell, I'd even seen him order a salad to go with the boys' mediocre offering of cheesy goodness.

A salad!

While the women had consumed their body weight in cheese and crispy, fried breading, myself included.

I wasn't sure I could waddle out of CeCe's, let alone walk.

A nudge at my arm had me turning, Beth's laser focus on me. Shit. Maybe the cornering wasn't going to happen at some point in the future.

Maybe it was going to happen now.

And I wasn't sure I was on my game enough to avoid a full-frontal attack.

Beth was...a lot and intense and really fucking cool, and I wanted to be friends with her, wanted to be friends with these women who were kind and welcoming and didn't worry about consuming their body weight in said cheese.

So...

I braced, waited for Beth to pounce.

But the curvy redhead just lightly squeezed my forearm. "I just wanted to say that I don't know what it's like to be you, and I don't know what put that haunted look in your eyes."

I inhaled sharply.

"But I *do* know what it's like to feel like I'm not good

enough, not worthy enough, not *doing* enough for the people I love—and I know how heavy that burden can be to carry by yourself." She released the hold on my arm, dropped her hand back to her lap, and her eyes went just the slightest bit playful. "And I also know what it's like to let a sexy, sweet hockey player step in and share the burden."

I released the breath I'd taken.

A small nod, indicating something behind my shoulder and I looked, saw Theo was closing in on us, my coat in his hands.

My stomach fluttered, and my heart pulsed. What would it be like?

To have what Beth had?

Could I?

Could it be more than just a fantasy?

"*And* I happen to know *that*"—another nod at Theo—"sexy, sweet hockey player is strong enough to help." A wink at Theo, who moved up behind me, fitting his front to my back, his arm coming around my middle. "Plus," Beth said, changing the subject to something lighter—for which I was grateful, considering I had enough spiraling through my head—"he has a great ass."

Theo chuckled, pressed a kiss to the side of my throat, murmured, "I might have heard that from someone before." He glanced up at Beth, voice increasing in volume. "Should I circle around again so I can get another compliment?"

Warmth invaded my cheeks—from Beth's knowing glance and Theo's close body and the fact that I'd told him the very same thing.

But I didn't pull away, just settled back against his chest as Beth bantered back.

As the conversation continued and swirled and, eventually, wound down.

We paid and bundled up and went home.

And all through the teasing and banter and conversation and quiet drive home and Theo keeping me close as we slept in his bed, I thought.

Hoped.

That maybe Beth could be right.

# THIRTY-EIGHT

Theo

"FUCK YOU!" the asshole on the other team shouted, shoving me hard in the chest.

"Fuck *you!*" I shouted back.

Because—one—fuck that asshole. He'd taken a cheap shot on our goaltender, Martin, after the whistle and he deserved being leveled to the ice.

Even *if* it had caused a scrum in front of the net that Martin had to slip away from so he didn't get trampled.

"*Fuck you!*" the asshole shouted back.

I snorted. "Really?" I yelled over the din of the crowd. "*That's* all you have?"

The asshole shoved me, sending me stumbling back, but I was a good skater and I was strong and I had great fucking reflexes. I could take a hit and keep my feet.

Especially when it came from someone who was a hell of a lot smaller than Lake fucking Jordan.

And I could shove the motherfucker in return.

Hard enough that the weak little bitch boy toppled backward onto the ice.

Which...started the scrum up again, and I was pushed and punched.

But, like I said, I could hold my own, and I could push and punch—and deliver a couple of face washes—in return.

Little Bitch Boy didn't like that, jumping up to his feet and getting in my face again. "You wanna go, motherfucker?" He shoved at my chest and the refs—thoroughly busy trying to separate the rest of my teammates and the opposing players—didn't step in.

That was okay.

I could handle myself.

*And* Little Bitch Boy—who was at least four inches shorter and thirty pounds lighter.

He was fast and a good skater, but there was no way he could take me. It was simple physics...and the fact that I had handled myself in more than a few fights and Little Bitch Boy had played maybe a dozen games in the big leagues and was only on the ice because one of the fourth-liners had gotten hurt.

Trying to make a name for himself.

But he wasn't going to do that with me.

Unless it was Turtle—as in, being one of those fuckers who loved starting shit but when it came to actually finishing it, they dropped to the ice and covered their head.

Like a fucking turtle.

My fist flying toward his face would be about as real as finishing this shit got.

"You *really* wanna go?" I asked dryly, brows lifting, my mouth twisting up into a smile. "With *me?*"

"Yeah," Little Bitch Boy snapped, skating forward, bumping his chest to mine. "Yeah, I fucking want to go."

That had me busting up—

At least until the gloved fist swung for my face.

I dodged, gripped the fucker's arm, and shook the glove off like I was controlling a puppet. If we were doing this, we were going to do it properly. Gentleman like. I grinned and shoved the fucker back, dropped my own gloves, ripped my helmet off, and tossed it to the side then yanked the helmet from Little Bitch Boy's head when the asshole lurched toward me again.

Barehanded.

No helmets.

*That* was a hockey fight.

And I laughed again as the fear entered Little Bitch Boy's eyes.

Maybe I should have backed down, let him have that play, save him that embarrassment, but...Little Bitch Boy needed to be taught a lesson—and that lesson wouldn't be me backing down, letting him use that fact as fodder or motivation or material to chirp about.

Plus, it wouldn't take much.

I caught the neck of Little Bitch Boy's jersey and swung back.

Then let my arm fly.

*Crunch.*

My fist connected.

Blood began to pour from Little Bitch Boy's nose.

And...it didn't take more than that.

Little Bitch Boy dropped to the ice, hands clamped to his face.

"Turtle," I muttered, shaking out my fist, pain radiating up my knuckles, the back of my hand, my forearm, "fucking knew it."

Then I skated my ass to the penalty box.

My hand still hurt after the game, but since the rest of my body was just as sore—eighty-two games in the regular season and two rounds of playoffs would do that to a man—I just ignored it as I got dressed.

Up two games to one.

Two more wins. Then two more rounds.

Then, hopefully, hefting that big silver Cup.

I shoved down my underwear, wrapped a towel around my waist, and started to head for the showers.

"Theo!"

I turned back, saw two of the rookies—Sam and Aiden—standing there like mischievous toddlers. Ah, to be eighteen or nineteen again. That felt like an eternity ago—though, I figured with my upbringing, I'd never been this young.

Or at least not since shit imploded with my dad.

Not wanting to think about that, I lifted my brows, asked, "What's up?"

They just thrust a phone into my hands, coming behind me and hitting the screen.

"What's—" I froze as the video started playing and a woman in a truly sinful bikini began...*what the fuck?* "Uh..."

"Hot, isn't it?" Sam said as I found his eyes glued to the video, brows lifting higher and higher as the woman sat on the cake in a sexy—?—fashion. Was that possible? Certainly, her body was gorgeous and the way she moved sinful, but watching that ass plunk down repeatedly on a perfectly good cake was...

Not doing it for me.

"I mean," I said, passing the phone back. "Fly that freak flag, man."

Disappointment on Sam's face. "Didn't you see it?"

I frowned, shook my head.

The phone found its way in front of my face again.

"Look"—Sam pointed—"right there."

I squinted, saw that on top of the cake was written *Nice Finish.*

"Because Raph said he was going to get CakeGirl28 to make you a special message for that sick-ass goal last round, and he didn't, so Aiden and I took care of it for you."

He looked so earnest that I didn't have the heart to give him a hard time.

But I really wished that Coach hadn't backed down from the No Phones in the Locker Room thing.

"Right," I said. "Uh. Thanks."

Aiden crowded closer, sandwiching me between the rookies and blocking my escape. I glanced up and saw Smitty and Raph busting up, but neither of my supposed friends came to save me. "I gotta shower," I muttered, stepping back.

Aiden and Sam were too enthralled with their gift to me to notice. "That chick's body is fucking amazing," Aiden said.

"Yeah, it's hot," Sam replied, "but she never shows her face, man."

Aiden cackled. "Probably because she's a troll."

"Nah," Sam countered, holding up his cell as though showing off the best prize ever. "Look at that body. Her face has *got* to match."

I didn't know about her face.

The woman's body *was* hot—something I couldn't help but notice (don't tell Eva) because the phone was right in my fucking face again. But Eva's body was every bit as hot as the woman's on the screen. Hell, I'd even wager to say that her ass was bet—

I froze.

Because the woman shifted, still not showing her face, but her arm passed in front of the camera, and—

Fury and terror boiling, making war in my belly.

Not butterflies.

Not anything close to *squishy*.

The camera had caught almost all of the woman, sans her face and whatever flesh was covered by that skimpy bikini, and when she shifted, that arm passing in front of the lens, it also captured her wrist.

And what was *on* that slender wrist.

A bracelet of string and gemstones.

Intended to bring good luck.

And identical to the one that was still currently tied around *my* wrist.

# THIRTY-NINE

Eva

"DO you want me to come back to the arena?" I asked, worry settling heavy in my stomach. "I can meet you and drive you home, so you can rest your hand."

"No," Theo said quickly. "They just want to do a quick X-ray, but I can tell it's not broken."

I'd just pulled into my apartment complex when he'd called.

But I would go back in an instant.

"I—" A flash of headlights as a car passed next to mine, slowing to a crawl, the driver turning and staring at me, but it was too dark for me to see the other person's face, and I was too worried about Theo to really give them more than a passing glance.

Theo's hand might be *broken*.

How could he play if it was broken?

Though, I supposed, hockey players regularly played with all sorts of injuries—including broken bones in the playoffs.

It was just—my heart pulsed—his hand might be *broken*.

"I'm fine," he said distractedly. "Look, I've got to go. I just wanted to let you know that I wasn't going to make it to your place tonight."

"Should I go to yours instead?" I asked, glancing behind me, staring to turn the steering wheel.

A pause, long enough for me to freeze. Then, "You've got to be home by now."

"I just pulled into the lot—"

"Then go up and get some sleep," he said. "It's late. I'll catch up with you some time tomorrow."

*I'll catch up with you some time tomorrow?*

What the fuck?

For weeks now, we hadn't spent a night apart—minus his travel with the Breakers, of course.

"I—" I took a breath.

"Look, sweetheart," he said with a thread of annoyance, "it's late and I have shit to do."

"Are you sure you don't want me to come over?" I pressed. "I can make you something to eat." I clenched the steering wheel, worry swirling in my belly. "I know you're always hungry after games."

"I'm fine."

My stomach convulsed. "Okay," I whispered, hurt coursing through me.

Silence then, "I really need to go. I've got to get this done. It's already late and I need to pick up my parents and sisters from the airport early tomorrow."

Right. The visit I'd nearly had a panic attack over. The visit that still scared me but I was going to get through anyway.

"Do you want me to pick them up so you can sleep in?"

Another pause, long enough for my belly to twist again.

"Thanks, sweetheart," he said, his voice gentling, that

thread of annoyance disappearing. "But I've got it covered. Talk tomorrow, yeah?" he added before clicking off.

Before I had a chance to say goodbye.

Which...

Well, it didn't feel good, but I did my best not to dwell on it as I pulled forward again, parked in my spot, and hurried up the stairs, feeling cold and uncomfortable and a little off.

Had I done something?

Messed this up?

I thought carefully, going through every moment of the last twenty-four hours as I unlocked my apartment door and stepped inside.

Closed and locked it, but my legs wouldn't carry me forward, my body slumping back against the panel of wood as my mind raced and my heart pounded and as I *thought*.

I hadn't done anything that I could think of.

Hadn't ruined anything.

Hadn't messed up.

He'd been fine before the game. And fine after, when I'd gone through the process of recording sound bites and interviewing the guys. Hell, when I'd headed out once I'd gotten what I needed, he'd wound an arm around my middle and hauled me in for a kiss that had made the guys whoop and Smitty declare he was the best matchmaker in the history of matchmakers.

The steel door that had slammed into my face.

Smitty's booming voice and nosy demeanor.

I figured the two were a toss-up.

But none of that really explained why Theo had been distant on the phone.

"Because it's late and his hand hurts, you moron," I muttered, forcing myself to push off the door and head for the bedroom.

That was it.

A simple explanation.

Nothing to worry about. Nothing to see here.

I went into the bathroom and washed off my face and then spent an absurdly long time planning my outfit for the next day.

Meeting his parents.

A terrifying prospect because I liked Theo so much and I didn't want to fuck it up and...because I loved him.

Had never felt a love like this before.

But he'd been weird, and there was that odd note in his voice tonight, and the whole not wanting to spend time together thing, and—

Sighing, I dropped my toothbrush into the holder and made short work of flossing my teeth and moisturizing my face, brushing my hair and oiling the ends...and crawling into an empty bed. Across from which sat my ring light, propped up in the corner.

Staring at me.

Accusingly.

Uncomfortable, my gaze slid away but, worse, it caught on my rolled up backdrop sitting on the floor of my closet.

Shoved into the back.

But not completely hidden.

Especially, with my little plug-in nightlight illuminating my sins.

"What are you doing, Eva?" I whispered, sitting up and clutching the covers to my chest.

Logically, I knew I deserved to be happy.

Deserved to *do* what made me happy.

So, why was I still sitting on cakes? And doing it feeling ashamed and sick and hating myself? Why was I worried that Theo would hate *me* for putting him at risk of exposure?

Why was my fucking ring light still sitting in the corner?

"Yeah, Eva," I muttered. "Why?"

The future I wanted was right there, on the tips of my fingers and my hand closing, capturing it. A man I loved, who I'd gotten to know. He'd shared and kept promises and was fucking amazing. No missing puzzle pieces to slot in place. Nothing unexpected that would come up and slap me in the face.

Nothing—

Except *my* secrets.

Secrets I didn't need to keep because I'd fucking made it.

That dream. That career. That future.

It. Was. Mine.

Rage boiled up—at myself, at my idiocy and wavering and shame—and spilled over, exploding out of me as I tossed the covers back.

Because, despite all of those truths, as I'd been sitting in bed, my ring light staring at me from the corner of the room, the temptation to pick up my camera had been there.

To numb.

To hurt myself.

To be fucking stupid doing something I didn't want.

Disgusted, I threw the covers back and marched across the room. I took the ring light, the banner, the skimpy bikinis I'd never worn anywhere else but on camera, and I kept marching.

Into my kitchen.

Grabbing a black plastic bag and shoving everything inside.

Then marching to my bathroom and shoving *myself* into my robe, pulling it tight, and knotting the tie.

Flip-flops on.

Keys in my pocket. Phone in the other.

My heart was pounding and my hands shaking.

But I commenced marching—out my front door, down the stairs, and straight to the dumpster behind the apartments.

It was hard to throw the bag away.

And not just because it was a bitch to get the lid open and the trash inside.

But because it was like I was tossing out my security blanket.

But then it was inside and the lid was closed, and I wasn't marching back to my apartment, but I *was* moving determinedly to my door.

And inside.

To a future that wouldn't make me feel bad about myself.

And...I felt a fuck-ton lighter than the weight of that bag I'd just thrown out.

So much so, that I missed the shadows down the hall shifting as I let myself back into my apartment.

*That* I wouldn't process until much later.

# FORTY



ROGER SNAGGED my arm just outside the automatic doors of the airport, drawing me to a halt and letting my sisters and mom walk ahead of us. "What's going on?"

Great. A private talk.

"Nothing," I muttered.

Roger tilted his head to the side, studying me with a bland expression. "This is about the girl."

Fucking hell, why did my stepdad have to pay attention?

"No," I lied. "It's not about Eva."

Even though it was. It absolutely fucking was.

And I'd stayed up all night last night trying to figure out how I felt about it.

Conflicted. Jealous. Upset. Hurt.

The bottom line was...that I was hurt.

Because I'd given her everything, and she hadn't shared the fact that she made money by sitting on fucking cakes in bikinis.

I wanted to understand why she did it and if it made her happy and if she wanted to keep doing it.

I *needed* to know that.

Because if she did...

Could I be with someone who did that?

Not even because I had a problem with her making money off dumbasses like Aiden and Sam, but if people found out and I had to go through what I'd gone through again...

I wasn't sure I could do *that*.

Even though I loved her.

Even though I'd told her she was more important than everything else.

It was just...the *everything else* was fucking big and...I wasn't sure I could hack it.

Which—*fuck*—made me question the kind of person I was, the one I'd promised to be. If I was thinking of cutting and running *now*—

"Yeah," Roger said dryly. "Totally *not* about a woman." He laughed when I scowled. "Let me level with you, bud. No man ever has the expression you're sporting and *doesn't* have woman trouble." He clapped me on the back, rolled his shoulders. "Okay, I'm ready. Lay it on me."

"Like, I said," I lied again. "We're fine."

Yup. We were fine. Totally fine. Nothing was wrong. Nothing to see here. Nothing to—

Amusement on Roger's face, but thankfully, he started to walk again, letting me off the hook. "Yeah, bud, I can totally see that. You're fine. And your relationship is fine. No hiccups whatsoever."

Nope.

No hiccups.

Because I'd forget about the urge to run, and I'd process what I'd discovered and what it might mean and—

"Is it life-changing?" Roger asked suddenly.

It would all be fine.

It. Would. All. Be. Fine.

"What?"

"The shit that's got you all in knots," Roger expounded. "Is it life-changing?"

I inhaled but didn't answer.

Though, I supposed, my inhalation was enough. Roger heard or saw the change in my expression. "Think about it this way," my stepdad said. "Is it enough of a dealbreaker that if you let her go, you'll look back on it and won't wish you'd handled things differently?"

I didn't answer right away.

Partly because we were following my mom and sisters across the crosswalk, hauling a shit-ton of luggage—far too much for a freaking short visit. Partly because I already knew what I felt.

It was just...terrifying.

I wanted to run—but wasn't sure I could.

I wanted to stay—but wasn't sure I could.

"This is a time you can choose to fuck up and have to fix it," Roger said, catching My gaze on the far side of the crosswalk. "Let her go, realize you fucked up—because someone isn't as conflicted as you are right now without knowing that you're about to make a dumbass mistake—and then try to patch things up later."

Leaving because I was hurt.

Because she'd held back.

Because I wanted *everything*.

"Or," Roger said, nodding for me to keep moving into the parking garage, "you can skip the whole fucking-up part and *just call* your woman."

My fingers tightened on the luggage as I wheeled it to my

car, as I bleeped the locks and let the girls into the back seat. As Roger and I crammed the bags into the trunk, playing fucking Tetris to get them all to fit—all while thinking that I really needed to upsize.

Mostly because I didn't want to think about what Roger said.

Because...I knew Roger was right.

"I just realized you're dating someone!" my mom called from the back seat, her voice carrying through the plethora of suitcases, her statement slicing at my heart. "Does that mean you're out of condoms and we should stop by the drugstore and pick you up some more?"

I groaned, slammed the trunk, and dropped my head to my chest. "Christ."

Roger huffed out a laugh as he got into the passenger's seat.

"Or not," she said, still talking way too fucking loud for how early it was in the morning, her voice now echoing out through Roger's open door. Okay, it was way too fucking loud for *any* time of day. "Though, maybe I should throw all the condoms out! I do want to be a grandma sooner rather than later!"

Kids.

Christ.

I'd never thought I would be in the position to have them.

Never thought I'd *want* them.

But...I couldn't imagine having them with anyone but Eva.

Which was why I didn't get in the car, why I didn't get in the car and drive to the fucking drug store to stock up on enough condoms to get me through the next century.

Instead, I paused, thought about a little girl with Eva's pretty blond hair and my gray eyes. I thought about coming home to Eva every night and seeing her smile at me, the special smile she only gave me—warm and soft and *mine*. I thought about what I wanted my future to look like and the man I wanted to be.

And I knew.

I didn't give a fuck if she wrote a hundred shitty stories about me on her blog. I didn't give a fuck about the OnlyFans and making a living sitting on cakes in tiny bikinis.

I didn't give a fuck if the world found out and paparazzi showed up at my door and we were in every news story in the world.

I just...wanted Eva.

She'd share when she was ready and then we'd talk about it. We'd figure it out. I'd share that I was hurt and why. I'd be a fucking grown-up with a relationship that worked.

Because *that* was what the man I wanted to be did.

Which was why I didn't get in the car, didn't do anything but take Roger's advice.

I pulled out my cell and called her.

And like I knew she would, she picked up on the first ring.

And like I knew she would, she promised to be at my place in an hour.

And like I knew she would, when she hung up, the love in my heart for her was even bigger than it had been before.

## FORTY-ONE

Eva

I KNOCKED ON THE DOOR, worry clogging my throat, barely resisting the urge to turn around and sprint away.

To hide in my apartment for an eternity.

To avoid *this*.

"No," I whispered, digging my toes into the soles of my shoes. "You're going to make this work—"

The door swung open so quickly that I jumped.

Two girls stood just inside, bouncing up and down on the wooden floor.

They were fucking adorable—and way more put together than I had ever been at their age. Hell, their makeup looked better than my carefully applied face full of contour and high-lighter, liner and shadow and blush and mascara and...

They squealed—and the sound defied expectations—but then they were each grabbing one of my arms and dragging me inside.

"Oh, my God," the younger one, Rose, said. "Your eyeshadow is so pretty."

I'd gone a little smokey with a dash of simmer.

"I love your jeans," the older one, Lana, told me—a light wash high-waisted boyfriend style that was both extremely comfortable, but also nice enough for Meeting the Parents.

"And your jacket—OMG the *fringe!*" Rose reached out and fluttered her fingers through the strips of leather.

"I saw your video with..." Lana said, naming a popular influencer who I had collaborated with not long before. "Was she nice?"

"Yes," I told her, head jerking from side to side as I tried to keep up with the rapid-fire questions. "Really nice."

That set off more squealing and more peppering of questions about my videos and what other influencers were like. I'd met very few that weren't in the sports world, but the couple I *had* met were enough to bolster Lana and Rose's excitement.

And my credibility with the young ones.

Well, I'd take my victories where I could get them.

"What about—"

"Will you let me say hello to my woman?"

I glanced up, saw that Theo was leaning against the wall, arms and ankles crossed, looking like the yummy, hot hockey player snack he was. Only there was something in his eyes that had my stomach doing a flip—and not because he was looking so delicious.

"No," another voice said, drawing my focus to a woman who was tall and slender and had Theo's eyes. His mother. My stomach did another flip. *Crap.* Here we went. "We get to say hi first." Then, before I could brace, the woman was coming close, wrapping her arms tightly around my shoulders, and squeezing. "Hi, honey," she said softly. "It's nice to meet you. I'm Emily."

"It's nice to meet you too," I whispered. I'm Eva."

"I know." She pulled back, lightly cupped my cheek, her mouth curving. "You sure are pretty."

I inhaled.

"And from what I've seen on TV," Emily added. "Also, smart and funny." A wink. "I'm so glad my son convinced you to give him a chance."

That was...well, it was weird, mostly because I couldn't ever remember anyone calling me pretty—and certainly not a maternal figure—but also...there was pride in Emily's voice. Pride for *me.* And she didn't even know me, not really, and she was being nice and—

I didn't know what to do with that.

Movement out of the corner of my eye had me shifting, and Emily's hand dropped to my shoulder—which she gave a little squeeze before she backed up.

Then there was a man moving in front of me, handsome and in shape with salt-and-pepper hair and a well-trimmed beard. He extended a hand. "Eva," he said. "I'm Roger, Theo's stepdad. It's nice to meet you."

We shook hands, exchanged nice-to-meet-yous and then he began asking me about my commentating, which got me talking about hockey and my job and the players and behind-the-scenes funny moments and...well, it got me talking about all the things I loved. That sense of family and teamwork and never being alone, even though we all had our own jobs to do because each job was a cog in the wheel that rolled us to the playoffs. To the Cup.

And now I was part of that wheel.

So, in fairness, *that* had started me off blabbering and when I realized that I'd been doing said blabbering for near on ten minutes while standing two feet inside Theo's front door the first time I was meeting his family, doing that blabbering when

I was supposed to be learning about them and impressing them and not making it about me...

My words stoppered up and my cheeks went hot. "I-uh—" I cleared my throat. "I'm sorry, I didn't even ask. How was your flight? Did you guys want to go sit down? I'm sure you're tired and I—*oh*, I forgot I made you all some cookies, but they're in my car—" I backed up a step. "Oh—or I can get you something to drink and—"

Theo, probably sensing the nearing implosion of my psyche, pushed off the wall then and strolled toward me, nudging his sisters and parents aside.

He put a finger beneath my chin, lightly pressed up to close my mouth, thankfully cutting off the flow of words as he wrapped his arms around me and pulled me close. "Breathe, sweetheart," he ordered softly.

I exhaled.

"Good." He pulled back slightly, touched that finger to my cheek, just below my eyes. "You sleep okay?"

"Yeah," I whispered.

"Good," he whispered back.

"Is your hand okay?"

A blink, that blip in his eyes that had made my stomach twist making another appearance. But a heartbeat later, it was gone and he was smiling at me.

"It's fine."

Which meant that it hurt, but he wasn't going to admit it.

*Fine.*

"Okay," I murmured, giving him that play as I reached for that hand, needing to see it with my own two eyes before I could move on.

"I'm *fine*, sweetheart."

Hmm. Well, I'd just check up on him later and bully him into either an ice pack, pain meds, or a visit to the team's trainer, Samantha. Yeah, guys played through major injuries all the time in the playoffs, but that didn't mean I wasn't going to do my best to look out for my man.

My man.

*My. Man.*

Surprisingly, that didn't make me panic. Mostly, because of my decision the night before. But also because of Theo.

He was different.

He was *mine*.

"Plus, it serves me right for punching that asshole in the face," he said lightly.

"Branchard deserved it," I grumbled, gently touching the abraded skin. "He's an annoying fuck."

Theo smiled proudly. "Who's now sporting a broken nose."

Okay, that made me feel a *little* better.

I dropped my hand to his chest, felt the steady beat of his heart beneath, and that made me feel a *lot* better.

His face gentled, and he touched my nose.

I leaned in.

*He* leaned in.

Our lips were a hairsbreadth apart. OUr bodies pressed tightly together, pinning my arm between us as his hand dropped to my waist, fingers gripping my flesh.

"I'll get the cookies," came a soft voice.

Not Theo.

Slowly, I turned my head, saw that Theo's family was unabashedly watching us.

Roger was the one who'd spoken, and he slipped my keys from the fingers of my free hand, moved past us, and walked out the front door.

"They're in the trunk," I called.

He lifted a hand, telling me he'd heard, and as I turned back, the three women in Theo's life—aside from me, I thought with a blip of pleasure—were still studying me and Theo like they were bugs.

"I don't know if they're romantic," Rose said. "Or gross."

Lana's mouth curved. "Romantic. Definitely romantic."

Emily's expression was gentle. "Yeah, baby," she said softly. "They're definitely romantic. Now," she added louder before I could melt into the floor—or my cheeks catch fire, "Theo's promised us pancakes at Donna's. You're going to join us, right?"

# FORTY-TWO

Theo

"I WANTED TO TALK TO YOU," she murmured, curled up to my side, her leg tossed over mine, her arm over my middle.

I braced.

Waited for her to confide in me.

Something I'd done for the last two weeks, through the second round of the playoffs, and now as I was getting ready to leave for the first two games of the conference finals.

Waiting for her to talk to me, explain, and yet knowing she didn't owe me an explanation.

Dumb, huh?

I needed to tell her I knew.

I just...wanted her to confide in me.

But this might be it, the final barrier falling away, her telling me everything—and, God, I just wanted to fucking tell this woman I loved her, no matter what.

"Theo?" she asked again, arm squeezing. "Are you sleeping?"

That had my lips turning up—because if I *had* been sleeping, the question and squeeze would have woken me up. "No, sweetheart," I murmured. "I'm not asleep."

"Oh," she whispered. "Right."

"Eva?" I asked when she didn't go on.

"What?"

I chuckled. "You said you wanted to talk to me?"

"Oh. Right," she said again, though not in a whisper this time. She pushed up, and I braced, readying the speech I'd been thinking about the last two weeks—the one that told her I loved her and didn't give a shit about what she'd done in her past or if she still wanted to keep making the cake-smashing videos.

I'd even buy her a new bikini.

And remind her to take off her bracelet if she wanted to remain anonymous. Or tell her to fuck it all and leave it on if she didn't.

I'd—

Her hands came to my arm, lifted it so my hand wasn't cupping her ass. "What does this tattoo mean?"

Okay, so I liked the feel of her fingers on my arm, on my skin.

But I couldn't stop the disappointment from sliding through me.

Because I was no longer cupping her ass.

And because...she'd asked me about my tattoo. My *tattoo*.

I exhaled, realized I'd gone very still.

"It's okay if you don't want to talk about it," she murmured. "I can wait until you're ready."

The fact that was basically the mantra I'd been repeating to myself for two weeks didn't escape my notice. Oh, the irony. Unfortunately, my tattoo wasn't anything deep.

"It's okay," I told her.

She shifted, folded her arms and plunked them on my chest, resting her chin on top of them. "No, really," she said.

"No, really *really*," I teased. "It really is nothing serious."

Her brows lifted.

"It's the classification chart for dogs."

A blink. "Um, what?"

"I had a dog growing up," I said. "His name was Dog."

Her lips twitched. "Original."

"Yup."

"And that's a classification chart for Dog?" She nodded at the array of lines on my bicep.

"For dogs in general." A nod. "Yup."

"But..." Her brows pulled together. "Why?"

"You know I went back to school, yeah?"

Now her face warmed. "Yeah, I know. You went back to school for *funsies*." A beat. "Like a sociopath."

I laughed. "Hey, easy, now. I'm just a man who likes to learn." I stroked a hand through her hair. "I was actually thinking about going back to school again— getting my master's."

"Really?"

"Really *really*."

Her mouth curved. "In what?"

I shrugged—or attempted one, considering I was lying down. "Chemistry."

Her brows lifted. "*Chemistry?*" She laughed. "I like how you offer that up all casually." She stretched and brushed her lips over mine. "Chemistry. Like it's a throwaway class on knitting or something."

"Hey, I hear that knitting is hard."

She giggled, brushed her mouth over mine again. "But, yeah, you could definitely do it, honey. I know you could."

"The issue is the lab work." Another half-hearted shrug.

"You can't really do that from home, so it might have to wait until after I'm done with hockey."

She settled back onto her crossed arms. "I do like a man with a plan. Though," she added, "I still don't know what a classification graph is."

That had me laughing.

"Or why you have one that represents a dog on your arm," she went on.

"Well, I had Dog the dog, and he was living with my mom. I didn't want to have to move him multiple times until I had a steady contract, and by the time I got that with the Breakers, he was too old. I didn't want to uproot him."

The sound she made—pained, sorrowful—cut right through me.

Brought me back to the time when I'd lost my furry best friend.

"He died a couple of days before I learned about the charts, and when the teacher gave the dog one—okay, the chart for *canine lupus familiaris*—as an example during class, I nearly broke down." I stroked a hand through her hair again, taking solace in the silken strands. "Anyway, so it's a simple story. I thought the charts without the words were really cool, like something that might mean nothing to anyone else, but meant something to me, so I got a recommendation for a tattoo artist from Smitty and took the graph in and she stylized it for me." My throat went a little tight. "So, I've got Dog with me— literally."

She sniffed. "Dammit, Theo," she whispered, swiping at her eyes. "That is fucking beautiful, Squishy."

"I try." I tugged lightly on her hair. "Now, not to be a party pooper, sweetheart"—and dammit, I really needed to circle back to the nickname creation—"but it's late and I have practice tomorrow."

A sigh, her bottom lip sliding out. "Fine." She wrinkled her nose and dammit, she was fucking cute, and I loved her so much and—

She uncrossed her arms, wrapped them around my middle and hugged me tight. "I'm so sorry about Dog."

My throat went tight again. "Thanks, sweetheart."

"And you'll totally rock chemistry when you get around to it." She pressed a kiss to my pec. "Mostly because I know you'll look adorable in the white coat and safety goggles."

God, if Smitty caught wind of that—

I shuddered.

Maybe I needed to rethink my choice of degrees.

Ecology didn't need safety goggles, right?

"Theo?" she asked a while later, her voice groggy.

My heavy eyelids had begun to slide closed. "Yeah?" I managed to reply sleepily.

A sigh. Her words barely audible. "I love you."

My eyes flew open, every muscle in my body going tight. *God.* Hearing that never got old. "I love you too." I started to shift, to roll her to her back, suddenly wide awake and ready to show her exactly how much I liked those words on her lips.

But just as I started to move, I heard it.

The soft snore.

Carefully, I glanced down, saw that her eyes were closed, her lips parted to allow her steady breaths to slip through. To puff against my chest.

Asleep.

She'd fallen asleep and I was ready to—

I huffed out a silent laugh, sat in the moment, in the love that she'd given, that had come from patience and just being myself with her...

And I didn't sleep right away.

But, for once, it wasn't from worry eating away at my insides.

It was because I was so fucking happy, I never wanted to forget this moment.

# FORTY-THREE

Eva

## THIS HAD BEEN A TERRIBLE MISTAKE.

I should have known this.

But I'd made the cookies—shaped like the letter B—and painstakingly decorated them with cute little waves and...I wanted to see Theo. This playoff series had become a string of battles, a long, drawn-out *war,* and I'd wanted to give them a little boost after their light skate today.

They'd flown home yesterday—taking one out of two games on the road, about as good as they could hope because their opponent in the conference finals was tough—but their plane had been delayed and they'd gotten in so late, he'd gone straight back to his place.

I would have joined him, no matter how late.

But—my gaze slid to the side—I'd had things to do today.

That included driving my mom to her doctor's appointment.

Not because my mom couldn't drive herself—she was working and driving herself *there* every day—but because I didn't trust her.

The hospital visit had scared her enough that she'd been good about taking her medication and following her doctors' orders for a little while, but I could already see the shift happening, the slide back into older habits—the too-full pill bottles and food she wasn't supposed to be eating in the fridge and not doing her physical therapy exercises and the meals I cooked going uneaten.

Hell, she'd been huffing and puffing just walking out to the car.

And she'd had to stop and catch her breath on the way into the doctor's office.

I bit back a sigh.

I knew that, ultimately, there wasn't one fucking thing I could do about my mom, that I could kill myself going over to the house multiple times a day, stand there and make sure she took her meds, could keep cooking and filling the fridge with healthy meals and snacks. I could vacuum and clean the windows, and Theo could weed the planter beds. I could do what I'd done this morning and sit in a waiting room and then a doctor's office and listen to medical professionals telling my mom baldly that her decisions were shortening her life and if she wanted to be around to see her youngest son graduate from high school, she needed to make some changes.

My mom had said all the right things, but I had seen through the bullshit.

Right there in the doctor's office...and on the way home when my mom wanted me to stop at a fast-food place for a hamburger and fries.

Who gave a fuck about her heart?

Low salt? Meh.

Veggies and whole foods? Nah.

Normally, I would have made it an argument, would have refused to pull in and buy food that was essentially killing my mother, but as I'd sat in that office, watching the bullshit perpetuate and my mom not giving one *fuck,* I'd had enough.

Because I'd seen how Emily treated her kids.

Hell, I'd *felt* how Emily and Roger had treated *me*—like I was smart and nice and *welcome,* not a burden or an annoyance.

Me.

A woman they were just meeting.

Meanwhile...my mom—

"So stupid," my mom said, greedily digging through the grease-stained bag and shoving French fries into her mouth. "I don't see why you can't just drop me off at home, baby."

"The rink is on the way to your house, Mom," I reminded her as I pulled into the lot.

"Stupid girl," my mom muttered. "Making her sick mother wait in the car when you could just drop me off and come back."

Across town.

Through rush hour traffic.

Taking more time out of my day, doing shit I didn't want to do, while putting off the one thing I *wanted* to do.

I parked in a spot behind the rink, spotting Theo's car nearby. "This'll just take a minute—"

"Don't be stupid, Eva," my mother snapped, shoving a fry into her mouth. "It never just takes a minute."

An inhale. Exhale. "I'll be right back." I popped the door, started to push it wide.

"You treat your mother like this, you stupid girl. You—"

I froze.

And then something snapped inside me.

Fingers tightening on the handle, I whispered, "Shut up."

Silence, then, "*Excuse* me?"

I ignored her as I pushed the button to unbuckle my seat belt, allowing it to fly past my chest, to retract into the side of my car. All while trying to control my temper.

Because I didn't lose it often.

But I was there—near implosion, tempted to launch my mom from the car, drive off, and never look back.

Unfortunately, that might impact my plans of coming to this rink.

Or having a happy future with my man.

*Breathe.*

I swung my feet out, started to stand—

Was jerked back with a rough grasp, a surprisingly strong yank. The steering wheel jabbed into my side and my head hit the frame of my car.

I jerked myself out of my mother's grasp, whirled around, bending and glaring at her. "Don't," I ground out.

"What the fuck do you think you're doing?" My mom's chin came up and the glistening of grease on her lips from the fries she'd eaten sent my temper spiking further. "Get back in the car, stupid. Let's—"

*Snap.*

That tiny thread of control I'd managed to hang on to broke.

"What the fuck do I think *I'm* doing?" I screamed, the sound loud enough to startle myself.

But not loud enough to stop.

"What the fuck do I think *I'm* doing?" I yelled again, slamming a fist to my chest. "This coming from the woman who's spent the last decade making a goddamned sport out of being a shitty mother? From the woman who'd rather gorge herself on French fries and shit food instead of seeing her son graduate from high school? Who doesn't give a fuck that her daughter was traumatized by finding her with her lips turning blue on the goddamned floor? Who has *never* once gone to a show at her other son's art school?"

My mom narrowed her eyes. "That's not my fault."

"Oh, really?" I asked, clenching the frame of the car. "Then whose is it?"

"I can't help that I'm sick or that your father died."

"No," I said. "Which is why I didn't care about helping, why I was happy to do it! But do you even know what *I* do?"

A pause. "Always on that phone of yours."

That. Right. There.

"Yeah, I'm always on my phone, researching, making videos, working my ass off to get a contract to do what I wanted. Something I told you about and you sniffed at because it was only for three years." I threw up my hands. "Three years is amazing! Three years of consistent pay and stability and doing what I fucking love! And you couldn't even say congratulations."

"I—"

"And you know what? I don't fucking care!" I bent again, jabbed a finger in my mother's direction. "Because you're the old, bitter, pathetic crone who looks down on her daughter, on *me*"—another slam of my fist to my chest—"the woman who has paid your mortgage and utilities too many times to count over the last years, who has filled your fridge at the expense of my own so my siblings could eat. Meanwhile, you've slowly and surely turned into an awful person who doesn't give a shit that you're hurting your kids over and over again and"—I tossed up my hands—"I'm done. Eat whatever the fuck you want. Don't take your medicine. Stop going to work and lose the house. I don't care."

"But Jeremy—"

I shrugged. "Can come live with me."

My mom's eyes narrowed. "You ungrateful little bitch."

I leaned in until I was less than an inch away from my mother. "You horrible, hateful, piece of shit."

My mother gasped.

I leaned back again. "Even with all of this"—I waved a hand between us—"you don't get it, *do you?* I've done every-fucking-thing to help us survive. Cook. Clean. Parent. Worry. Not eat. Not sleep. Live on pennies so my siblings didn't go without! I even sold myself!"

My mom clamped a hand to her chest. Then she shoved open the door, staggered out. "I'm leaving."

Honestly, that had a blip of worry sliding through me, cooling my temper.

It wasn't always easy to turn off love.

Even the unhealthy variety.

But then my mom spun around, words a whiplike lash. "You're a terrible person. Talking to your mother that way."

And my temper boiled over again. And I knew I wasn't going to go back to the person I'd been before.

That I wasn't going to continue catering to this *woman.*

And, sure as shit, I wasn't going to let Dommie or Gabe or Jer do the same.

They *all* had lives to live.

No longer would I allow them to be held back by the past.

"You're not even going to question what I mean, are you?" I asked, rounding the hood and stepping close. "You don't even give a fuck that I sold myself, sold my body for views and likes and cash, that I did things that made me feel like shit about myself just so you could stream your favorite show or Jer could play lacrosse or Gabe could pay for the supplies he needed for school or Dommie didn't have to cripple herself with loans like *I* had to do."

My mom just turned away, muscle in her jaw flexing.

But she hadn't forgotten her fries, was still clutching the greasy bag like it was a goddamned security blanket.

I wanted to rip it out of my mother's hands, to toss it to the ground and jump up and down on it. Had actually taken a step forward to do just that when I caught a flash of movement out of the corner of my eye.

Slowly, my stomach filling with dread, I turned my head.

And saw Theo standing there, his expression thunderous.

"I-I—" My temper was gone in an instant, horror searing through me. My stomach twisted and my eyes filled with tears.

He crossed over to me, face harder than I'd ever seen it.

"I-I was going to tell you," I whispered.

He shook his head, started to reach for me, and I couldn't. I just...*couldn't—*

See his expression change. Watch the love leave his face. Witness the hate and disappointment and disgust take its place.

I stumbled back a step.

His eyes widened. "Eva—"

"I-I—" My mind blanked.

And I took another step backward.

"Sweetheart—"

That broke something inside and...I turned on my heel and took off.

Running through the parking lot, sticking to the shadows.

Doing it for long enough—weaving without sense, without thinking about direction, running through streets and alleys, down sidewalks and up between big buildings with darkness clinging to their eves—that my lungs were sawing by the time my panic and anger, shame and horror had faded enough for me to really process what I was doing.

And how *stupid* it was.

But I'd no sooner realized my mistake than a hand gripped my arm in a bruising grip and yanked me down a narrow alley.

I fought against the hold.

Screamed and clawed and hit.

But the blackness still surrounded me anyway.

# FORTY-FOUR

Theo

I TOOK off running a heartbeat after Eva had, but then her mom wavered, looked like she was going to pass out, and I knew that as pissed and hurt as Eva was, she'd never forgive herself if something happened to her mom.

If she got hurt because of Eva.

A quick step brought me close enough to catch Carmen's arm, to steady her when she wavered.

She leaned heavily against me instead of fighting my hold, and I sighed, gaze going to where Eva was just disappearing behind the rink, taking note of her direction.

"My baby," her mom whispered. "My—"

Yeah, considering all I'd learned through Eva about this woman, what I'd witnessed in the hospital and while helping my woman at her mother's house, and I wasn't buying the remorse in her tone.

Maybe it was real.

Likely, it was bullshit I didn't have time for.

"Come on," I muttered, scooping her up and carrying her back toward the rink, toward the door that was the team's private entrance to the practice facility, and was just reaching it —and pondering how I'd use my badge to unlock it with an armful of Carmen—when it swung open to reveal Walker.

Who paused, but only for a second, his eyes widening.

Then narrowing.

"What happened?" he asked.

"What do you think?" I muttered, widening my eyes at the man who'd been spending time—and trying to do it on the sly —with Dommie and thus, had to know *exactly* what was going on with the snake of a woman I was schlepping across the parking lot. "I need to go after Eva. Can you keep an eye on her?"

Walker didn't hesitate, just nodded, steadying Carmen when I set her down. "I'll call Dommie."

I nodded, said a quick "Thanks," then turned and took off in the direction Eva had run, searching the shadows as I sprinted, unease growing in my belly as the distance from the rink increased.

She'd been panicked and not thinking and the neighborhood around the rink wasn't always great.

And it was getting dark.

And—

A shriek rent the air.

"*Fuck.*"

I searched, tilting my head, trying to figure out what direction the sound had come from.

Then the scream came again. And again. And a-*fucking*-gain. I moved even faster, sprinting along sidewalks, cutting through alleys, cursing when I had to backtrack, closing in on the voice that was growing hoarser and quieter by the moment.

The voice that then cut off completely.

"Fuck," I hissed, eyes searching the shadows as I pulled my phone out and turned on the flashlight.

Nothing.

Nothing.

No—

A scuffle to the right, toward a narrow gap in the buildings I hadn't noticed.

I lurched forward, turned to look down the opening—

And saw fucking *red*.

Illuminated in the flashlight of my phone was a man.

On top.

Of Eva.

I didn't remember moving. One second, I was at the mouth of the alley and the next I was right there, shoving the man off, getting Eva to her feet and propelling her behind me. Words literally wouldn't come as I moved again, gripping the man's shirt and shaking him, losing my phone in the process, distantly hearing it clatter to the concrete, the light disappearing as I dropped it.

That was okay.

I had the man by the collar, and tightly, by the sounds of the man's gurgling, and that had my throat loosening.

"Eva?" I rasped.

"I-I—" I heard footsteps, saw her shadow move as my eyes began to adjust, watched as she picked up my phone, the flashlight arrowing in on me and the man.

"Can you walk to the end of the alley, sweetheart?" I asked, not wanting to let go of the man, trying to keep my tone as gentle as possible.

"Ye-yeah."

"Okay, go first, sweetheart." The phone bounced as she nodded and started walking.

"Can't. Breathe," the man wheezed.

"I don't give one fuck," I snapped, tightening my hold, dragging the man forward, every single cell in my body demanding I just start pummeling the man, turning his face to pulp.

Maybe I would have.

But Eva needed me calm first.

Something that was a goddamned struggle when we reached the end of the gap between the buildings and walked into the alley, and I caught sight of her face. Something that was harder when we made it out onto the sidewalk and I saw the rest of her—face already bruising, clothes torn, one shoe missing, lip split.

"Theo!" Smitty appeared out of nowhere, voice booming down the sidewalk and making Eva jump.

"Call 9-1-1," I ordered.

Smitty pulled out his phone, dialed, and seconds later was talking to a dispatcher.

"Hang in there with me, sweetheart," I said softly.

She nodded, but she was shaking, and I didn't know how much longer she would be able to keep it together. Luckily, Walker pulled up in his car then, screeching up to the curb and throwing open the door.

He jumped out, halted, looking between us.

"Take this," I muttered, shoving the man at him.

Thankfully, Walker had quick hands, and he caught the fucker, yanking him to a halt when he tried to run off, holding him tight, and considering the yelp of pain the man made, Walker had clocked what had happened—or almost happened

—or—

I turned to Eva, who was shaking violently now.

I made it to her just as she collapsed, catching her before she hit the sidewalk.

"I've got you," I murmured, holding her tightly. "You're safe now." And I repeated the words as sirens closed in and the cops came, and the man was put into cuffs.

"It's him," she whispered as the officers shoved the man into the back of a squad car.

"Who, sweetheart?" I asked.

"The man from my apartment complex," she said, still whispering and I didn't miss the other officer pulling out a notebook and writing furiously. "I've seen him there."

"Okay," I said, smoothing my hand up and down her back. "Okay."

Yeah, no, she wasn't ever going back to that apartment without me.

Hell, she was moving in with me.

And I was getting a security system. Or maybe I was moving into a gated community and she was going to live there with me—

"And I saw him that night you helped me with my tire. Remember I was freaked out when you pulled over?"

I *did* remember that.

"He was in the shadows, but I couldn't make out his face. I just...well, it creeped me out, but I guess I convinced myself it was just my imagination and—"

The man started shouting.

She jumped.

The officer by the car ordered the man to quiet down while the other asked Eva if she was okay to answer some further questions about what the man had done and what he'd said.

And as she recited the sequence of events, what the man had hissed in her ear as he tried to tear off her clothes, the names he'd called her, I realized that the guy was some creep who'd watched her on her socials.

Her *hockey* socials.

Christ.

Maybe the anonymous OnlyFans account was better.

At least then she wouldn't have deal with creepy fuckers tracking her down.

"And then he said I was a whore because I let my boyfriend sleep over and—" Her voice broke and she shuddered.

I rubbed her arm. "We don't have to do this right now."

But she just lifted her chin and straightened, releasing a long slow breath. "I'm okay," she whispered. "Then"—her voice grew stronger—"he hit me and put his hands around my throat, choking me, and I screamed, but then I couldn't a-and then he tried to rip off my clothes, but Theo got there before he could—"

I held her tighter. "And we came out here, my teammate found us, called you guys, and now we're *here*," I said when she broke off on a hitching breath. "I think you have enough for now," I told the officer. "If you need more, we can come down to the station later."

The officer nodded, pocketed her pen and notebook, and passed me a card. "We just need to take some pictures."

Eva stilled.

I wanted to protest, wanted to protect her from that. But I knew the pictures would be important.

So, when she was ready, I stepped back, let them take the pictures, and held her close when they were done.

"I'd recommend taking her to the hospital to get her checked out before you take her home," the officer said. "That's quite a bump on her head."

"I'm fine," Eva protested.

"I'll take her," I promised, overruling her and earning an approving nod from the officer.

"We'll be in contact," she said before she disappeared and moved into the alley to continue taking pictures.

"I'm—"

"Don't even try it, Evie," Walker said, moving to his car and opening the back door.

"Yeah, babe." Smitty lightly touched her cheek. "Don't bother protesting. You're not winning on this one."

I chuckled, even though I shouldn't be the least bit amused.

But the mutinous look on Eva's face was just so...Eva.

She sighed but got in the back seat.

And she let three annoying—her words, not mine, but I couldn't disagree—hockey players take her to the hospital to get checked out.

---

I TUCKED her into my bed, resisting the urge to go through the house and check the windows and doors again.

Security system was happening fucking yesterday.

And maybe I'd hire a big ass bodyguard for her and—

"Theo?" she whispered.

I glanced up, saw that she was clenching at the blankets so tightly that her knuckles had gone white. "Yeah, sweetheart?"

Her throat worked. "You're probably wondering about what I said in the parking lot."

My lungs froze, but I moved to the bed, sat on the edge of the mattress, forced my voice to be casual. "I heard a lot of stuff."

She sighed, looked down at her hands.

But didn't speak.

"Just so you know," I told her gently, "Raph and Cas dropped your car off at your apartment for you. I have the keys in the kitchen, so don't worry about either of those things."

"That was nice of them," she said quietly.

"And Dommie came and picked your mom up," I told her carefully. "She's fine."

Eva sighed again, her eyes coming up to mine, a flash of fire in the deep brown depths. "I'm done with her, done with the way she treats all of us, done with how she talks to me and done with putting my life on hold for her." She sucked in a breath, released it in a rush. "I'm done with doing things that make me feel like shit. Done with allowing her to sacrifice everyone else for her own benefit."

"When you say you're done with doing things that make you feel like shit, what do you mean?"

She stiffened, throat working.

"Do you mean things like cake-smashing videos?" I asked, keeping my voice completely even.

She still jerked like I'd smacked her. "I was going to tell you." Words barely above a whisper.

"Eva—"

"And, more importantly, I deleted it weeks ago," she said, louder, the words coming in a hurry. "With the new contract, I have steady money if my siblings need help and I don't have to do that—" A sob. "I don't have to do that any longer," she said in a hurry. "And I know that you're probably worried with every-thing that happened with your dad and us going viral with the whole Squishy thing, but I never showed my face on those videos and it's deleted now and—and there shouldn't be anything connecting you to it."

"I don't care."

"And I didn't like doing it," she went on like she hadn't heard me. And maybe she hadn't. Maybe she just needed to get this all out. "So, deleted it wasn't all about you—though I *am* sorry I potentially put you at risk—"

"Eva—"

"But, more importantly, it made me feel yucky to do it and sick when I'd pull out my camera or the bikinis, and I think if I'd made the choice initially, things might have been different but because I had to make the videos or I wouldn't be able to pay rent or Jer wouldn't have food or water or power, or my mom would lose the house, and I—"

"Sweetheart."

"I get that you'd be upset about it. I'm your girlfriend—or, hopefully, I'm *still* your girlfriend—and other people saw my body and I-I made videos for a bunch of weirdos who liked me sitting on—"

"Cakes."

She froze, probably realizing that was twice now I'd mentioned cakes.

So, I tried to break it to her gently.

That the rookies were into it. That one of the videos she'd made was for me. That many of the others had been a topic of conversation in the locker room more than once.

Her tears in response soaked the material of my shirt.

There wasn't really anything gentle about this conversation.

"I'm so embarrassed," she whispered long moments later.

I didn't want to have this in her head, to be eating at her, to make her feel uncomfortable. "First of all, *I* only noticed because of a one-second moment in a video made specifically for me."

Her head lifted.

I tapped her wrist. "You left the bracelet on."

She blanched. "I never wore jewelry in them before." She rubbed her head. "I'm sure of it. I always took it off. I just…I was conflicted about making the video in the first place, but it was a lot of money and—"

Right. I needed to nip this in the bud.

"—I struggled for so long that—"

I cupped her jaw, tilted her head up, holding her steady, keeping my eyes on hers. "I am so *fucking* proud of you."

She stilled. "What?"

"Look," I admitted. "I can't say I love that other people saw your body." I shrugged. "But that's just because I'm feeling all caveman-she's-mine about you."

She exhaled.

"And yes, it took me a bit to think it through, to make peace with it, to understand."

"Understand what?"

"Understand that it's not about the videos or the bikinis or the cakes. It's about my woman doing what she had to. It was you stepping up and taking care of your family and being unselfish enough to do it in a way that maybe you didn't like." I tucked her hair behind her ear. "But, sweetheart, you want to keep making videos, go for it. You wanna fleece some dumbasses out of their money without ever having to show them this beautiful face, *go for it*. You want to do something else, fine. Show your face. Forget the bikini. Change to fucking pies. I don't care."

Her mouth fell open.

But I kept going. I *had* to keep going, had to make sure she understood. "You want to write a shit talk post about me on your blog or make a hundred TikToks or waste dozens of perfectly tasty cakes, and *I don't care.* I love you and that means loving *all* of you."

"Honey," she whispered. "I-I—" A shake of her head. "I don't know what to say."

"You don't *need* to say anything." I tugged lightly at her hair. "Look, your day was shit, so we're going to lay in this bed, watch shitty TV or sports highlights—your choice—and then we're going to order tacos. And you're going to sleep easy, knowing I'm here with you, holding you, *loving* you. You're going to sleep easy knowing that you're safe and you don't have to worry about a secret tearing us apart and if you do happen to have a nightmare, I'm not going anywhere, yeah?"

Her exhale was shaky. "Okay."

I started to stand, intending to grab my phone so I could order those tacos.

"Theo?"

"Yeah, sweetheart?"

"I'm so sorry for not telling you."

I wiped at a stray tear on her lashes. "We're good, sweetheart. I promise."

"I love you." Her palm came to my chest, rested above my heart.

*Her* heart.

It belonged to her.

Just as hers belonged to me. Because I didn't have any doubts of that. Not now. Not after all we'd been through.

"I love you too." I touched her cheek. "Now, hockey or trash TV?"

She smiled, finally she gave me *her* smile. "As if that's even a real choice."

Then she snagged the remote.

And turned on the game.

This woman.

Fucking perfect.

# EPILOGUE

Eva, Two Months Later

THE TEAM'S run for the Cup had ended in Game Seven of the Eastern Conference Finals after a heartbreaking own goal.

They'd had a great season.

Made it deep into the playoffs.

But none of that meant anything, not when they weren't hefting the Cup.

Not when they had to watch another team get the pleasure.

Still, the sting of losing eventually wore off and the guys regrouped, going off to spend time with their families and their kids and wives—or their girlfriends in my case. They'd begun the slow process of healing injuries and getting back into beginning of the season shape.

Having a built-in hockey player boyfriend meant I had a lot of great content for my socials.

Having the contract with the team meant I'd even gotten to work with the team's social media manager to do some fun crossovers.

To make videos *I* wanted to make.

No pressure. No shame.

Just...me.

I zipped up my suitcase, thinking of the beach vacation that Theo and I were getting ready to leave for. We were flying to San Diego and his family was going to meet us for a couple of days so Theo could check out the zoo and wildlife park (my man vicariously living his zoology days) and we'd hang with the girls while Roger and Emily had an extended weekend. Then Theo and I were heading to Hawaii for a five-day trip.

Five days. A beach. By ourselves.

With lots of bikinis I'd bought for Theo and Theo alone.

I couldn't wait.

"Ready, sweetheart?"

"Yup!" I chirped, starting to lift my suitcase off Theo's bed —really, *my* bed now since we were living together now by his demand—but he took it from me before I could, carried it to the door. He hadn't cared about my moonlighting as an OnlyFans girl or releasing content on my social media accounts about him, but he'd put his foot down about me returning to my apartment by myself.

Because the man who'd assaulted me had been arrested and charged and was currently in jail.

But he'd been at my place, and as the terror had faded and time had passed and I *thought*...I'd remembered all of the weird things—the doorbell ditches, the slow car passing me, the door being open when I'd thought I'd closed it, the shadows feeling like they were watching me, the night with the flat tire and the piece of paper on my windshield and more shadows hiding a man. The visit to the repair shop the next day, the technician telling me the tire looked intentionally punctured.

All the things I'd explained away.

Discounted.

Things I'd made the mistake of telling Theo, giving him ammunition for his demand that I move in.

In the end, I hadn't fought too hard.

Theo wanted it.

And I wanted to be here. With him.

So, I'd broken my lease, and moved in, and we'd spent pretty much every moment together since.

And it had been happy. Smooth sailing. Peaceful.

Except when his dad had shown up and my mom had tried to pull her same shit, seemingly not caring that her daughter had been assaulted.

*"How could you be so stupid, baby?"* she'd tsked. *"Running off like that."*

That was the last time I felt guilty about yelling at me.

That was the *first* time I'd begun erecting a careful distance that would ensure I did right by my siblings but wouldn't be sucked into my mom's cyclone of making me feel like shit.

I was taking a page out of Theo's book.

Do. *Not.* Engage.

He'd slammed the door on his dad and ignored the subsequent rings and knocking.

Then had later filed a restraining order.

Minimal drama. Effective.

My man was smart.

I was lucky—not just because of the smart and the minimal drama and him being okay with every part of me.

But because he loved me.

No strings. No changes requested.

Just *me*.

I followed him down the stairs, climbed into his car, and we headed for the airport.

"Reach into the back seat and grab the bag for me, will you?" he asked as we turned onto the highway.

Frowning, I turned, saw a small black gift bag, and snagged it, setting it in my lap, smothering my curiosity.

He chuckled, no doubt at my poor efforts of said smothering. "It's for you, sweetheart."

Pressies!

I loved pressies.

I tugged out the tissue paper then the wrapped parcel below, shoving the former back into the bag and setting it on the floor mat. Then I placed the present on my lap and looked at him.

He glanced from the road. "What?" Then back.

"What's this?"

Another glance at me then back to the road. "Just a little first trip together present."

I stilled, heart squeezing. This man.

Sweet.

Totally *not* an asshole.

"But I didn't buy you anything," I whispered.

He grinned at me. "How about you do me a favor and wear what's in that present?"

"Oh." I lifted my brows, judging the box's size. It wasn't that big. Maybe it was a special icing bag? *Heh.* "Are we getting sticky on this trip, Squishy?"

He winked at me. "Since we're always getting sticky normally with all of our *cookie-making*, this trip is going to reach superglue level."

I giggled.

"Now, quit bantering with me and just open it, sweetheart," he ordered.

My thighs pressed together—because I was a little hussy who liked it when he got commanding—and began tearing at the paper, yanking it off and shoving it into the bag at my feet. It was...a T-shirt.

Uh…

T-shirts were *sticky* now?

But I kept my thoughts to myself. Maybe he wanted me to wear it without any panties and he'd reach under and—

Okay, yeah, I could count that as *sticky*.

Yet, even as I was thinking that, I unfolded the shirt, lifting the material up to see what was printed on the front.

Wifey.

I blinked. Eyes closed. Opened again.

Nope. It still said *Wifey*.

"Um," I began, glancing over at Theo then back at the shirt. Then out the window on my side, seeing we were pulling into long-term parking at the airport.

He grabbed a ticket, pulled through the barrier gate, and parked.

Only then did he look over at me. "What do you think?" he asked softly.

I just…blinked. Again.

The shirt still said Wifey.

We were still parked. At the airport.

But now Theo wasn't just sitting across the console from me, hands on the steering wheel. One of those hands was extended in my direction.

Holding a diamond ring between thumb and forefinger.

"I've really failed in the creative nickname department," he said softly, stroking the knuckles of his free hand over my cheek, tucking a strand of hair behind my ear. "So, I thought we could make a pitstop in Vegas and then I could call you Wifey."

I froze, heart beating a million miles per hour.

*Breathe.*

Then I reached across the console, gripped his cheeks with both hands, and kissed him with every bit of love in my heart.

When we broke apart, chests heaving, I let him slip the ring on my finger and said—

"I guess it's a good thing I know *your* T-shirt size, Squishy."

------

Dommie

I gently squeezed the piping bag, spinning the turntable on which the perfectly iced cake sat on, sending a thin thread of icing out of the metal tip, draping it carefully.

Decorating the top edge of the wedding cake that would be the biggest I'd ever made.

Six tiers.

Coated in fluffy white buttercream.

Each tier decorated differently with royal icing in an elegant white-on-white pattern that had my hands aching.

And my neck.

And my shoulders.

And my legs and ankles and feet.

Because—one more squeeze and I carefully pulled away, set the piping bag on the metal table—I'd been at this since three in the morning.

It was noon now.

And though I'd been squeezing in the rest of my duties that came from opening the bakery—namely baking the items that filled the cases so people could buy them and eat them and the business made enough money so that *I* had a job—the rest of the time had been spent decorating the cake.

Busy.

Always.

The job. The bakery itself. My life.

*Always* busy.

Now I had less than an hour to box up the cake, stow it safely in the walk-in, and get my butt over to class.

I loved decorating cakes.

It was a steady job that paid decent for a college student.

But it wasn't my dream.

It wasn't—

"Did you leave any icing *on* the cake?"

I'd just finished boxing said cake—or the top tier of *said cake*. Luckily. Because the man's voice had me jerking, my hand bumping into the cardboard.

And if the *man*—who, unfortunately, I knew just from that single silken question, whose voice I knew (and maybe heard in my dreams)—had made me ruin this cake—or even just one layer of it—I might very well commit hockeycide.

As in, murder of the sexy, annoying hockey player currently leaning against the doorway that led out into the front part of the bakery.

Walker Laine standing there looking sexy, with a big, strong body, tattoos and a beard, and jeans that encased his thick thighs in a way that should be illegal.

And *annoying,* with his kissable lips turned up at the edges into a smirk.

And his arms crossed.

And his freaking ankles crossed too.

Looking totally comfortable in my space. *Invading* my space.

Again.

For a man who supposedly didn't like making connections with women, he seemed to be doing that a lot. Crowding me in the waiting room of the hospital when I'd been too upset to know what I was doing, to keep him at arm's length. Driving me home. Showing up at my place, at my mom's house, at...

My work.

I narrowed my eyes, picked up the boxed cake, and carried it to the walk-in, stowing it on the shelf with the rest of the tiers. Tomorrow I'd stay late, and then would go with Roy, our delivery guy, to the venue to set up the cake.

Then live with my hands in ice buckets for the following twenty-four hours.

Sighing, I wiped those aching hands on my apron which—as a certain annoying hockey player had pointed out—was covered in a fair amount of icing.

Okay, a *lot* of icing.

Probably it was a comment on me, that I worked so messily. God knew, my mom would say so. Messy life, messy mind. Which was fucking hilarious. Because my mom was...

Not a good person.

So, I just shoved that away and embraced my messiness.

My apartment was clean. My car was immaculate. My aprons...trashed. But, more importantly, my cakes were perfect, even if I wore a piping bag's worth of icing each and every time I finish—

"*Ack!*"

I'd run into a brick wall.

No. Okay, fine. I'd run into a brick-*headed* hockey player.

"What the fuck, Walker?" I snapped, brushing off his hands, which had come up to steady me—*ugh, why did he have to be nice?*—and started to move by him.

Even though he was smaller than a lot of the guys on the Breakers, Walker still took up a lot of space. Or maybe that was only in my head. It was just...he seemed big, *too* big, and he sucked all the air out of the room, and he made me feel—

It didn't matter.

What I felt didn't matter.

Not when it came to one Walker Laine.

"I need to talk to you," he said.

"I think we've done all the talking we need to do," I snapped.

Regret careening across his face, marring the beautiful features.

Because once I'd thought that his invading my life meant something, that he might want something special with me.

That he might want...just me.

Just *me*.

Just a girl who was no one special being wanted by a man who was—

Who'd made it abundantly clear a future that included wanting me wasn't in the cards.

"Sunlight—"

Yeah, no.

That he'd called me *that*, now, after what'd he'd said and how he'd pushed me away and...how he'd made me feel?

I could deal with the invading my life, the annoying presence when I was capable of handling my own shit. I could even deal with him showing up at my place. He wanted to fix my sink? Sure, knock himself out.

But calling me *Sunlight?*

*That* couldn't happen.

And certainly not in that gentle voice and paired with his hand lifting, fingers trailing down my throat.

*That* was what had given me the stupid hope, the thoughts of a future that might be.

*That* was what had hurt so fucking much when reality had smacked me back into my place.

"Don't," I snapped.

His eyes flared with annoyance. "Dommie—"

I didn't focus on that. Couldn't. Not when my gaze slid over his shoulder and I saw the door to the walk-in slowly swinging closed.

*Shit.*

I lurched for it but was too late.

It closed with a soft *click.*

One that couldn't even begin to demonstrate how fucked I was.

Because the door to the walk-in was broken. Because the freaking handle that was supposed to function to let someone out if the door shut on them didn't work.

Because I was now trapped in this goddamned giant refrigerator with Walker Laine.

"Shit!" I hissed, moving over to the handle and jabbing at it anyway.

No surprise, the door didn't move.

"What's wrong?" Walker asked.

I glared over my shoulder at him, hoping he could see it in the dim overhead lights. "We're trapped," I snapped. "The handle is broken, so we can't get out."

His brows dragged together. "That seems dangerous. What if you were stuck in here and nobody was working?"

I let my glare intensify. "Well, I'm not normally confronted by annoying hockey players in the walk-in."

A beat as he appeared unfazed by my laser eyes. "Didn't really answer my question, sweetheart."

Sweetheart. *Ugh.* Why did that send a flutter through my insides?

I turned back, wrestled with the handle again. "I'm always just in and out."

Those brows flicked up, seeming to say, *"That didn't answer my question either."*

I huffed out a sigh. "Normally I'd just call for help and one of the other bakers would come in and let me out."

"So why don't you do that?"

Silence.

Annoying, long silence before I admitted, "I don't have my phone."

His mouth quirked.

I hated him.

Detested him.

And I *still* thought his little smirk was the sexiest thing I'd ever seen.

"I have my phone," he said, pulling it out of his pocket.

Thank God.

I wasn't sure my could yell loudly enough for them to hear me out front.

"But..." He tucked it away again, voice like velvet.

"What?" I asked dread gathering in my belly.

"I'll only let you use it if you agree to go on a date with me."

---

THANK YOU FOR READING! I hope you loved Theo and Eva as much as I did! The next book in the Breakers Hockey series is BLAZED. **He'd never wanted to settle down. Until he'd she'd careened into his life.**

CLICK HERE TO READ BLAZED NOW>

---

**WANT to know what happened when Theo and Lake went out for that beer?**

Check out my Sierra hockey novella, SNOWED, the prequel of the Sierra Hockey series.

---

And if you enjoyed BREATHE, pick up book one in my brand

new Grizzlies Hockey series, MARRIED TO NUMBER TWENTY-TWO. **I signed the contract. I just didn't expect her to show up ten years later, ready to cash it in.**

CLICK HERE TO READ MARRIED TO NUMBER TWENTY-TWO NOW>

READ on for a sneak peek below!

Aiden

I wake up to a heavy knock on my condo's front door and glare blearily at my phone in the charger.

"Two in the fucking morning," I mutter, grabbing a pillow and clamping it over my ears. "It's two o'clock in the morning on my fucking birthday, and I have to deal with this shit."

This shit being my neighbors.

It's not the first time they've pounded drunk on my door, desperate for their roommate to let them in to what they think is their apartment.

This was sort of funny the first time.

I remember those days, drinking too much, being dumb.

But after the second and the third—where I gained status into the inner circle and a code to the keypad to their apartment door—it was no longer cute.

Now, six months later and countless times of bailing them out, I'm *so* not in the mood.

Especially when it's my fucking birthday.

The knocking cuts off and I think—*pray*—that they've gotten the hint.

But it's approximately two seconds later when it starts up again.

I glance at my phone again, see that really five minutes have passed, making it two-seventeen and officially my birthday.

Some present.

I could try to ignore it—but that just means extending the torture. Sighing, I toss back the blankets and stomp to my apartment door, whipping it open to reveal a slender brunette on my doorstep.

"Ho, mama," she says, gaze taking a slow perusal down my body.

"Who the fuck are you?"

"It's me. Luna."

I stare at her, uncomprehendingly.

"From Rockfield?" she adds.

Recognition begins to dawn. "Luna Maybelle?"

"Yup! That's me." She nods, grinning, and I see it then, the glimpse of my best friend from the childhood rink I grew up playing at come out in her smile. Mischief and life. Joy and hard work.

Summers spent spending every spare moment together—her figure skating, me playing hockey.

But she's not little Luna anymore.

Christ, she's anything but—tall, beautiful, curves for days—and she's staring at me.

Because I'm staring at her.

Fucking hell.

I spur myself into motion.

"Luna! Oh my God!" I pull her into a hug. "What the hell are you doing here?"

"It's your birthday!" She holds up a piece of paper that looks faintly familiar. "And, well, it's mine too, remember?"

That's right.

We have the same birthday.

"We're both twenty-five, single, and—"

My eyes narrow in on the paper. It's crumpled and stained, as though it's years old.

A purple and pink swirl decorates the edges and suddenly I remember her painstakingly drawing it as we sat side-by-side at one of the high top tables of the ice rink, waiting for the Zamboni to finish cutting the ice.

Her brow had been furrowed. Her movements carefully controlled.

And I had been obsessing over how pink her lips were and what her butt looked like in her skating dress, so much so that I barely remember what we'd been drawing.

No, I think hard, grabbing on to those memories, not what we'd been *drawing*.

The contract we'd put together.

The contract my hormonal twelve-year-old self had signed.

With a sparkly pink colored pencil.

A giant boulder settles in my stomach, but before I can snap myself out of the horror of those memories, she shoves the paper in my hands then throws her arms around my neck.

"We're getting married!"


CLICK HERE TO READ MARRIED TO NUMBER TWENTY-TWO NOW>

BREAKERS HOCKEY SERIES

<u>Broken</u>
<u>Boldly</u>
<u>Breathless</u>
<u>Ballsy</u>
<u>Bewitched</u>
Blowout
Breathe
A Breakers Christmas
Blazed
Bound

Hate missing Elise's new releases? Love contests, exclusive excerpts and giveaways?
Then signup for Elise's newsletter here!

www.elisefaber.com/newsletter

---

And join Elise's fan group, the Fabinators (https://www.facebook.com/groups/fabinators) for insider information, sneak peaks at new releases, and fun freebies! Hope to see you there!

---

If you enjoy my series, considering supporting me on PATREON! Get access to early releases, bonus content, character art, audiobooks, special edition covers, swag, and much more!

CLICK HERE TO SUPPORT ME>

---

I so appreciate your help in spreading the word about my books, including sharing with friends! Please leave a review on your favorite book site!

Broken

Boldly

<u>Breathless</u>

<u>Ballsy</u>

<u>Bewitched</u>

Blowout

Breathe

A Breakers Christmas

Blazed

Bound

***Sierra Hockey Series***

Over the Line

Caught from Behind

The Big Skate

On the Fly

Attacking the Zone

Snowed

***Rush Hockey Trilogy #1***

Big Puck Energy

Filthy Puckboy

So Pucking Over It

***Rush Hockey Trilogy #2***

Love, Pucks, and Other Stories

All's Fair in Pucks and War

No Pucks Lost Between Us

***Rush Hockey Novellas***
Puck and Make Up

***Eagles Hockey Series (all stand alone)***
Broken Laces

Lace 'em Up

Knotted Laces

Loaded Laces

Lucky Laces

***Billionaire's Club* (all stand alone)**
Bad Night Stand

Bad Breakup

Bad Husband

Bad Hookup

Bad Divorce

Bad Fiancé

Bad Boyfriend

Bad Blind Date

Bad Wedding

Bad Engagement

Bad Bridesmaid

Bad Swipe

Bad Girlfriend

Bad Best Friend

Bad Rebound

Bad Romance

Bad Business

Bad Billionaire's Quickies

### *Love, Action, Camera* (all stand alone)

Dotted Line

Action Shot

Close-Up

End Scene

Meet Cute

### *Love After Midnight* (all stand alone)

Rum And Notes

Virgin Daiquiri

On The Rocks

Sex On The Seats

### *Life Sucks Series*

Train Wreck

Hot Mess

Dumpster Fire

Clusterf*@k

FUBAR

Perfect Storm

Free Fall

Lost Cause

### *Roosevelt Ranch Series* (all stand alone, series complete)

Disaster at Roosevelt Ranch

Heartbreak at Roosevelt Ranch

Collision at Roosevelt Ranch

Regret at Roosevelt Ranch

Desire at Roosevelt Ranch

**Phoenix Series (read in order)**

Phoenix Rising

Dark Phoenix

Phoenix Freed

**Phoenix: LexTal Chronicles (rereleasing soon, stand alone, Phoenix world)**

From Ashes

In Flames

To Smoke

**KTS Series (all stand alone, series complete)**

Riding The Edge

Crossing The Line

Leveling The Field

Scorching The Earth

**Cocky Heroes World**

Tattooed Troublemaker

# ABOUT THE AUTHOR

*USA Today bestselling author*, Elise Faber, loves chocolate, Star Wars, Harry Potter, and hockey (the order depending on the day and how well her team -- the Sharks! -- are playing). She and her husband also play as much hockey as they can squeeze into their schedules, so much so that their typical date night is spent on the ice. Elise is the mom to two exuberant boys and lives in Northern California. Connect with her in her Facebook group, the Fabinators or find more information about her books at www.elisefaber.com.

facebook.com/elisefaberauthor

amazon.com/author/elisefaber

bookbub.com/profile/elise-faber

instagram.com/elisefaber

tiktok.com/@elisefaberauthor

goodreads.com/elisefaber